PRAISE FOR **WING HAVEN**

"Wing Haven...is a beautifully imagined fairy tale
that feels both timeless and new."

"The book blended the charm of childhood imagination
with the weight of adult emotion."
—*Literary Titan*

"This is not a run-of-the-mill tale of Fae; it is a brilliant
lean into the issues that arise from authoritarianism."

"The settings are cinematically depicted...a story
I could easily read again and again."
—*Asher Syed for Readers' Favorite*

WING HAVEN

ISBN 979-8-9891388-5-2 (e-book)
ISBN 979-8-9891388-3-8 (paperback)
ISBN 979-8-9891388-4-5 (hardcover)

Visit the author's website at naomishibles.com

Visit the designer's website at carolinebounds.com

First edition: 2026

FOR
Rowan, Willow, and Averly
Treasure trusted friends.

WING haven

NAOMI SHIBLES

CHAPTER 1

That bug could drain half my blood in a blink. The thought made Almond shudder. She eyed the mosquito's winding sucker as it circled over a spot of marsh and bit back a scream. *If it doesn't kill me, it would give me swamp sickness, for sure,* she thought.

Ducking behind a crimson toadstool, she settled among the mushroom's white spots so that her gossamer shift camouflaged her. Trying to make herself smaller, she pulled her long, slender limbs against her body, but pressed too close, squishing her sling of fruit. A cloudberry quivering with juice spurted into her face. Blinded by the juice, she swiped at her golden eyes and floated out of the toadstool's shadow, not realizing she was exposed. For a moment, both Almond and the mosquito froze in the air.

She held her breath, gaze locked on the giant vampire bug. It drifted in her direction. Almond backed against the toadstool and the ruptured berry slipped from her sling. She watched in horror as it tumbled to the ground and winced when its thin juice splattered across a clump of clover. Almond's heart thudded in her throat. The mosquito didn't move.

Careful not to draw attention to herself, she shifted her gaze to check if the beast detected the sugary elixir spilled across the clover. It floated in the breeze, drawing closer, then wheeled around and zipped into the wet dawn. Almond squinted after it. Was it really gone? Once she was sure, she sagged against the toadstool. *One little mistake around here, and I'm just another notch on the Tree of Sorrow*, she thought. She bent her head to acknowledge the dead fairies tallied in the tree's hard bark. Almond flitted between the holly leaves, their sharp points scratching against her periwinkle arms, leaving sapphire trails. Morning dew slimed her wings and made them heavy. The sling of berries across her shoulders didn't help. Flexing her wings, she angled her body toward the Fairy Nook, but the delicate appendages strained to keep her in the air.

She hated foraging duty. The forest at night was always cold, the darkness full of terrifying monsters like raccoons and owls.

All around her, tree trunks soared from the loamy forest floor. They towered skyward—higher than fairy wings could go—before crashing together at the last moment into a photoprotective canopy. Despite offering cover, the trunks marked canyons of dangerous open forest. After several seasons of foraging duty, Almond held deep convictions about which trees were and weren't fairy-friendly. She knew that the bark of the redwoods was scored with crevices—natural hiding places for a fairy being stalked by a spotted cat. Try to blend in amongst fig leaves, however, and risk a full-body rash from the milky sap. She shuddered and rubbed her upper arms, remembering the burning sensation.

For obvious reasons, she steered clear of monkey-no-climb trees. If the jagged thorns marching up the tree trunk didn't pierce a wing, their bizarre exploding seedpods could pulverize a fairy. They were without question the most murderous trees in Rosepurse Wood.

Almond landed just over the jutting oak root that hemmed in the Fairy Nook and padded toward the hawthorn nicknamed the Teacup Tree. In its hollow sat a chipped, china teacup that some weary human placed there long ago. Her gaze swept the great furrows of ancient tree bark that soared to the leaves covering the sky. They formed walls around the Nook on three sides, while Rosepurse Stream tinkled and splashed over smooth stones, protecting the fourth. On the other side of the hawthorn, the wizened oak leaned its thick hide, forming a defensive wall. The carcasses of old pinecones stood like haunted sentinels in the early morning mist, making Almond jumpy.

Together, they created a natural fortress that had kept the Nook hidden for millennia. There were five adult humans in the world who could still see fairies, and none of them lived near Rosepurse Wood. Most children had the ability, but it had been five hundred and eighty-eight moons since the last one had ventured deep enough into the forest to stumble upon the Nook.

Other fairies returning from foraging duty peppered the ground surrounding the tree. Almond was on the cloudberry squad this moon—a mostly futile assignment so early in the season. Others gathered raw pollen and honey, sunflower seeds, blueberries, sweet peas, mock strawberries, and cowslip bells brimming with fresh dew water.

Lacy ferns sprang like ruffled collars from the bases of the tree trunks and hung overhead. Almond stepped into their deep corridors of shadow. A line of fairies carrying slings of seeds marched past her toward the hawthorn. Several of them looked at her askance as she plucked a pair of lady slipper blossoms and slid them over her feet. *Go ahead and get your feet muddy,* she thought as she slogged past them in her slippers.

Readjusting her sling, she merged into the crowds of exhausted fairies flowing toward the Teacup Tree to deposit their haul from the night forage. She glanced at the two cloudberries she carried—half the minimum that she was required to contribute to the Nook. It wasn't her fault that a mosquito almost quenched its thirst with her blood. She scowled as a ray of sunlight touched her face. *They're lucky to get two berries after what I've been through,* she thought, emerging into the heart of the Fairy Nook.

The old hawthorn stood low in the middle, casting its shadow and keeping the soil damp. Its twisted branches were bare from the white blossoms with their sprays of claret stamen that now littered the ground. Bright baby leaves sprouted in their place.

As she edged nearer, Almond stepped around the petals that curled brown at the edges from rot. Watching the other fairies stomp squarely into the decay, her stomach turned as the brown flecks splashed against their ankles.

The Nook teemed with fairies floating through the mist—returning from night duty or waking for the day shift; showering in the fallen stone waterfall; collecting rations in the new dining hall fashioned of pebbles; stringing fresh forget-me-not blossoms across the Nook's tiny plazas to form sky-blue streamers. Still, with all its busyness, loneliness managed to drape itself across Almond's life like a dead leaf. She was isolated in her revulsion at anything slimy, muddy, sticky—anything to do with the forest. Loving the forest was part of being a fairy. So, what kind of fairy was she?

She dumped her meager offering into the teacup and blew out a sigh, relieved that her night foraging duty was completed for a moon. Rolling her shoulders, she geared up for the short flight home to her length of ivy. She'd have the morning to sleep before her next day shift.

"Let me go!"

The voice sounded familiar. Noting the panicked tone, Almond paused in the air and scanned the clearing for its source. In the shade of a broken twig, one of the young Fairy King's guards held someone by his wings. A chill rolled up Almond's spine as she recognized the detained fairy—it was Sage Thornsmith, one of her squadmates from cloudberry duty. She had just seen him at the bend where Rosepurse Stream curved deeper into the forest. They had discussed venturing across the stream to check for honeysuckle blossoms but decided that it was too early in the season to take such a big risk.

"The queen says you didn't bring back enough cloudberries," said the guard. He struggled to keep a grip on Sage, whose biceps bulged as he wrenched at the guard's arm. With a scowl and a firmer grip, the guard pushed Sage forward, hissing, "Off to the pebble pit with you!"

The pebble pit? thought Almond. Why would Sage be sent to the gash in the ground full of pea pebbles that ran along Rosepurse Stream? Freezing groundwater filled the spaces between the pebbles and rose nearly to its brim. Many fairies had lost all feeling in their fingers while pulling the pebbles out for royal building projects. Only fairies who offended the royal legacy ended up on that duty.

Almond's lavender curls tightened at the base of her neck as her heart rate accelerated. Sage was a hard worker—much more so than she was, she admitted to herself with an inner eye roll. Why was he being detained? Watching the burly fairy struggle with the guard, she pulled her wings flush across her back, aphidbumps erupting across her arms. Sage, likely as exhausted from foraging as she was, sagged in the guard's grip when his feet lost purchase in the damp clover. She hugged herself as the guard hauled him into the gloom by his wings.

I can't stand by and watch this, she thought. Aiming her head, she zoomed after them. "Wait, please!"

The guard's fairy sight glowed red in the dawnlight. "This doesn't concern you, Almond Nettlesworth," he growled. He grunted as he wrestled Sage—still struggling—into a headlock.

"Let him go," Almond cried, hovering just out of reach. "I was on the same foraging squad and can vouch for him. The season is too early for cloudberries. We gathered all we could."

Sage nodded, despite the guard's forearm across his neck. "Listen to her, please!"

"Not according to the queen," said the guard. "The squad failed to perform their duty and there are consequences."

Almond blinked. *We don't have a queen yet. Do we?* As far as she knew, King Cornsilk had yet to choose a mate. She wished he would hurry in making his selection. Ever since he replaced his father as the Fairy King, the Nook had been a beehive droning with speculation and gossip.

"I was the one who lost part of the haul," she said to the guard. "There was a mosquito..." She twisted her hands together as she watched him force Sage to his knees.

Gripping his prisoner by the elbows behind his back, the guard yanked Sage to his feet, turning his back on Almond. "Like I said, this doesn't concern you."

She landed, helpless, as her squadmate lost whatever small amount of freedom he'd had. Bitterness spread in her mouth, and she spit out the thin strip of bark that she had stuffed inside her cheek without thinking—masticating like an egg-bearing fairy building her nest. Still gagging, she ran a hand down her face, ignoring the oily sensation in the pit of her stomach after the encounter with the guard.

Vibrating her wings, she rose from the ground as thick mist made the tiny glen cozy and spooky at the same time. Glimpses of other fairies starting their day peeked through the fog—a confusing contrast to what she'd just witnessed.

Why didn't the guard take me, too? she thought.

Even though she hated night foraging, Almond was usually happiest—if you could call it that—at this time of the morning. The crisp air invigorated her, and the dawn that trickled through the tree-tops was a velvety robe that she slipped on to hide in the shadows. This was the time when she could watch her community without fear of being noticed.

Because scrutiny in the Nook meant one of three things: you were being evaluated for joining—being forced to nest with a mate, which Almond intended to avoid—you were in big trouble with the royal legacy, or you were about to get extra work. She considered herself to be a clever fairy, and clever fairies kept their heads down in the Nook.

The mist dissolved into droplets of dew, slicking the leaves and rocks. Almond wrinkled her nose. The spell of daybreak was broken, and she was back in the 'puddle,' as she secretly thought of the Nook. It was full of mud and slime—her two least favorite things—with steps of rotten mushrooms clotting the tree trunks. Earthworms occasionally reared their harmless but disgusting heads out of the soil to her dismay. Still, she lingered.

In the heart of the Nook, toadstools lined pathways that led to various plazas. Each plaza catered to fairies in different phases of life. All of Almond's old school friends were in the nesting plaza now, bark chewing and sitting on eggs. She shuddered at the thought of such tedium. Fairy School was its own plaza, where young fairies were sent to live and learn about their place in the Nook.

Almond hadn't graduated from the fledgling plaza—mostly consisting of a sturdy vine of ivy whose curves and sheets of leaves served as barracks for the newly adult fairies who were assigned the most dangerous duties. She had hoped when she moved to the ivy after school that it would be one giant celebration, but the wingbreaking work that they performed left them exhausted and listless. Almond's friends had moved to the nesting plaza at the first opportunity. But as much as

Almond hated living in the ivy, she couldn't stomach the thought of joining. She'd rather be alone with her thoughts, free to imagine an ordered forest and a Nook free of grime.

Her wingtips vibrated, alerting her to a nuisance. She closed her eyes and cracked her neck. Without looking around, she asked: "Why are you awake this early, Pepper?"

"Two berries? That's seriously all you got?" asked her younger sister from behind her.

Almond didn't need to look over her shoulder—Pepper's drawling voice betrayed her perpetual sneer. Tall and lean, Almond towered over Pepper, but her petite sister's ferocious personality made her seem as overwhelming as a screaming cicada swarm.

"I wanted to see for myself if the rumors are true," said Pepper, closing the gap between them. She swept her silky cerulean hair back and locked gazes with her older sister.

"Rumors?" Almond tensed. She had been ready to curl into her nest, but thoughts of rest scattered with the morning mist. Facing Pepper, she plastered on a smile. "Tell me all about it over here, out of the way." She wrapped her fingers around Pepper's lime green wrist and float-walked to a massive, deserted pinecone.

"Everyone's talking about how you haven't been gathering as many berries as the other squads," said Pepper. "And it looks like they're right." She cut her eyes at the teacup in the tree holding her sister's two berries. "I'm tired of hearing everyone's complaints about how you think you're too good for the Nook."

"Everyone?" Almond's brow drew down in a vee, a dry cough escaping before her throat constricted. "Other fairies are gossiping about me? Why?" She leaned back on her shoulder but bounced away when a cold patch of mildew smeared down her arm from a jutting pinecone scale. "Ugh! I hate how dirty everything always is." She swiped at her grimy arm and scowled at the ground, embarrassed.

Pepper shook her head as if Almond had laid an egg during the Resting Moon. "It's not dirty. The forest is a place of coexisting. It's an enchanted sway of the wing."

Almond gaped at her and then turned away. "I'm going to my nest." She dragged her wings through the air and bumbled away from her sister. *Pepper seems way too into Nook life as she enters her pixie moon,* she thought.

"If you think the Nook is so dirty, why don't you find somewhere else to live?" Pepper's sharp words carried over the remaining ground fog and rang in her ears.

Almond squeezed her fists and clamped her lips together, but her retort burst undaunted into the morning, startling other fairies returning with full slings of acorn caps for the teacup. She rounded on her sister. "Maybe I will! Maybe I'll go someplace clean and tidy, where I can have my own things the way I like them, and I won't have to get chased by squirrels on a nocturnal suicide mission to gather cloudberries once a moon! Maybe..." Almond paused and looked Pepper up and down in an unspoken insult. "I'll go someplace where I don't have to listen to entitled nits like you!"

Pepper narrowed her gaze, unflinching. "Then go. You're embarrassing." The words dripped from her everlasting pout.

Almond took a breath to fling more careless barbs at Pepper but stopped at the disapproving stares of fairies who had paused to watch the argument. Two pips looked away from her, uneasy, as they fluttered wildly to haul half a walnut shell full of honey toward the Teacup Tree. A fairy matron swept the ground around the hawthorn with a stout dandelion, her lips pursed and wings rigid with reproach.

A fairy around Almond's age picked apart thin strips of bark as she sat cross-legged on a daisy's yellow pouf of florets. She cut her eyes at Almond while stuffing the bark strips into her cheek. Brown saliva dripped from the corner of her mouth as she softened them with her sharp teeth, preparing to build a nest for her imminent egg. Almond looked away, the recent memory of her own bark chewing souring her stomach.

"Well?" asked Pepper.

Almond clenched her jaw to keep silent as she examined her little sister, this time with interest. Pepper was no longer the pip Almond pictured in her mind's eye. This was not the little gnat who used to follow her around Fairy School, trying to join her group of friends despite how they treated her. Before her stood a poised fairy, self-possessed and full of conviction. Her lime skin glistened, mature and ripe, and shiny tresses cascaded down her erect posture.

When did she become stunning? Almond wondered.

A ray of light filtered through the overhead ferns and glinted on something iridescent at Pepper's throat. Almond stiffened. *It can't be,* she thought. Understanding broke through her cluttered mind. She pointed to the tiny emerald and cobalt featherlettes wrapped around Pepper's neck. "Is that from a peacock feather?"

She watched the smug child still inside her sister struggling to break free from the constraints of maturity—clearly gleeful.

There was only one peacock in all of Rosepurse Wood, and he shed just one long tail feather from his magical fan per year. Featherlettes from this one feather were the most coveted treasure in the forest, only to be worn by the Nook's royal legacy.

What was one doing around her little sister's neck?

Pepper touched the drape of silky, jewel-toned featherlettes that signified her membership in the royal fairies club. "Cornsilk joined me to his legacy last night. Which means—"

"Which means, you can tell me what to do," said Almond, interrupting.

"Correct. I am your new queen. But I won't make you kneel—this time." Pepper whipped a fresh sling from the hawthorn tree and tossed it to Almond, who caught it on reflex. "Don't come back until that sling is full of cloudberries."

Almond stared at the sling in her hand, and then at her little sister, who had morphed into her queen with dizzying swiftness. Her tired mind struggled to make sense of what was happening. "Right now? But, it's daylight, and—"

"Were you about to say you're tired?" asked Pepper. "Well, I'm tired of you lallygagging about in an untidy vine nest, soiling our legacy's reputation. You could have ruined my joining, you know. You're lucky I don't have you locked up with the rest of your worthless squad. I'm giving you a second chance to please me, big sister. Now, get back to work."

"You had the squad arrested?" Almond gaped like a trout. "Pepper! You know it's early in the season—there aren't many berries yet. We did our best."

Pepper smirked. "Maybe you belong in the pebble pit, after all."

Almond noted the gathered fairies nodding approval at Pepper's assessment of her. She had forgotten they had an audience. *Every fairy in the Nook hates me,* she thought miserably.

Raking the crowd for a sympathetic glance, her gaze stopped level with a hard line of topaz thigh. Perverse curiosity dragged her vision upward over a heaving chest as broad as an acorn. Her breath hitched as she stared into the deep clover eyes of Beechnut, the Knight of the Nook.

His chiseled face was stony, but his irises held her with their kaleidoscope of green hues—almost as if there were emotions warring beneath his stoic visage. But she knew that couldn't be true. The Knight of the Nook was incapable of feeling anything but the desire to protect and serve the royal legacy. Songs were written about his bravery—she knew one by heart. He was born into his position, sequestered from his family as a pip and trained to become the ultimate soldier. There was no time for family or friendship in the Knight's life—only the possibility of danger.

Rattled by his fame, Almond stood mute before the handsome fairy, unable to tear her gaze from his jawline; his stern, straight nose; the hollow under his neck where his collarbones met. Somehow, her lungs had filled with air that she whispered out through full, pursed lips.

There was one emotion that his shifting eyes settled on—disgust. His gaze raked the congealed filth coating her arm. She ran her palms down her shift, sticky with smeared pollen, and her cheeks flamed. Pulling her long, lavender curls in front of her shoulders, she tried to cover herself with her curtain of hair. She could feel his thoughts dripping over her head and down her spine—she was just another sloppy, lazy fairy. Pepper was right.

Pepper!

Almond's wings drooped toward the bracken at her feet and a thought pitted her stomach. *Beechnut is here as Pepper's escort.* The Knight of the Nook only accompanied royals. Pepper's newfound power was a reality—and it was going to be bad for everyone.

Still gazing into Beechnut's cold eyes, she knew that being Pepper's sister did not mean a thing to him. He glared down at her, taller than any fairy she'd seen. This was the closest she had ever been to him, and she flushed deep indigo as berry juice seeped from her shift and trickled down her leg.

His lip curled.

Fire leapt from the tips of her ears when Almond registered that he'd noticed the rivulet drip to her ankle. She swiped it from her calf with the bridge of her other foot, dragging her toes in the dirt. "It's just berry juice," she said.

He flicked his gaze to Pepper, awaiting orders.

The image of the guard hauling Sage to the pebble pit flashed in her mind. She'd been powerless to save him, and there was nothing she could do for herself now. Pepper was queen and she commanded the Knight of the Nook. Almond had to obey.

Too exhausted to fly, she dropped the sling over her head and trudged back into the thick forest, only using her wings once she got to the oak root wall. She glanced over her shoulder at the damp corner under the ferns teeming with morning fairies. Sprays of dew from their wings cast strange little arcs of color where sunlight collided with her home.

It almost looks pretty, she thought.

Over the root wall, she dropped to the ground and bounced along springy moss, unsure of where to forage at this time in the morning. Her thoughts were fragments like shattered ice that could not make sense of her new situation. All she knew was that she deeply regretted snubbing Pepper at school with her friends, but she regretted even more that she'd failed to keep an eye on her in recent years. She'd been a rotten excuse for a big sister.

Those friends were all feathering nests now or fulfilling important duties to the Nook. Only Almond had floundered when she moved to the ivy vine with the other fledglings. Pepper never even made it to the vine before becoming joined. *She only just finished school.* Almond's thoughts spun painfully.

She toed the thick, dry moss under her feet. Making herself still, she opened her thoughts to the forest, probing for danger. Activating her fairy sight, her golden eyes glowed white and she peered into the gloom, searching for camouflaged creatures. The air buzzed with emerging insects and the sodium whine of plant life, smelling verdant and steady. But only soil, wood, stone, and lichen surrounded her.

Satisfied that she was safe for the moment, she wrinkled her nose and slid between the soft moss, curling into a long overdue nap. As she drifted to sleep, she didn't care that moss flakes stuck in her curls or that Pepper plotted to make her life worse than it already was. She would rest, gather what she could before the sun blazed at the top of the sky, and return to the Nook triumphant.

CHAPTER 2

Someone grabbed Almond's wrists and ankles. Her stomach lurched and she thrashed out of her dreams, but it was only her limbs twined in the moss while she slept. She tore herself free, alone in the dim light while the tangle closed in on her, a crashing wave aimed at drowning her. *Why am I moving?* She scrabbled for the opening she had made to crawl in and the dry tendrils bit into her willowy fingers.

Almond strained to wiggle farther out, squeezing her wings close to her body and twisting her shoulders. She peered through the opening. Above her, spindly umber sticks stuck straight up, seemingly reaching to the clouds above. That didn't make sense, so she flipped onto her stomach. Moss grabbed at her like a malevolent weed. She swept her gaze around. Underneath her froth of vegetation were fathoms of clear air.

Looking up again, she realized the spindly sticks were the legs of a chickadee, and the cloud they touched was the bird's snowy under-feathers. Almond gulped and struggled in a frenzy to loosen herself from the clump of peat that was bound for cradling chickadee eggs.

I'm too high up. I'm too far from the Nook to find my way home. Sweat running wildly from her temples, her thoughts pounded at the inside of her skull as if they too were trying to escape through her pores.

She folded her wings against her back, careful to keep them tight as she pulled herself farther out of the moss. It crumbled under her hands. She swung her legs around to dangle over the edge of the clump, steadying herself. The bird soared higher than fairy wings were meant to go—or so Almond had always been told. But she couldn't let herself be carried off and lost forever. The only option was to leap into the sky and pray that her wings didn't tear.

If I can free fall long enough, it'll be safe to open my wings closer to the ground, she thought. But there was no way to know for sure. What if the velocity of her fall ripped them right out of their sockets? What if she crashed into a star? They were invisible during the day. Even in the sky, the world was full of danger.

Seated on the moss clump, Almond let the rhythm of the chickadee's flapping soothe her frayed nerves. The fastest way to get herself killed was by panicking. Her gaze swept the horizon. *I never realized how big Rosepurse Wood is,* she thought. She marveled at the view. Usually so overwhelming, the forest floor far below looked fairy-sized. *There's so much more out here than the Fairy Nook. Are there* other *fairy nooks? Are any of them clean?*

With each flap of the bird's wings, Almond's thoughts crystallized and burst forth, urging her to flow into the quest for her place in the forest. It hid teeming worlds in its vast carpet of benign green—some microscopic, but all mighty with the force of life. *Maybe I can find another nook where the fairies aren't so judgmental,* she thought. Her hand wound around the chickadee's leg, and she leaned her head against it, daydreaming of adventure.

The bird twitched, tried to shake her off, and when that failed, pecked her hair.

Almond slapped her hands on the crown of her head. "Sorry!" She craned her neck, meeting the bird's black eye, annoyance reflecting back at her. Just one more creature who found her irritating. She was already too far from home to daydream, anyway. If she didn't jump now, she could end up on the other side of the forest, away from everything she knew. The thought surprised her by sending a thrill up her spine.

"Farewell, then," she said to the chickadee, who ignored her. Before she had time to think about what she was doing, she slipped from the wad of moss, instinctively angling her body—wings tucked tight—so that her face aimed for the ground. Her fear blew away with the air rushing along her torso. The festival of greens, browns, and grays blazed toward her, and she grinned, exhilarated. Nothing this exciting had ever happened to her. She floated like a pip just learning to flutter. Twisting and coasting along the air currents, she drank in the expanse of timberland and strange piles of stones beyond.

She loved to swim in Rosepurse Stream and feel the cool water lick against her periwinkle skin, caressing her as she floated and dove. This felt even better. The air whispered against her—almost tickling her—while it carried her toward the treetops. Reaching the crowns of the tallest trees, she hesitated to use her pinions. Was she still too high? Would they hold?

Taking a deep breath, she unfurled her opalescent wings and flipped them perpendicular, slowing her descent. She was jerked up when they caught the air and then released to float like a silken seedpod. *I can't believe I just did that*, she thought. Panting, she scanned the forest as quickly as she could before sinking below the tree line, searching for something familiar that would lead her home.

She didn't recognize anything. Puffs of spring leaves foamed as far as she could see in every direction—everything looked the same. Panic bubbled in her stomach. Which way should she go? Her wings trembled and she dipped lower in the air.

And then there, to the left, she spotted the stream that wound through Rosepurse Wood.

The Fairy Nook crouched near Rosepurse Stream. She had just been there last night—with Sage. But there was no time to worry about him. Almond blew out the breath she'd been holding. *All I have to do is follow the stream and, one way or another, I'll find my way home.* It was a long way off, though, with vast meadows between her and the water. She drifted down to perch on a high branch and considered her options.

As she leaned against a crumbly fork in the branch, she entered one of those rare and wonderful states when she was exactly comfortable. Every part of her body felt easy and good, with no annoying kinks or awkward angles. She closed her eyes and turned her face to the sun.

"What are you doing? Are you crazy?"

Almond peeked from behind her curtain of curls at a very rattled adolescent chipmunk twisting her paws together next to her. "What?" she asked.

"You can't sleep out here like this," said the chipmunk, squeaking. She trembled from her long lashes to her stubby tail. "This territory belongs to Boscoe. It's not safe."

"I wasn't sleeping, I was just perfectly comfortable." Almond adjusted her back against the branch, trying to regain the blissful moment. No matter how she positioned herself, it was gone, elusive as morning mist burning off a stream. She gave up and scowled at the chipmunk. "It's been quite a day."

"Please come inside if you want to see the end of it," said the chipmunk, who threw furtive glances around her, clasping Almond's thin wrist and tugging her to her feet.

Despite its fuzziness, the animal's paw was surprisingly bony. Almond allowed herself to be hurried into a hole in the tree, the chipmunk pushing her from behind with squeaks of effort.

"Stop pushing. And I'm not that heavy, so you don't have to huff and puff like that," Almond whispered vehemently. She stumbled through the opening and stood in a tidy room with a respectably sized pile of nuts in the corner. The floor was swept clean, and a crusty brown leaf served as a meager doormat. Smooth twigs bound with strips of young tree bark formed a sturdy-looking chair. Its back sat flush against the far wall, near the nuts. In another corner, more leaves—these fresh and green—were piled into a passable nest. The room was otherwise bare. There were no special objects displayed. No drawings hung on the walls.

The chipmunk tumbled in after her, making *chip chip* sounds and knocking Almond further into the room. She slumped against the wall, gathering herself. Looking around again, something felt off.

The chipmunk crouched at the opening, apparently scanning the skies for Boscoe—whoever that was. Her rust-colored fur was grubby and matted, with a set of black stripes running down her back parallel with a white set. Almond examined her from across the room. Her stripes were the only things giving her structure. Her tail trembled as she ducked under the opening.

"What are you looking at?" Almond asked the nervous creature.

The chipmunk peeked over the sill of the opening. "Oh, nothing... just a cloud. I thought it might be Boscoe."

Almond approached the opening and peeked out. A lonely wisp of a cloud hung listlessly in the bluebell sky. She glanced down at the chipmunk sitting on the floor and slid down next to her.

"Who is Boscoe?"

The chipmunk shuddered. "A truly horrible bluebird who terrorizes this grove."

Almond thought for a moment. "But bluebirds don't eat chipmunks." She didn't mention that they were known to snack on fairies. Shivering, she examined the room. It occurred to her what seemed off. "What are you even doing up here? Chipmunks don't live in trees."

"Boscoe kidnapped me when I was a pup and flew me far from my family." The chipmunk scrubbed her face with her fawn paws. "He stopped to rest on the same branch where you were enjoying comfort, and I scurried into this nest. Boscoe was too fat to squeeze through the opening, but he kept watch every day so that I couldn't escape."

"How long have you been up here?"

"An entire season," the chipmunk wailed, throwing her ample fluff into Almond's arms.

Almond patted her head. "But whose nest is this?"

"I don't know. No one ever came back, so I live off of their nuts and rainwater." She sniffled against the fairy's tiny shoulder, making it damp.

Almond's heart ached for the chipmunk, but her new friend was also quite heavy, so she eased the furry head from her shoulder and stared into her cocoa eyes. "You're not alone anymore. We'll get out of here together."

"Easy for you to say," said the chipmunk. "You have wings and can hide easily. Every time I try to run down the tree, Boscoe swoops and chases me back here." She looked around her little prison. "I'm so sick of eating nuts."

"Look...what's your name?"

"Nutsie."

Almond nodded. "I feel like every chipmunk I meet is called Nutsie."

"It's a classic."

"My name is Almond Nettlesworth. Look, Nutsie, I have to get back to the Fairy Nook, and I'm not leaving you behind. You've already lost a season in a place you don't want to be. Let's get you home."

Nutsie shook her head, and her whiskers drooped. "I don't know where my home is."

"You still have to leave here and live your life. Let's have breakfast and then begin our escape." Almond crossed the room and grabbed a nut from the bottom of the pile, quickly realizing her mistake.

"Nooooo!" Nutsie shouted as an avalanche of nuts tumbled toward the fairy.

The deluge rolled over Almond, sweeping her toward the opening. Nutsie's eyes were round with shock as the riptide knocked her off of her paws. Together, they tumbled out of the hole onto the branch as a seemingly endless surge of nuts followed, falling from the tree and peppering the ground far below.

CHAPTER 3

Almond sat up and ran her fingers along her wings, checking for damage. Beside her, Nutsie clung to the branch with all four paws, flattening her plump body against the bark. The last of the nuts trickled to the edge of the opening and stayed there, as if waiting for the nest's real occupant to return.

"Get up, Nutsie. That's surely a sign that it's time to go," said Almond.

Nutsie ignored her and raised her head to scan the expanse of clear sky. *Chip chip*, she instinctively chirped, warning other chipmunks of the danger of a predator. No other chipmunk answered her call.

"We have to go right now," said Almond, shaking Nutsie's arm. "You climb down the tree trunk, and I'll float along with you. If anyone comes for us, I'll distract them." She vibrated her wings and rose above the branch.

Nutsie gulped. She released the branch with her front paws and sat on her haunches as if she would never move again.

"What are you waiting for?" Almond's heart pounded as she swept the skies, searching for the fearsome bluebird. *Anyone around had to hear all those nuts clinking against each other,* she thought. Adrenaline coursed through her, spring-loading her for trouble.

Nutsie remained planted, staring straight ahead as if the tree next door was spurting rainbows.

Almond faced her, still bobbing on the breeze, and took the chipmunk's paw, forcing her voice to sound calm. "You can't stay here, Nutsie. This isn't a life."

Nutsie pulled her paw away. "I've been up here so long, and the forest seems so big. Why shouldn't I stay put?"

"Because you need to be around friends."

"Do you have lots of friends?" asked Nutsie.

Almond's wings drooped and she settled onto the branch beside the chipmunk. "Not anymore. But I will again—soon. I just need to figure out my place in the Nook." She thought of her sister's disgusted scowl and slumped against Nutsie.

They sat in the caress of the breeze, stilled by the prospect of the vast forest pouring from the base of their tree in every direction. "Since we both have to find our place in the forest, perhaps we should journey together," said Nutsie in a small voice.

Almond breathed out a sigh of relief. "Let's go quickly. Trust me, I'll see old Boscoe coming if he turns up."

Nutsie shuddered and gave the fairy a weak smile. As she placed one tentative paw on the tree trunk, Almond hovered nearby and surveyed the forest before her. The land brimmed with vitality beneath the robin's egg blue sky as the sun climbed higher and hotter. Compared with its impossible scale, she was insignificant and helpless—a speck in the greater world. Panic welled inside her, filling her throat, and the weight of the world tumbled toward her.

"Almond!"

She shook her head, pulling herself back to reality.

Nutsie gnashed her long front teeth, already below her on the tree trunk. "What are you doing? You're supposed to keep watch for Boscoe, but you're just floating there, staring into space." Nutsie's squeaks were urgent, her gaze darting from branch to branch.

"I am!" said Almond, too fiercely.

Nutsie winced.

"Sorry for shouting. Just keep going," she said, this time gently, fluttering lower so that they were face-to-face. She focused her golden gaze on Nutsie's big doe eyes, forcing them to connect. "Trust me."

Nutsie nodded and continued her darting climb down the tree trunk.

Almond kept her back to the chipmunk and scanned the area around her in an arc, watching for any sign of movement involving blue feathers. A strange wind kicked up and whipped the small branches so that rustling leaves spiraled to the dense carpet of flora below. The back of Almond's neck tingled, her curls tightening, and she spun to face Nutsie. The chipmunk darted in a halting zigzag down the bark. Almond flitted behind the tree to check for danger, but there was nothing.

"We're halfway down," said Nutsie, keeping her focus on her paw placement. "I can't believe it. I haven't been this close to the ground since I was a pup."

"Wait until you taste toadstools," Almond replied, keeping her talking.

Nutsie wrinkled her nose. "That sounds gross."

"Lots of good things sound gross." Almond's head swiveled as she scanned for Boscoe. The world around them now consisted of mostly leafless, bark-covered masts that dropped into a gloaming of shadows. As they descended into the forest's shade, Almond's eyes glowed white and her fairy sight adjusted to the gloom.

Nutsie's legs trembled. "I'm tired of climbing. Let's rest."

"No, we have to get to the bottom and find cover," said Almond. "We're almost there." The feeling of apprehension on the back of her neck—like her curls tightening—urged her toward the ground. But she forced herself to stay next to Nutsie as the chipmunk picked her way down the tree trunk. She could almost hear the flap of feathers that would signal Boscoe's attack. Her wings were taut; her muscles flexed. Easing her hand out, she snapped off a sharp-looking twig from the tree, holding it like a spear.

"I need to stop," said Nutsie. She made a *chuck chuck* sound, exposing her creeping fear with the deepened warning call.

Almond dragged her gaze from her surveillance and regarded Nutsie, taking in the chipmunk trembling on the verge of convulsions.

Her fur splayed with static, and her eyes bulged. Almond sensed that Nutsie was about to unravel into a spiral of panic. She couldn't be pushed much farther.

"Okay," she said, resting a hand on Nutsie's shoulder. "I'll keep watch while you rest." She stroked the matted fur and murmured soothingly while her gaze danced and skittered, scanning for Boscoe. Any minute could be their last. One hand still on Nutsie and the other gripping her spear, Almond coiled to defend them from a keen beak, eager to peck them to bits. "I'm going to fly out, just a little, to find a landmark on the ground while I can still see the stream, or else we won't know which way to travel."

The chipmunk shook violently, her eyelids squeezed shut and nose pressed to the tree bark. Almond took that as an assent and fluttered to the end of a branch to get her bearings. She zipped back and whispered into Nutsie's ear: "I promise to be right back." This time, the chipmunk nodded.

With the feeling of being exposed to danger and skin crawling, Almond peeked from behind a clutch of infant leaves and located the stream glinting like a thread of ice sewn across the verdant quilt below. She flew toward it, careful not to veer from her flight path. When she cleared the tree's drip line, she looked straight down for something that would stand out to them when they reached the ground.

A late coming chickadee sang, "Hey, sweetie," in the distance and Almond reeled. Realizing her overreaction, she fumbled to find her spot in the air where she could mark their journey.

"Hurry," Nutsie squeaked behind her from the tree trunk.

Almond flitted back to the chipmunk. "Shhhhh." Her back to the bark next to Nutsie, Almond pressed her palms against the tree, chest heaving. "I didn't see anything to aim for. I have to go back out there."

"No, don't leave me," said Nutsie. "I can climb the rest of the way now."

"I have to," said Almond, noticing for the first time the scars across Nutsie's shoulders that gleamed from her fur like glimpses of bone. "Are those scars from…"

"Where Boscoe pecked me when I tried to escape." Nutsie nodded. *Chip chip.* "Where is he? I've never made it this far before."

"Maybe he's gone," said Almond, trying to hide her hitching breath. "Stay here and blend in with the bark." She flexed her shoulder blades to flap her wings in two hard pushes, gaze fixed on the winding stream. At the tip of a branch, she looked down and cast about for anything to mark the stream's direction on the ground.

There. Her heart flipped in her chest. Below, an unbroken line of stone wall snaked between the trees and brush on its way toward the water.

Almond zoomed back to Nutsie. "Hurry, let's go. I see a way to the stream. From there, we can navigate our way to the Fairy Nook."

Nutsie steeled herself and raised her whiskers to the air. "I'm ready." Now that the base of the tree was visible, she was able to place one paw in front of the other more quickly than when she had climbed before.

Almond returned to sentinel duty, her apprehension dwindling as they neared the ground. If Boscoe hadn't seen them by now, chances were, he really was gone, and the silly chipmunk had been alone in the tree for no reason. Almond allowed her breathing to slow and deepen, no longer tensed for battle.

In a twinkle, Nutsie reached the ground and gingerly placed her paws in the spongy moss. "It's so soft," she marveled. The cache of nuts that fell from her nest lay scattered across the ground like boulders. She scampered to one and kicked it hard, sending it skipping into a clump of ferns. "I'm never eating nuts again!"

Almond dropped to the forest floor and folded her wings away. "You'll have to change your name." She dug her toes into the moss—the best way to get her ground legs back—and grimaced as mud seeped between them. "Ugh, I almost forgot how gross everything is on the ground."

Nutsie tested the springiness of her moss patch, hopping on all fours. "It's not gross—it's wonderful!"

Almond huffed. No one understood her wanting someplace clean and orderly. She searched for the line of stones that led to the stream to their left. "Help me look for those stones." When no one answered, she looked behind her at Nutsie, whose face was buried in the purple center of a wild geranium. Almond dragged her out of the flower. "You have a lot to catch up on, I know, but we need to get to cover quickly."

Nutsie scooped up a froth of fern moss and rubbed it on her cheeks before plopping it on her head for a hat. "This is better than I imagined!" She twirled around, arms flung wide, wearing a wide grin.

"Nutsie!" Almond's voice rose with urgency.

The chipmunk stopped spinning and stood unsteadily.

Almond pointed. "Look, the stones are there. It's an old human wall. Let's hide in its shadow—we're too exposed here." She froze. "Did you hear that?"

Nutsie cocked her ear and concentrated. *Chip chip.* "I hear rustling."

Almond raised her twig spear above her head, poised to defend her larger but less athletic companion. The rustling deepened. She held her breath and raised a finger for Nutsie to be silent. A moment later, she dropped her arm and put her hands on her knees, laughing with relief as a black snake slithered through a patch of brush. "I thought it was B—"

An explosion of leaves sent them scurrying for the rambling stone wall. Almond looked over her shoulder. A mangy bluebird rocketed after them, trailing debris.

Nutsie unleashed a keening screech as she bolted from her tormentor.

Nutsie! The anguish in her friend's voice rocketed Almond into the air. There was no time for fear. She rounded on the bluebird—the dreaded Boscoe—and pointed her spear at him as he barreled toward her.

Just when she was sure that he was going to impale her with his beak, he peeled off from his trajectory before reaching the jagged end of Almond's twig. In the moment before he rounded on her, she zipped in the opposite direction from Nutsie and then paused in the air, keeping the bird's focus on her. She stared up at him, trying to hide her ragged breathing.

What is this bluebird's problem? she thought, examining the creature. She had never seen a bird so disheveled. From finch to falcon, every bird she had ever observed in her corner of Rosepurse Wood had kept neat, tidy feathers and were economical in their delicate movements. This bluebird was an anomaly—cannoning through the air, snagging his tender under-feathers on branches as if he didn't notice.

"Why are you doing this?" Her shout seemed to float away on a cottonwood seed.

"I enjoyed seeing you fumbling your way down the tree," snarled Boscoe as he wheeled around to face her midair, ragged wings flapping. "But it would have been too easy to pick you off. Ha! You should have seen your faces when I surged you."

The bird was clearly unhinged. His waxy feathers puffed around eyes that gleamed too brightly, making his cherubic face seem sinister. He compulsively swung his head from side to side as he stared her down first with one eye, then with the opposite one.

Outrage bubbled up from somewhere deep inside of Almond. "Why are you tormenting poor Nutsie?"

Boscoe's beak curved upward. "I like the taste of her. I just lack the teeth to take a really good bite."

Almond shuddered. She gazed past Boscoe at Nutsie's progress, blowing out a sigh that the chipmunk was faster on the ground than she was in the tree. *Just get to the stone wall, Nutsie,* she thought. Refocusing on Boscoe, she bobbed in the air, trying to make him dizzy. "So, did your egg fall out of the nest and crack or something?" she asked.

"Hold still!"

"Sorry, Boscoe. About your egg? Was it cracked too early?"

The bluebird's gaze narrowed; a predator's gleam reflected in his eyes. He turned toward Nutsie as she scampered toward the wall's deep shadow. Almond had to do something to stop him from giving her more scars—or worse.

She was never the strongest fairy in the Nook. Her patrol experience had been cut short when she failed to stop a baby bunny from nibbling St. John's Wort's sod roof. And back in Fairy School, the mandatory flight course to qualify for the cadets proved more than her shoulders could bear.

But she had persevered and finished the course—barely—in order to graduate. And she would finish this deranged bluebird if she had to. She raised her twig spear over her head and let out a sharp peal of laughter. When Boscoe's attention shifted from Nutsie's retreating rump to her, Almond fluttered higher, forcing him to look up.

"What kind of bird are you—toying with flightless animals? You must not be very good at flying."

Boscoe clicked his beak. "Nice try, but I'm not going to let you distract me. I'm in charge here."

A chill whipped through the grove just then. Gray clouds crowded out the light and branches clacked against each other, creating menacing applause that mocked Almond's efforts to stay alive. Hovering above his head, she shrugged and released the twig-spear with a sudden thrust that sent it whizzing to the crown of Boscoe's head. It bounced off of the bird's dirty feathers and fell to the ground.

Boscoe shook his head and chuckled, still fixing her with alternating eyes. "Foolish little fairy. You might as well be flightless yourself with those puny wings." After a look around to locate Nutsie, Boscoe threw his head back and laughed in Almond's face.

The bluebird's words stung, especially after the inconceivable day she had already endured, and Almond felt the heaviness of her circumstances. Between her sister's shifting power, being far from the familiar, and worrying about poor Nutsie, she did feel puny.

But Boscoe couldn't be allowed to win. He was just another bully in the forest, making himself big by convincing other creatures that they were small. *Not so different from Pepper,* she thought. As he gloated, Almond gradually descended to the ground. Boscoe wiped his streaming eyes on a wing and cast about for her. "Where did you go?"

"I'm right where I'm supposed to be," she said from between his clawed feet. She jabbed up into his threadbare belly feathers with her recovered spear until the tip touched flesh.

He maneuvered his wings backward like a swimmer in reverse to stumble out of her reach. "Ow! You nicked me." His brow gathered like a thunderhead.

"Just a peck," called Almond over her shoulder as she zipped away, her wings streamlined for speed. "My spear liked the taste of you but lacks teeth to take a proper bite!"

Boscoe unleashed a screech and soared after her. Finally, being smaller than him was an asset: she zoomed over roots and under ferns, aiming for openings barely large enough for her to fit through. Their second lap around a tree, she spotted what she was looking for and bent her head toward it.

Risking a glance over her shoulder, Almond confirmed that Boscoe's entire focus was aimed at her. When his beak was a mere hair from her toe, she was overcome by the feeling of being prey—an ugly, gray tingle deep in her stomach. Using the fumes of her strength to boost her speed, she tucked her chin, cut her eyes, and hoped that this wasn't her last moment.

Air *whooshed* along her body as she sailed through the space between two intertwined branches. She targeted a tangle of creeping roses for her crash landing. Bouncing into the soft petals, she heard a satisfying screech and didn't have to look to know that Boscoe was stuck up to his wings in the twined branches.

He struggled to break free, but his wooden chains held fast. Almond lay back on the rosebuds to catch her breath. Her wings were folded awkwardly beneath her, and she sat up to resettle them against her back.

"Don't you dare leave me here," Boscoe screamed, his neck feathers clotting around his throat.

She gave him a hard stare and then slowly turned her back on him.

"I'll find you and gobble you up for this." Boscoe's promise leaked from his beak in a hiss.

The words chilled the backs of Almond's arms, and they erupted in aphidbumps. She forced herself to walk away at a leisurely pace, letting her wings rest. No way would she let him see her rattled.

The stone wall was closer than she thought, and she set off in search of Nutsie. She had assumed that her new friend would wait for her at the base of the stones, but she was alone. Wandering along the wall, she occasionally checked behind her for bluebirds, certain that she would stumble across the podgy chipmunk. She cocked her pointed ear, straining to pick up a *chip chip*.

Almond walked until her legs wobbled. She stopped to slurp some old rainwater from a cowslip cup, and then slumped against the base of the wall, her chin in her hands. Should she keep looking for Nutsie or head for the stream?

The shadows along the forest floor were long and she had far to go. The extent of her exhaustion overcame her after foraging duty the previous night, being inadvertently kidnapped by a chickadee, helping Nutsie down the tree, fighting Boscoe, and walking aside the stone wall. Arcs of dirt caked under her fingernails, and she grimaced, feeling a viscous combination of sweat, pollen, and sap when she rubbed her arms.

She itched.

Longing for a bath in the clear stream, she knew she wouldn't make it there before dark. She hauled herself up and plucked a cowslip blossom, careful not to spill the rainwater from its bell. Delirious with fatigue, she rinsed herself before climbing into a fold of leaves and was asleep before she closed her eyes.

CHAPTER 4

Something soft yet bony wrapped around Almond's arm and shook it. With a gulp, she sat up and yanked her arm free. She was groggy, still in a terrifying dreamscape of bluebirds, chickadees, and the Rosepurse peacock—tossing her in the air like a toy and plucking off her wings with razor sharp beaks.

"Hush," said Nutsie, grunting as she grappled with the startled fairy. "You're having a bad dream. It's me, Nutsie. Be quiet, will you?"

Almond relaxed her fists and looked up at the chipmunk like a lost child. Then, she threw her arms around Nutsie's neck and buried her face in a pillow of soft fur.

Nutsie patted her back. "There, there. You're not alone." She gently held Almond's shoulders and pulled her back to look in her face. "Not that you need me. You were magnificent the way you handled that beast, Boscoe. I've never been so happy." She crushed Almond in another embrace.

"Where were you?" Almond allowed herself to be led to the base of the human wall. Last night, it had looked cold and dark, but in the morning light, mustardy egg yolk lichen brightened the dowdy stone.

"I looked for you for a long time before night came."

Nutsie nodded. "I waited for you at the base of the wall, like you said. When I saw you trap Boscoe, I scampered a little way down, in case he got free, but you never came."

"That's not true! I came straightaway and couldn't find you." Hurt crept into Almond's voice.

Nutsie continued: "And I waited until dark and never saw you."

Almond shook her head. She risked her life for this chipmunk—twice! How could she think Almond would abandon her at the last minute? It wasn't fair.

Nutsie held up her paw. "Relax. It turns out that we never saw each other because I accidentally ran down the far side of the wall and didn't realize it."

Almond's mouth formed a circle as understanding dawned on her. "We were walking next to each other all along? Just on opposite sides of the wall?" Laughter burst from her throat like a dam breaking. It was like she had been holding her breath for days and could finally exhale. She leaned her hand against the stones and then jumped back, clapping away lichen scales. "Yuck." She pursed her lips, thinking. "How did you find me?"

"I found a place to sleep—wait until you see it—and when light came, I backtracked along the wall to look for you. I thought I'd have to go all the way to the end in order to come around to this side. That's when I found this." Nutsie stepped aside to reveal a hole bored through the stones of the wall—possibly the work of generations of vigorous earthworms.

"You squeezed through that?" Almond gave the narrow tunnel a critical look. She hated enclosed spaces, as the episode in the chickadee's nesting material had made apparent. The tight, moist tunnel made her skin crawl.

Nutsie huffed. "Yes, I fit through! Go on." She nudged Almond with her nose.

"What for? Let's just stay on this side of the wall and follow it to the stream. The way looks clear enough." Her voice trailed off as she peered down the line of stones into thick mist.

Nutsie nudged her again. "Trust me, you want to see what's on the other side. Plus, I don't like this side—Boscoe could still find us."

Almond shivered at the thought and dropped to her hands and knees, tucking her wings close. She didn't like the look of the rough stone. But dawning light shone at the other end, so she crawled in. Nutsie followed, rippling the fur on her loose skin to creep forward.

Once inside, the tunnel wasn't as narrow as it looked. But nubs of wet rock brushed Almond's wings—so cold that they switched elements and felt like embers. Down the length of the hole, she focused on a firefly wrapping up his nighttime carousing, light winking as he disappeared into a collection of tall grasses. Reaching the end, Almond popped out and stretched, gulping air.

She planted her feet and closed her eyes, probing for danger. Peaceful daybreak surrounded them. She lifted her eyelids and stood next to Nutsie—their backs to the wall—scanning the area. Daylight creatures trundled from their nests. A line of ants at the far end of the clearing shook sleep from their antennae. Songbirds accompanied the dawn from high in the trees.

The view on this side of the wall was nearly identical to the other, except for a shining, white structure rising from the clover and violets, its back flush with the stone wall. A willow tree bent like a dancer and dangled its branches overhead. Its leaves filtered a gauzy atmosphere that gave the clearly foreign structure a sense of belonging to that spot—as if its placement had been carefully planned and executed. Almond's feet carried her toward it as she admired its clean, square lines—so contrary to the surrounding tumbled stones and beading dew.

She faced the front of the structure, a fuzz of loose pollen scratching her ankles. With the bridge of one foot, she scratched the back of her calf while gazing at the snowy rectangle before her. Two rows of smaller rectangles dissected it, forming manageable rooms like tidy nests. It was a dollhouse—set against the wall by some human and forgotten.

Nutsie scampered into one of the lower rooms and kicked a fresh pile of willow leaves into a corner. "Isn't this great?" She spread her paws wide and spun in place. "I slept here last night, and it was warm and dry."

Almond craned her neck to see the whole of the edifice without moving away from it. Overhanging rock polypody ferns crowned the structure. They sprouted from between the stones of the wall and shaded the front of the dollhouse like a royal canopy. She imagined a queen nesting here, high above the mud—someone like her sister, Pepper.

It was out of a dream: solid as a boulder but pristine as a cloud and the most beautiful thing Almond had ever seen.

The rows of rooms reminded her of the cells of a giant honeycomb. She unfurled her wings to explore them and drifted from the forest floor, rubbing the soles of her feet together to shake off the grit. Openings between the rooms allowed passage through them without having to exit the building's open face. The dollhouse's framework was smooth to her touch, almost slippery, and mostly dry despite the morning dew that softened the rest of the world into a damp sponge.

She ran satisfied fingers along the impossibly straight, almost sharp lines of one of the middle rooms on the top floor. There were no bumps or warts. Nothing oozed or splattered under her hand or crouched in a puddle of slime in the deep corners.

A small amount of dirt had carried in on a breeze and gathered, but she easily swiped it away from the smooth material, leaving it absurdly clean. Almond leaned her head over the edge to look down at Nutsie. "What is this place? What is it made of?"

"I don't know, but it feels like it's been waiting for us." Nutsie hoisted herself up to sit next to Almond, legs dangling over the edge. "The insects seem to avoid it—no food in here for them, I suppose." She inhaled deeply. "But I don't smell anything toxic. I feel safe."

"It's glorious," said Almond, leaning back to look at the stark ceiling. "There is nothing icky, nothing stinging, nothing gross!" She sat up. "Did Boscoe get us, after all? Is this the Spirit Meadow?"

Nutsie tweaked Almond's wing.

"Ow! Why did you do that?" Almond cradled her wingtip and scowled at the chipmunk.

Nutsie laughed. "You wouldn't have felt that if we were in the Spirit Meadow. It's just clean. I knew you'd love it. Do you want this nest, or do you want to explore the others?"

Almond stared at her. What did Nutsie mean? She had to get back to the Fairy Nook. In fact, she was probably already deeply in trouble for not returning with a sack brimming with berries. She smacked her forehead. *The sack!* It was probably part of the chickadee nest by now. And no one was going to believe this story. She was doubly in trouble.

"I think I'll move into a corner space up here on the second floor," said Nutsie. "It was dark when I found the dollhouse last night—I bumped right into the side. And I just stumbled into the closest room. But I like the view up here." She grabbed Almond's wrist and pulled her up. "Look, each nest is a different size. One could even be a storeroom, where we keep the seeds and berries that we gather."

Envy crept up on Almond like a cat as she followed the chattering chipmunk through the openings between rooms. She coveted where Nutsie pointed out a larger space that could be used as a parlor, and a low, triangular space below the eaves of the house that could be a bolthole in case of danger. *You can live here, too, and make plans for the space,* whispering voices breathed into her thoughts.

Almond couldn't open her eyelids wide enough to take it all in. Sorrow dragged at her chest when she thought of the sticky length of ivy that was her quarters in the Fairy Nook. Her head felt like it floated above her body as she wondered how she would cope with going back after discovering this Xanadu. "It's so...perfectly clean," she said.

"Wait until you see this." Nutsie scampered through two doorways to the far side of the house and hooked her paw on the outer wall to lean far out into space. With her free paw, she pointed. Almond fluttered after her and hovered in the air, following her paw finger.

The source of a soothing, tinkling sound that Almond realized had been in the background the entire time revealed itself to be a gentle trickle of accumulated dew. It flowed between the ancient stones of the wall into a wide, shallow ceramic bowl—another human artifact— squatting on a flat boulder like a plinth next to the dollhouse. The steady stream filled the bowl and dribbled water over its edges so that the liquid inside remained clear and clean. Almond noticed that where Nutsie's fur had been matted and grubby, it now lay against her body, smooth and glossy.

"Did you have a bath?" she asked.

The chipmunk preened. "It feels delicious. Quickly, I'll keep watch while you take a turn."

Almond rushed to the edge of the bowl, alighting on its brim, and let the flowing water tickle the backs of her legs. She plunged her toes into the bowl and marveled at the pool of dirt, pollen, sap, and slime that spread around her as she slid her body into the water. The gunk was quickly swept over the edge of the bowl as fresh water flowed from above.

When Almond emerged from her bath, Nutsie jaw dropped. "Your wings...they're like rainbows."

Almond pulled them around her to see and was shocked at how they gleamed without a layer of debris coating them. It had been too long since her last shower. They were iridescent as dragonfly wings, and she understood why those insects congregated around pools. "I feel gorgeous," she cried, spinning in the air to shake herself dry.

"Me too!" Nutsie gamboled in a circle and stopped in front of Almond, hugging herself. "I never imagined that life could be so wonderful. Thank you for getting me away from Boscoe. You've made my life worth living."

Almond flushed, feeling pride and wonder—possibly for the first time in her life. She marveled at the steadfast dollhouse, agleam under the willow branches.

"Look over here," said Nutsie, drawing her attention to a twisting vine burrowing through the stones and surrounding the flat rock and pool. Nutsie reached between the leaves shaped like scalloped kites, pulling out a fat, glistening berry. "Blackberries!" She took a huge bite, bursting its taut drupelets, and chittered as purple juice ran down her chin. "Now I need another bath."

Laughter erupted from Almond's throat—warm and tingly. She rushed to pluck a berry and plunged her finger in, cleanly piercing a drupelet, and suckled the juice without spilling. She repeated the process until the entire blackberry was deflated and her belly full.

Nutsie swiped the back of her paw across her mouth and scampered back to the water bowl for another rinse. She shook herself dry and led Almond back into the house, slumping against a pristine wall. "After searching for you, I could use another sleep. How about a nap before we kit out our nests?"

Almond stared at the blank walls, mesmerized. In her most vivid dreams of a spotless world, nothing came close to being this perfect. Picturing herself in the largest of the top floor nests, she imagined washing a pad of thick moss for a mattress, setting it atop the wall to dry in the sun. Only then would she use it to furnish her nest. She would line one side of the room with walnut shells to use as bins to keep her things tidy.

I can't let myself think this way—I know that I can't stay here. The Nook will be searching for me by now. Sorrow pierced her heart.

Next to the trunk of the willow tree, a patch of plum-colored violets sprang from the ground. She imagined hanging the blooms from her ceiling for decoration, but only on the outside so that dried petals wouldn't litter her floor. Her reverie was shattered by Nutsie's snores bleating from her willow leaf poof. Almond shook the chipmunk's shoulder, but she only curled more tightly into a furry ball.

Shrugging, she snuggled into Nutsie's newly washed fur, warm and comfortable. Almond was in no hurry to get dirty again with a long journey home. Being clean felt too glorious. And her belly was perfectly full of nourishing blackberry juice. *I'll set off for the Nook in a little while. A bit more time won't matter,* she thought, allowing her eyelids to droop.

"I can't stay here." Almond paced the large, ground floor room that they called the parlor. She had woken from her nap that afternoon like a cloud bobbing on the breeze. But then the dread of having to leave washed over her. "I have to get back to the Fairy Nook."

Nutsie sat up from her willow nest and stretched her paws wide. She yawned and the auburn fur around her mouth bristled. "What do you think is happening there? Do you reckon the other fairies are looking for you?"

Almond looked at her twice, shocked by the question. "Of course! Of course, they are. I've never been away from home this long. Someone must be worried." She trailed off, uncertain.

The last time she'd been in the Nook, the King's guards were carting most of her foraging squad to the pebble pit. And no fairy had stood up for her when Pepper sent her into the forest in the dangerous daylight. She gazed at the willow tree that embraced their little clearing. The sun was still high, yet it proved no more dangerous than at night.

Almond thought about the lessons she had learned at Fairy School that were now proving untrue: that fairy wings couldn't fly above the treetops; that daylight increased the danger in Rosepurse Wood. What other lies had she been told?

"No one looked for me when I was lost," said Nutsie.

Almond faced the chipmunk. "You don't know that. I'll bet your family searched for you."

Nutsie shrugged. "Maybe so, but no one kept me safe."

Almond felt the weight of Nutsie's words and wanted to fling her arms around the lonely chipmunk, covering her with her wings. "I guess that's true. But I'll keep you safe, Nutsie."

"How? When you're not staying?"

Almond gulped. "It's just that fairies can't leave the Nook without permission from the royal legacy. They might think I left on purpose. I might be in big trouble."

Silence marked the moments that passed.

"You could still come with me," said Almond. "That was sort of our plan from the start, wasn't it?"

"Do you really think the fairies would welcome me? I don't know how to do anything."

Almond wished that she could assure Nutsie that the Nook fairies would take her in as one of their own and train her in their ways. But she didn't even know what she believed about the Nook anymore. All she had to go on was a dread deep in her bones that she was the focus of intense fairy scrutiny.

Nutsie kept her face turned away. "It's just that I really love it here. And I know you do, too."

Almond glanced around the empty dollhouse, picturing how she would decorate it. Maybe she couldn't enjoy it, but Nutsie would. "Look, I feel terrible about leaving you after all we've been through, so how about I help you kit out this fabulous palace before I go?"

Nutsie swept the floor with her paw toes, not meeting her gaze.

Almond flitted to the violet patch and filled her arms with blossoms. "Look at these, Nutsie, they'll make your nest beautiful and smell amazing. Which one did you say you wanted? The top right corner?" She settled on the lip of the room and wove a streamer of flowers to hang from Nutsie's ceiling.

"Those are lovely," said Nutsie, sniffling. "I'd love your help, thank you." She scurried to her pile of willow leaves and hauled them up to her new room. "But what will happen to you, if the other fairies really think you ran away?"

Almond fluttered down from hanging the streamer and settled next to Nutsie. "I don't know of anyone who left, but they taught us in Fairy School that running away was forbidden. I've been thinking. I don't actually know if anyone is looking for me. I'm not really a popular fairy anymore. One more day with you in our dream home won't make a difference to anyone."

"Except me," said Nutsie.

Almond smiled. "What we need are some empty walnut shells to hold your things."

As the afternoon deepened, they stood in Nutsie's new nest, admiring their work. Dotted thyme moss carpeted her floor and tiny trout lilies in colors like the sun draped her walls. Almond had cleared out Nutsie's bedding of wilting willow leaves and replaced them with tidy pillows of mountain laurel blossoms, their shallow, white cups bursting with pink-tipped stamen holding found bunny fluff.

Near the pillows stood half of a deep walnut shell filled to the brim with seeds. The other half sat between Almond and Nutsie, piled with blackberries.

"It's beautiful—I love it," said Nutsie. Purple juice stained her arm fur up to her elbows.

"It is perfect," said Almond, leaning back with a sigh. "Tomorrow, we'll do the parlor."

Nutsie leaned against her own pillow and stared across the dollhouse's lawn at aster and goldenrod mingling in a shaft of waning sunlight. "What's it like to have a family?"

Almond shrugged. "My parents have traveled on."

Nutsie frowned. "To the Spirit Meadow?" Her voice was cautious.

"No, just up to the gourd huts at the top of the great yew tree. That's where fairies go to live when they grow old and their wings fall off." Seeing Nutsie's alarmed look, Almond hurried to say: "They're safe up there, but I only get to see them when I'm on Gourd Huts duty. We take turns bringing them supplies and sweeping out the huts while telling them tales of the Nook."

"How often do you do that?"

"Every first quarter moon," said Almond. "But they mostly just lay there."

Nutsie busied herself with a patch of rump fur, the pairs of black and white stripes on either side of her back rippling. "Do you have litter mates?"

Almond shook her head, curls bouncing around her shoulders like lavender sea foam. "Fairies hatch from eggs. I suppose some of my siblings hatched at the same time as me, but I was focused on figuring out my wings right away." Her laugh tinkled. "I'm not even sure if I know who all of my siblings are."

"Aren't you close with anyone?" asked Nutsie.

Almond cast a dark look at the floor. "Not really. Every day, we have a duty to fulfill. It's a lot of work and there's not much time for socializing." She hesitated, not sure if she wanted to examine a thorny problem. "My sister, Pepper..."

"Are you and Pepper close?"

Almond shook her head. "She's from a subsequent nest of eggs, but we were at Fairy School together. I gave her a hard time there." Her shoulders slumped. "She's our new queen."

"Queen? What does that make you?" asked Nutsie.

"I don't know yet. I must return to the Nook and make things right with her or else she could have me mucking out hummingbird stalls until my wings fall off."

"Your own sister would do that?" *Chip chip.*

Almond's gaze traced the sweeping willow branches. "Fairies are cold-hearted creatures."

"You're not," said Nutsie, offering her another berry.

Almond took it and shrugged one shoulder. "Maybe I've always wanted a warmer community." She yawned. "But the Nook is my home. In fact, I would be smart to start my journey at daybreak."

"But you said tomorrow we'd decorate the parlor!" Nutsie sat upright and placed her paws on her hips.

"Nutsie! I just helped you so much. Can't you be grateful?" *And can't I change my mind?* thought Almond.

The chipmunk scrambled to her paws and glared at her. Almond jumped up and faced her. They stood staring at each other, breathing hard.

Then, Nutsie nodded. "You're right. And thank you for all of your help. It's just that I'm so excited to be free that I want to share it with someone."

Almond flung her arms wide. "I understand. I'd love to stay here and have fun with you in our new palace. But I can't."

Nutsie browsed along the walls of her newly decorated nest, taking in every detail. "But why? It's perfect here."

Almond's skin prickled. Why did Nutsie keep bringing this up? Of course she wanted to stay in this beautiful dollhouse. But she had no choice. She had to go home. "You're not listening to me. The Nook is complicated and there are consequences for misbehaving. You wouldn't understand."

"I understand that you're the only friend I've ever had, and I want you to stay," Nutsie wheedled.

This is getting insulting, thought Almond. *She doesn't appreciate anything that I've done for her. And she clearly doesn't care what happens to me. All she cares about is herself!* She stood and straightened her wings. "I should be with my own kind."

Nutsie's shoulders tensed, and she spun to face Almond. "I'm not with my own kind and I feel okay."

Almond scowled. "You've never been with anyone, Nutsie, so how would you know?"

The chipmunk's lower lip trembled. "Well, who wants you back at your Nook? You said yourself that you're not popular. That means the other fairies don't even like you."

The pointed tips of Almond's ears flushed a dangerous shade of sapphire. "If it wasn't for me, you would still be up that tree—all alone."

Tears gathered at the corners of Nutsie's eyes. "Well if it wasn't for me, Boscoe would have had you for a snack while you were asleep!"

Almond kicked a stray acorn cap across the room, and it skittered into a corner. "You don't know that."

Nutsie cringed at the clatter when the cap hit the wall. *Chip chip.*

"Well, you don't know that I would still be up the tree," she said, balling her paws.

Exasperation exploded out of Almond's mouth. "I've done enough for you, Nutsie!" She couldn't stop yelling, despite the devastated look on Nutsie's face. "You can't expect me to keep taking care of you just because we escaped from a crazy bluebird together. I have to go home."

"Then go!"

Before she had time to make a plan, Almond flexed her shoulder blades, unfurled her wings, and zoomed toward the rushing stream. She knew without looking that Nutsie was gaping at her retreating form, but she didn't care. *That dumb chipmunk is not my problem. I can't even take care of myself—how can I be responsible for anyone else?*

She flew through the forest, absorbed in her own tempest, following the stream's beckoning burble. *Nutsie wouldn't care if I lost my Berry Moon privileges or got reassigned as Pepper's servant!* She nearly choked on that thought and shimmered with anger.

Her outrage gave her a boost of energy and she flashed between shades of light that found its way through the dim tree canopy. If she kept up this pace, maybe she'd reach the stream by nightfall and would only need to spend one more night away from the security of the Nook.

"Ugh!" A second too late to turn away, Almond rushed into a dusty, abandoned cobweb. She broke free of the tacky mire, but it stuck to her wingtips. *Disgusting!* she thought.

Spiraling to the ground, she flicked her wings to rid them of the filthy detritus stuck to her. Without looking, she landed on a pile of pebbles, slimy with mold. They tumbled beneath her toes, and she fell on her rump, sliding with the gravelly torrent. She was powerless, except for tucking her wings as tightly against her back as the clumps of cobweb allowed. The tumble dumped her into a mud puddle that had dried and thickened into viscous paste.

Her foot sunk into the goop, which held it and sucked her in as far as her ankle. Panting, Almond struggled to keep her wings above the muck and grabbed a flimsy root that tiptoed over the edge of the puddle. Her arm scraped along the fibrous root, but she was able to grab the end before it slid out of her reach. Sweat beaded on her brow.

She couldn't call for help. Hungry predators could be nearby, waiting for a juicy fairy to be trapped in the mud. Or for a plump chipmunk to come save her. Scowling, she wrapped the root tip around her hand.

Stretching her free leg behind her, she pointed her toe upward like a dancer, trying to reach the rim of the puddle. Her toe hooked it, and she arched her back to slide her foot farther along solid ground. Her ankle touched turf, and she let out her breath.

Using the edge of the puddle to leverage her body, Almond yanked her stuck foot, trying to free herself. She clung to the pale root, but it slipped in its earthen bed, pulling farther over the mud. Almond's free leg slipped from the edge of the crater as her stuck foot sank deeper, capturing her firmly up to her knee.

She was in too deep to swing her free foot back up to the rim and the rough root pulled at the delicate skin between her fingers. Almond's muscles trembled. If she couldn't hold on, or if her wings got muddy, she would never break free.

Gripping the slipping root, she scanned the ground—now at eye level—for anything useful. A scattering of buckled and timid dewberry petals reminded her how much she hated getting her wings muddy—it made them feel warped and fragile.

Almond's root disengaged further from the soft earth. The last thing she saw before she slipped beneath the rim of the puddle was a green caterpillar reclining under the shade of a mayapple blossom. A red azalea perched, upside down, on his head like a jaunty trilby. Motionless, he held a hot pink trumpet honeysuckle blossom to his mouth, watching her struggle.

CHAPTER 6

Pepper pulled her navel toward her spine and threw her lime shoulders back, ramrod posture displaying the new tiara crowning her sleek, cerulean hair. The laurel leaves tickled the pointed tips of her ears, but she didn't flinch. No display of weakness would be tolerated—especially not in herself if she was going to take over the Nook completely.

She savored the moment. The thought of her status had been driving her since her first year at Fairy School and she had taken carefully planned steps to elevate herself ever since. The last stupid thing she ever did was believe that her big sister, Almond, would allow her into her group of friends when she started school. Pepper hadn't been interested in wasting time with fairies her own age. Why hang with Freshmen when she had access to Seniors?

But that didn't happen. Almond had acted shocked when Pepper first approached her, as if she didn't know her. But they were from the same legacy! Never mind that their eggs had hatched years apart.

Pepper's lip curled at the memory. She had been a fool to chase after them. They lost all respect for her and treated her like a joke. Once

she woke up and realized that they would never accept her, she spun plans and schemes to make sure that no one ever disrespected her again.

Alone, Pepper adjusted her satchel over her freshly washed shift and approached Fairy School for the first time. She scanned the crowd of pips flowing toward the entrance for her older sister, Almond. They were the closest in age of their siblings since every other egg in Pepper's clutch had mysteriously been crushed before they hatched. She had broken through her own eggshell after the tragedy happened, as she'd told their mother, who never laid eggs again. Pepper smirked. She was possibly the closest fairy the Nook had to an only child.

The front doors to the school loomed as she approached. She cast about for her sister, still hoping to enter school riding a crest of glory by showing up on her first day with a Senior. *There she is.* Pepper shouldered across the crowd to get to Almond, who sat atop a low branch laughing with her best friends.

She took in Almond's thick lavender curls which fell perfectly against her athletic figure—the envy of every fairy girl Pepper knew. Almond's periwinkle legs twined over the branch, graceful and shapely. Pepper tugged at her own shift, which strained against her curves that had come too early. She hurried toward Almond's laugh tinkling across the quad.

"Are we ready for the first day of school?" she asked, squeezing between Apricot, the prettiest fairy in school and thought to be top choice for the next Fairy Queen, and Amaryllis, captain of the aerialist team.

Almond glowered down at her from her perch on the branch, silent.

Pepper glanced around at the other girls. They stared at the tips of their noses, haughty, ignoring her question.

"Almond? You must not recognize your own sister. I'm all grown up," said Pepper, smoothing her sleek azure locks. She looked at Apricot, then Amaryllis, Cherry, and Paprika, searching for a glimmer of friendship.

The fairies observed Almond, waiting for her cue. She would decide how they would all respond. Her big sister would choose

Pepper's fate for the rest of the school year: popular or...not.

She held her breath, willing Almond to acknowledge her as part of the group, as her sister—anything. *Come on, you snot-nosed troll,* she thought, gaze boring into Almond's and holding it. *Just give me a smile. That's all I need.*

Almond stared back at her with an impassive face and then cut her eyes to her friends, exhaling an obnoxious, sputtering laugh. Laughing right in her face! The other fairies joined in, and their giggles rang across the quad, drawing everyone's attention.

Pepper's lips itched from holding them still, willing them not to tremble. Her response could still save this. She struggled to keep her voice light, but it stuck in her throat. For a terrible moment, tears gathered in the corners of her eyes.

Almond's friends weren't looking at her anyway as they gathered their satchels for school. Pepper stood rooted and mute while her sister fluttered from her branch and led her gaggle of friends into Fairy School—without her.

That toad of a sister will regret this, she thought. *Watch me steal her friends and then she'll be the one standing alone.*

Within three moons, every pip in her class followed Pepper around Fairy School like beetles. But it wasn't enough. Her only objective was popularity with the Senior fairies. Almond's friends ignored her despite all of her tricks. She tried gifts, flattery, feats of daring, and sparkled her eyes at the Senior boys, but the fairies she looked up to only treated her like a patch of mildew. They made fun of her, undermining her self-esteem, and played cruel tricks on her. Worse, they remained loyal to Almond.

Why was she chasing after them? What was she trying to achieve?

What do I actually want? she asked herself during lunch as she perched on a toadstool in the quad. A fellow Freshman pip fluttered to her, handing her a cloudberry. Pepper accepted it like a princess on a throne. *No, like a queen,* she thought, grinning. *That's it. I'm going to be the next Fairy Queen. Now I just need a plan.*

Pepper crouched in the moonlight beneath the foxglove shrub. It was her second time outside of the Nook. The first had been two days ago when she had followed the hedgie witch here to see where she lived. She'd been picking violet blossoms on the edge of the Nook behind the school when she'd spotted the prickly medicine woman trundle by. In a flash, she had the answer to her conundrum for the past few weeks—how to get the future Fairy King to notice her over all of the beautiful older fairies during his speech at Fairy School.

She'd already decided that the fulcrum of her ascension to the throne would be the upcoming school visit by Prince Cornsilk. A member of the royal legacy spoke at Fairy School every year—usually a chance for pips to sneak extra nectar or take a nap. But this year, the entire school was eager to see the soon-to-be king. Pepper was eager for the future king to see her—and only her.

She peered through the gloom, hoping the hedgie witch was awake. Sweeping the area, she saw that nothing hid in the shadows, waiting to snatch her with deadly jaws. Using her wings, she rose from the ground and zipped to the hedgehog's door.

"Who's there?" The hedgie witch's voice rasped from the other side when Pepper knocked.

"Let me in," she whispered. "I'm a fairy."

The door rattled and swung inward. The hedgehog reached around it, grasping Pepper's shoulder, and yanked her inside. She looked the fairy up and down, her quills rippling. Giving her a sniff, the hedgie witch sat up and shook her head. "You're too young to be out. You can't protect yourself."

"Don't bet on it," said Pepper. "I need a love potion, quickly."

The hedgie witch snorted. "Fairy tales. There's no such thing."

Pepper reached into her satchel and withdrew a packet. "I don't have time for games, hedgie witch. You're right. I shouldn't be out of bed, so let's make this a fast transaction." She opened the packet and unfurled a long opalescent sheaf that crinkled like paper. A prism of colors shot through it.

The hedgehog drew back. "A dried fairy wing? It is forbidden."

"Don't be coy," said Pepper. "You know you want it. Think of all the spells you'll spin with its fibers."

The hedgie witch shook her head.

Pepper edged the desiccated wing under the hedgehog's nose. "No one will miss it," she whispered. "No one saw me steal it. There are many old fairies losing their wings this moon."

The hedgie witch's paw crept out to finger the fine fibers. She peered at Pepper and pointed her gnarled paw at her. "You are a bad fairy. But you're right. I do want the wing." She padded to a chest of drawers and drew out a small gourd. "This is the closest thing to love potion that you'll find. Spread it on yourself precisely before you encounter the fairy you want. They will be yours."

Pepper took the gourd and sniffed it. "What is it?"

"Fairy pheromones. It will make whoever smells it want to mate—with you. Are you sure that's what you want, young one?"

Pepper nodded. "Don't worry about me, witch." She fluttered out of the door into the darkness without looking back.

Pepper brimmed with confidence as she pushed past the older fairies on the day of Prince Cornsilk's speech. She positioned herself close to the stage in front of Apricot, the gorgeous fairy gaping at her. *Not so smug that the prince will choose you, Apricot?* she thought, indulging in a private smile. She patted the satchel at her hip containing the gourd full of love potion—her guarantee that she would someday be the Fairy Queen.

A ladybug tapped her mallet halfheartedly across the shell of a snail grazing on dried grass, signaling that the prince was taking the stage.

Apricot tapped on her shoulder, her pointed nail digging into Pepper's lime skin and leaving a forest green mark. She ignored the Senior, laser focused on the prince stepping in front of the audience. Even though he was barely older than her, he wasn't nervous—which she respected—and immediately opened his mouth to address the school.

Pepper had decided not to risk dousing herself with the hedgie witch's love potion while she was around male students and teachers. There was no telling how intense their reaction might be. Now that she was up front with the prince only three acorns away, she removed the gourd from her satchel and tipped it down her chest. She rubbed it into her neck, under her arms, and between her legs, never looking away from him. A heady floral aroma filled her nose. Then a rolling wave of flower scents washed over her. First tuberose, then lilac, peony, and honeysuckle—she loved honeysuckle.

Softness fuzzed the edges of her vision, and the rays of sunlight through the windows sparkled golden with rainbow flecks. Her chest swelled, lifting her bosom. The lines of muscle along her arms and legs hardened, taut and waiting. The other fairies in the audience surrounded her with waves of flowing hair. Cornsilk's own mahogany curls glowed around the edges as if a dawn ray erupted behind him. In Pepper's eyes, he was chiseled and noble.

Cornsilk, mouth open to begin his speech, remained silent and stared into the middle distance. Pepper watched his pupils dilate. His eyes momentarily glowed royal blue and his gaze jerked across the audience with frantic movements until it landed on her. She beamed a dazzling smile at him, fully prepared to meet him.

The murmuring behind her fell away as she felt the power of nature surge through her. Here she was, commanding the attention of a future king. *Almond is about to be sorry she messed with me,* she thought.

"Beechnut," said Queen Pepper from her toadstool throne. The peacock tail featherlette gleamed at her throat.

The Knight of the Nook stepped forward, looming and stoic. He did not display the customary subservience to a ruler by averting his gaze from Pepper's. "Yes?" he asked, staring at the middle of her forehead.

Pepper ignored his insolence, mesmerized by his eyes that glowed like green opals. "You are aware that my sister, Almond, has defected from the Nook," she said.

Beechnut nodded once.

"While I have enjoyed her absence, the other fairies noticed that she has escaped consequences for going rogue," she said.

Beechnut opened his mouth, but Pepper continued before he could speak: "Because of this, there has been an uptick in slovenly behavior. Other fairies are acting like Almond—lazy and selfish. They think they can get away with it since she did. I cannot allow it."

Beechnut bit the inside of his cheek, waiting a beat before speaking in case Pepper wasn't finished. She was a long-winded fairy, fond of her own voice. He wondered at the wisdom of Cornsilk giving power to one so young and...mean. "How may I be of service?"

Pepper's smile was sly. "Find Almond, and bring her back to face her consequences, of course. We'll make an example out of her in front of the entire Nook. When we're done with her, no fairy will ever disobey me again."

Beechnut curled his lip. He, the Knight of the Nook, carrying out sorority vengeance like a pip—his wings quivered with rage. Before he spoke, he stilled his breathing. This new queenlette was objectionable, but Beechnut was loyal to the Nook. "Of course." He forced himself to incline his head to Pepper and turned to go pack his gear.

Pepper eyed his rippling iridescent wings as he retreated. A pair of ladybugs settled on either side of her toadstool. She languidly caressed their heads, focused on the middle space before her, and then abruptly slapped their antennae. "Follow him," she commanded.

CHAPTER 7

"Help me!" Almond's sweaty fingers slipped farther down the useless root, and her free foot sank into the thick mud.

The grass green caterpillar startled, as if surprised Almond could speak. He dropped his honeysuckle blossom, and the bottom half of his plump body undulated, the foot nubs gathering force to propel his bulk along the forest floor. Once he got going, Almond was surprised and relieved at the speed at which he arrived at the edge of the mud puddle.

"Blunderman, at your service," said the caterpillar, with a head bob. "Er, aren't you magical? Fairies, I mean. Can't you just magic your way out of your predicament?"

Sweat ran into Almond's eyes. "No...that's just a...tale. Please! I'm slipping."

The caterpillar chuckled. "A fairy tale?"

The mud sucked at Almond's leg, cold and ugly as old possum scat. She clung to her root stub—itself repulsive with creeping hairs and clots of muck—and wished that she were nestled in a bed of freshly washed moss, safe at Nutsie's dollhouse. When she returned to the Fairy Nook, her bit of ivy would be as clammy and slick as the day she left.

Her hands slipped to the furred tip of the root. "Do something!" *What is wrong with this caterpillar? I'm going to drown!* "Hurry, find a stick," she urged the creature. A sloppy piece of turf broke off and her root tumbled into the mud.

Almond turned her face away from the repulsive cake of goo, bracing herself to be sucked in. It reached up and wrapped around her waist to pull her into its lair of secrets. "Where did you come from?" she asked when she came face-to-face with Blunderman.

"Just a moment," said the caterpillar, whose back half was still on level ground, while his front half had traveled down the side of the mud hole.

Almond realized that the belt around her waist was actually Blunderman's plump caterpillar arms pulling her up. Her slow ascent from the hole stopped when the mud refused to give up her stuck leg. Blunderman gave a tug hard enough to pop her leg out of her hip. "Thank you—ow! Mind the wings."

"Sorry." Blunderman grunted. "Just another...tug. There we go."

Almond's foot emerged with an obscene sucking sound and she bungeed out of the hole, landing on the prone caterpillar. She sat up and rubbed dirt from her elbows.

Wobbling, Blunderman rose and nodded. "Are you alright?"

Her lips trembled. She peeked over her shoulder at the mud hole that almost pulled her underground for good. Hot, salty tears spilled from the corners of her eyes, leaving tracks on her filthy cheeks. She put her head in her hands. "I almost died." Her voice was muffled, and her shoulders shook.

When her tears ran out, she lifted her face to the caterpillar. "You saved my life!" She wiped her tears on the back of her hand and hopped to her feet, flinging herself at him. He chuckled and she backed up, embarrassed by her display of emotion. She swiped her tiny foot through the grass, trying to remove the sticky mud. "Thank you so much. Sorry about using you for a landing cushion."

"No harm done," said Blunderman.

Almond checked the light in the sky. "I'll never make it to the stream before dark. I better find a safe place to nest." *Do I really want to go back to the Fairy Nook?* She pushed the thought away.

"I'm partial to underneath that sturdy leaf over there," said Blunderman. "You are welcome to share it."

"You are very kind. Maybe I'll have a look—hey what's this?"

Under a shrub near the mud puddle lay a package as long as the caterpillar wrapped in red striped flax cloth. It was secured by a round, black button.

"That looks human," said Blunderman.

"Sure does," said Almond. "Let's see what's inside." She lifted one corner of the packet's buttonhole and slid it over the ebony button.

The striped cloth fell open, revealing two sewing needles stuck through a flap of jute and a silver thimble. One of the needles had its eye still threaded with thick twine. To Almond, the twine was as sturdy as vine.

"It's a sewing kit," said Blunderman. "Part of one, anyway. Humans carry them to mend things while on the move. I once had a spool of thread that I used as a cafe table. This kit doesn't have that."

Almond drew a needle from its cotton sheath and held it aloft like a sword. "This beats a sharp twig any day."

Blunderman undulated backward. "I'll say. Careful, don't slash that thing around like that. You do know that you're bleeding, don't you?"

Almond stopped swaggering and checked her arms, then her legs. An angry scrape gaped on her left leg, dribbling rivulets of bright orange fairy blood that ran into the dried mud on her foot. It was sure to become infected if she didn't clean it out right away. She stuck the needle back into its cloth packet. "Blunderman, this treasure is ours to share, so let's take it to my...a nest I know of, and I can attend to my wound."

"Delighted," he said, cocking his crimson azalea over his brow.

"Almond!" Nutsie scampered from her nest in the dollhouse and squeezed the fairy in an embrace. "You're hurt."

"Mmph," said Almond, her voice muffled by Nutsie's fur. She let the sewing kit tumble to the ground and struggled to extract herself.

"Sorry." Nutsie released her and bent to inspect the coagulated orange blood on her leg. "This needs to be cleaned."

Two brown beetles with apple-red faces trailed Nutsie from the house.

"Hello," said Almond. "Who are you?"

At the same time, Nutsie saw Blunderman and asked: "Who's that?"

"This is Blunderman," said Almond.

The caterpillar doffed his azalea hat and bowed his head to Nutsie.

"I almost died and he saved me," said Almond. She jerked her thumb at the beetles. "What about them?"

Nutsie swept her arm to include the two silent bugs. "Meet Aksel and Bo. They stopped to rest, and I invited them to stay as long as they like."

"It didn't take you long to replace me," said Almond with a sulky lip.

Nutsie rolled her eyes toward Blunderman, who had wandered away to inspect the blackberry bramble.

"He saved my life," Almond hissed. She pointed to the boots of dried clay that caked her feet, leftover from the deadly mud puddle. "And helped me get back here."

Nutsie eyed the clot of dried mud encasing the fairy's right foot. She picked up a pebble and tapped it against the casing until it crumbled, freeing Almond's foot before doing the same on the other one.

Almond bowed her head. "Thank you. I'm sorry, Nutsie. I've been a troll."

Nutsie scooped her up in another furry squeeze. "I'm sorry I pushed you away. Will you and..."

"Blunderman," said Almond.

"Will you both come inside?" asked Nutsie.

Almond threw herself on the chipmunk, returning the hug. She realized how alone she had been, trapped in the mud puddle. With a sick feeling, she discovered that as she had inched closer to a mucky doom, she never once longed for the Fairy Nook. At her most afraid moment, Almond wanted her friend, Nutsie.

"Here's what we have to do," said Almond, once they were settled in the dollhouse's sparsely furnished parlor. Three cotton pods lay on the floor like forlorn tumbleweeds. A flat stone served as a low table and held two empty acorn caps.

Nutsie's whiskers twitched, and she stared into the middle distance, stuffing seeds into her cheek pouches.

"Let's pitch in and get this place kitted out and then we can relax and enjoy it," said Almond. Dusk settled into the corners. She tilted her head as Aksel and Bo climbed into the two acorn caps. "Is that comfortable?" she asked the beetles. "There's plenty of room for you to sleep in your own nests."

"Give them a minute," said Nutsie, flapping her paw at Almond. As the light faded from the room, the beetles' derrieres popped on and cast a warm glow into the room, turning the acorn caps into lamps.

Almond gasped. "Fireflies!"

Nutsie nodded. "The fellas agreed to light the night for us while they're staying at the dollhouse. Isn't it spectacular?"

"Like sitting amongst the stars," Almond breathed.

"Excuse me."

Almond jumped. "Blunderman! I forgot you were outside."

The caterpillar peeked his head and first four arm nubs over the front ledge of the dollhouse. He tipped his azalea hat in greeting.

"Come inside and enjoy the lights," said Almond.

Blunderman undulated backward. "No, thank you. It is my time to be on the ground. I like it here and came to ask if I may set up my quarters in the blackberry bramble by the pool of water?"

"Of course," said Nutsie. "Make yourself comfortable." She leaned against a stray cotton pod, her cheeks bulging comically.

"I brought berries for supper." Blunderman handed the blackberries from nub to nub until they tumbled into the house and Almond gathered them, passing them around the table.

Nutsie sprang to the ground next to him and scampered around the corner of the dollhouse. She returned with a fresh pawpaw leaf, which she added to the three large blackberries on top of the make-shift table. Then she sat with her hind paws dangling over the edge of the dollhouse floor and handed him a corner of leaf. "Where is it that you're from, Blunderman?"

"I came from a meadow downstream from here," he said, chewing the leaf's edge and tipping his azalea hat to her in thanks. "It's a generally forgotten place where caterpillars have built a vast village known as Wriggler's Rest."

"How vast?" asked Almond.

"Stretching from Rosepurse Stream to a very large ash that marks the center of the meadow." Blunderman's deep eyes twinkled with pride. "It is a beautiful village, artfully crafted from the freshest foliage and reinforced with sun-dried hay. My grandmother designed the northern quadrant nearest the stream, herself. That is where my family home lies."

"How did you end up all the way up here?" asked Nutsie.

Blunderman's naturally mournful eyes became black pools of sorrow. "There was no place for me in Wriggler's Rest. You see, I like architecture, but it is not my passion like it is for the rest of my family. I prefer to craft sculptures rather than buildings."

"They made you leave?" asked Almond, her periwinkle hand rising to her throat as she remembered her own sister's words to her: *Why don't you find somewhere else to live?*

Blunderman swung his head back and forth. "No, of course not. But I tired of the arguments—they made it difficult to create my art. So, I crawled onto a leaf on the bank of the stream one day and pushed off. I didn't think much about it at the time—just did it. The journey was quite pleasant with the sun warming my body and a steady breeze sailing me upstream in my little vessel. But when I saw a knot of rocks in the stream grow closer, I leapt to shore."

"Good thing you did." Bo nodded. "Those rocks form treacherous rapids."

Blunderman inclined his head, still munching his leaf. "I watched my leaf capsize when it hit them. Then I meandered inland, following the line of our friend, the wall." He waved his front nubs at the stone barrier that protected the dollhouse and bramble pool from the rear.

"I made my way to the marsh of mud puddles, being careful to avoid their brims, when I encountered the most perfect creamy white honeysuckle blossom that I'd ever seen." He heaved a sigh and let his eyelids droop. "Inhaling its magical aroma, I thought I fell into a dream. Especially while observing this tempestuous fairy zoom straight into a cobweb." He turned to Almond. "I honestly didn't think you were real for a moment when you first fell into the mud puddle. Please forgive me for not acting immediately to save you." He bowed his head.

Almond's gaze widened. "Forgive you? Blunderman, you saved my life!" She threw her arms around the surprised caterpillar's squishy green body and squeezed. "I'll owe you forever and ever."

"*Oof.* No need for that." He gently pulled out of her grasp and looked around at his companions. "I'll do it again if necessary. For any of you. I am quite happy here."

Nutsie clutched her heart and beamed at Blunderman.

The fireflies bent low. "As we will for you, brother," said Aksel, and Bo nodded.

The caterpillar's green body flushed mauve. "Thank you, friends. Perhaps family isn't so far away, after all."

The following morning, Almond worried at her scraped leg as she hung dew-fresh spiderwebs across the parlor opening. The webs formed handy curtains that filtered the sunlight and kept the rooms cool. The cotton pod cushions were upgraded to mounds of found bunny fluff, and she plopped onto one to examine her wound.

"How does it look?" asked Nutsie. She had found the thimble in the sewing kit and placed it as a chair in the parlor. Moving it from place to place, she examined it with a critical eye.

"It hurts. I think it might be infected," said Almond.

Nutsie padded to Almond's side and put her face close to the scrape, sniffing. It was an angry orange and puffed up around the edges. Nutsie drew back. "Oh, I see. Follow me."

Almond fluttered after the scampering chipmunk. Nutsie led her from the parlor into the next room. It was on the house's ground floor where a room littered with things she had gathered from outside had turned into a storeroom. Flower clippings were tossed in one corner and a pile of nut shells teetered nearby.

Nutsie hopped over to one of the shells and sniffed it. "This is the one," she said, handing it to Almond.

Almond took the shell and grimaced. "Ugh! It's sticky." She dropped it and wiped her hand on her shift.

"Careful," said Nutsie. "I had to trade two paws-full of pollen to a very surly bee for that honey."

"Meeting the neighbors already?" Almond covered her wound with her hands.

Nutsie picked up the shell and plunged her paw into the amber gunk inside. "Come here."

Almond shook her head. "Nope."

Nutsie shrugged one shoulder. "This will heal your wound. Stop acting like a pup and come here or we'll just have to chop off your leg."

"Yeah, right." Almond shuffled toward Nutsie and groaned when the chipmunk smeared thick honey across her scraped leg. "So gross. Listen, Nutsie, I'm sorry for the way I spoke to you when we argued. No one deserves to be yelled at like that."

Nutsie plastered a strip of willow leaf over the honey and smiled. "I forgive you."

Almond stared at the pile of shells in the gloaming corner. "When I thought that I wasn't going to survive that mud puddle, I wanted to be here with you, not back at the Fairy Nook. I've decided to stay, if you don't mind."

Nutsie hopped on her back paws and scooped Almond into her arms, careful not to crush her wings. "Mind? I'm so happy to hear that my best friend in the whole forest is staying. We're going to have so much fun!"

Almond squirmed out of Nutsie's grasp and laughed. "We are absolutely going to have so much fun."

Nutsie spun around like a dancer. "And with Aksel and Bo, and your Mr. Blunderman, we nearly have a full house."

"I got the feeling that Aksel and Bo weren't staying for good," said Almond.

Nutsie shrugged. "I was thinking. We have so much space, maybe we could turn the dollhouse into an inn. The Dollhouse Inn."

Almond picked up one of the discarded flowers and inhaled its sweet scent. "What do you mean?"

"We should make it a safe place where anyone traveling by can stop and rest and enjoy charming company." Nutsie buffed her nails on her shoulder fur.

Almond brightened. "I love that idea. We'll kit out the house—the inn—with lots of places to visit, and to sleep."

"Pardon me," said Blunderman from outside the storeroom. He held a brown figurine in his front nubs like an offering. "I heard your conversation and thought you could use some artwork for the illustrious Dollhouse Inn."

"What do you have there, Blunderman?" Almond took the figurine and examined it from every angle. It was comprised of clay chunks cleverly fitted together to form the shape of a chipmunk.

"I love it," said Nutsie, clasping her paws together.

"This is wonderful, Blunderman. Are these pieces of clay from the mud that dried on my foot?" Almond shuddered, thinking of the blood.

Blunderman inclined his head. "I like to make good things from the bad."

"I know the perfect place for it." Almond carried the figurine into the parlor and set it on the thimble, as if on a plinth.

Aksel and Bo flew in front of the dollhouse, each trailing a papery strip. The strips fluttered to the ground as the fireflies landed, revealing long washes of rainbow colors along their lengths.

"What are those?" asked Nutsie.

"They are bark strips from a rainbow eucalyptus tree," said Aksel.

"We gathered them to use for rugs," said Bo.

"They're beautiful." Nutsie nosed closer to the narrow channels of red, green, and blue.

The fireflies guided one of the strips into the parlor and draped it across the floor. They flew the second rug into one of the small rooms upstairs, where they bedded down for their midday nap.

"I'm glad they're comfortable," said Nutsie. "If the rest of our guests are as helpful as they are, the Dollhouse Inn will run itself." She hoisted herself up to her top-floor nest, her hind legs cycling in the air before she heaved herself inside.

"There has to be an easier way for you to get up and down, Nutsie." Almond cast about the sun-dappled area in front of their new home. "Look over there. See those flat stones piled at the base of that tree? If we find the right sizes, we can build you a staircase."

Almond revved her wings into hyper-speed, and by the time she and Nutsie stacked the stones ascending to Nutsie's nest—with Blunderman lifting the high steps—Aksel and Bo flew out of their quarters in lazy circles. The fireflies immediately set off into the forest, collecting pinecones that they brought back to line a path leading to the parlor.

"What about you, Blunderman?" asked Almond. "How are your quarters?"

The caterpillar's face lit up and he pushed his azalea hat forward. "I have created a yurt using fern fronds."

They followed him to the blackberry bramble and admired his leafy hut. Outside of the conical structure, Almond noticed a pile of broken clay pieces. "This must be your sculpting studio."

"Indeed." Blunderman bowed and then inched to his rubble as if already forgetting the others were there.

Almond and the fireflies buzzed back to the dollhouse, with Nutsie padding below them.

"What is that?" Aksel floated ahead of them and landed next to the discarded sewing kit.

"They are called needles and thread," said Almond. "I found them yesterday, along with the thimble in the parlor, after Blunderman saved me from that dreadful mud puddle."

Aksel and Bo each drew a needle from the rough cloth of the kit and swung them like swords, cutting the air with a duo *whoosh*. "*En garde*," said Bo and zoomed at his comrade.

"Ha!" Aksel evaded Bo's charge and swung around to slash at him with his own needle.

"What are you doing?" Nutsie cried. *Chip chip.*

"They are sparring," said Blunderman, joining Almond and Nutsie.

"It is just a dance—nothing serious." The caterpillar clapped his front nubs. "Hooray! May I try?"

Aksel flew to Blunderman and offered his weapon. Blunderman squeezed his nub into the needle's eye, but the stumpy appendage could not find purchase. Again and again, the needle tumbled out of his grasp onto the ground. "Blast. I cannot spar."

Almond observed them, tapping her foot.

"What's that look?" asked Nutsie.

"This dance fighting has me thinking. We need defenses."

Nutsie scratched her head. "We do? Why?"

"Because of creatures like Boscoe who go around with bad intentions. If we really want to offer travelers a safe place to rest, we have to be able to defend the Dollhouse Inn."

"I can give fencing lessons," said Aksel.

"Yes, Aksel fences very well," said Bo.

"I want to learn to dance fight," said Nutsie.

"What about me?" asked Blunderman. "What can I do?"

"I know!" said Almond. "Boobytraps."

Blunderman spread his nubs wide. "What is boobytraps?"

"Boobytraps ambush your enemies before they can get you," she said.

Blunderman's face glowed. "Ooooo. I will have to think of one." He wandered toward his bramble, nudging at and discarding sticks and pebbles in his path as if considering elements for his snare.

"Another thing," said Almond.

Aksel and Bo rolled their eyes along with Nutsie. "There is more?" asked Aksel. "Housekeeping, defense, what else must we do?"

"Farming." Almond's golden eyes gleamed.

Bo dropped his sword.

Nutsie scratched her belly. "What are you talking about? We don't farm. We forage."

Almond turned to her with arms akimbo. "Why must we always forage? Back at the Fairy Nook, I loathed foraging duty. It was always boring or scary. We can grow our own food and sustain ourselves."

Nutsie gestured toward the bramble. "We have the blackberries."

Almond shook her head, lavender curls flying around her face.

"Those blackberries won't last forever, not if we have many guests in our inn. You said you wanted to offer a safe place to stay."

"And good company," said Nutsie, looking alarmed.

Almond flapped her hand at the chipmunk. "Yes, but none of that matters if we can't offer a safe meal, defended by our swords."

"And boobytraps," called Blunderman from his yurt.

Aksel zoomed around the dollhouse in a circle. "Fencing lessons will begin at dawn!"

At daybreak, they learned that he meant every dawn and followed his glow to the middle of the twilit yard for drills.

Nutsie, Blunderman, Almond, and the fireflies reclined in the pool, soaking their sore muscles after a full day of sparring and toiling. Since Blunderman's nubs were too short, Almond dug his boobytrap holes after she finished her own. She examined her arms, ropy with use, liking the way the lines of muscle looked.

"How do you two know each other?" Nutsie asked the fireflies. "Are you littermates?"

"No, we're not related. But Aksel and I pupated under the same sheet of tree bark," said Bo, sharpening his needle on a flint stone. He sipped from an acorn cap of nectar. "We emerged at the same time and decided to travel together, relying on each other's skills. Like brothers."

"That stuff is going to your head," said Aksel, laughing as he grabbed the cap of nectar. He took a deep draught, smacked his lips, and wiped his mouth. "We've had adventures with many sparkles, but our light flashes have never synchronized with theirs."

"What's a sparkle?" asked Blunderman.

"A 'sparkle' is what we call a group of fireflies who fly together," said Bo, hiccuping.

"When we find the correct sparkle for us, our flashes will become one with theirs," said Aksel. "We'll flash the same color in the same pattern. It means we belong."

Almond twisted a lavender curl around her finger. "I never knew firefly flashes were so meaningful. Are your two flashes synchronized?" she asked.

"Yes, of course," said Aksel. "Bo and I have been together our entire adult lives."

"So you two are a sparkle!" Nutsie jumped up and twirled, splashing water onto Almond's wings.

"Watch out," she said, scooting away from the chipmunk.

"Sorry." Nutsie plopped into the water and turned to the fireflies. "It's true, though. You are a sparkle—just a tiny one. Good thing the Dollhouse Inn is a haven in the forest for tiny creatures."

"I love that," said Blunderman.

"Our own tiny sparkle?" Bo grinned and threw his arm around Aksel. "It is my honor to be in your sparkle."

"And my honor to be in yours," he replied, chortling. "We have learned much in the ways of survival and taught each other what we know. It is better to have a companion in the forest."

Almond's gaze found Nutsie and she smiled at the fuzzy chipmunk—her own sweet partner in navigating the secrets of Rosepurse Wood.

CHAPTER 8

Queen Pepper crept behind the school, skirting the campus to retrace her steps from all those moons ago when she set her plan in motion to take over the Fairy Nook. She passed the fragrant violet patch where she found solitude as a pip and squared her shoulders, unafraid. The forest was unsettled, screeches and cries drifting from the darkness. But nothing could touch her. She was one of the creatures to fear—one of the causes of the screeches and cries.

Ahead of her, Cornsilk's bright tangerine skin flashed in the shadows as he fluttered under the shaggy caps of a clump of parasol mushrooms. She kept her husband in sight, but hung back, letting him lead her to the foxglove shrub where the hedgie witch kept her cottage. Crouching in a buttercup, a smirk slid across her face as Cornsilk raked a hand through his short mahogany curls and then knocked on the hedgehog's door. Pepper detected the door easing open and ducked down. It swung wide to admit the Fairy King.

The door closed after him but remained open a crack.

Perfect, thought Pepper. She flitted to the cottage and turned a pointed ear toward the conversation within.

"How can I help you, wee king?" asked the hedgie witch in her sleepy, rasping voice.

Pepper peeked inside to see Cornsilk draw himself up before the fire crackling in the hearth as if this homestead belonged to his realm. "I found a gourd belonging to you in my possession," he told the hedgehog.

The hedgie witch rippled her quills. "How can you be certain that it's mine?"

Cornsilk held up his hand. "Fear not. I only want to ask you about its contents. There will be no consequences if you are honest with me."

Pepper rolled her eyes. *Idiot*, she thought. Cornsilk didn't quite grasp that although he was king of the fairies, he was not the king of Rosepurse Wood. He'd never seen battle and had no idea how to use the sword at his thigh. He didn't even have a guard accompanying him.

"Do you have this gourd with you?" The hedgie witch's voice was sly. Pepper imagined that she heard the clever gears in her brain spinning a tale for this tiny imbecile interrupting her slumber.

Cornsilk pulled the gourd from his tunic and Pepper covered her mouth and nose, gagging at the potent stink of fermented pheromones. When they were fresh, they had caused him to become enamored with her. They were the tool she used to become the Fairy Queen. Now they were rotten and useless.

The hedgie witch drew back and covered her snoot. She held out her paw to take the gourd. "This is quite a nice gourd. I did lose one like it moons ago, but how can you be sure that this one is mine?"

"The clasp," said Cornsilk, drawling the word. "It's made from the tip of a hedgehog quill. And you are the only hedgehog that I know of."

The hedgie witch chuckled. "My, but you are cleverer than we—" She barked a cough. "That is, I think you might be right. I do sometimes use my shed quills for various needs. Why don't you have a seat?" She pointed to a chair with one paw while placing the gourd smoothly onto a shelf. "Would you care for a soothing brew?" She produced an acorn cap of tea and placed it in Cornsilk's hands while pushing him into the chair.

"But what is that foul odor coming from the gourd?" asked Cornsilk. "It's familiar but disorienting at the same time." He sipped his drink.

The hedgie witch watched him with glittering eyes. "How is your tea?"

"Good, very gooood." Cornsilk drew out the last word, slumping back in the chair.

It was time for Pepper to make herself known. She threw the door open and zipped into the room, landing beside the hedgehog. "Go ahead and tell him," she demanded.

The witch rubbed her paws together. "The gourd contained what we're calling a love potion, your majesty." She bent into a mocking bow and then turned to Pepper. "It took him long enough to find it."

Cornsilk rolled his head across the chair back, giggling to himself. "I knew it. I knew I didn't really love you." He pointed to Pepper and his eyes glowed royal blue. Tears streamed from them as his giggle grew into chortling.

"How much did you give him?" Pepper asked the hedgie witch.

"Enough to make him forget this conversation, now that you've had your moment." The hedgehog handed Pepper a fresh gourd. "This foxglove powder will keep him drunk and incoherent. Put a grain of it in his tea in the morning and again after the sun sets. Don't touch it yourself. It's highly addictive to fairies. Drop hints to everyone that he's developed a habit. Tell them that you don't think he can make sound decisions for the Nook."

Pepper grinned. "And then I take over."

Thud.

Cornsilk rolled on the ground, hysterically laughing. "I knew it!" he howled.

Pepper's upper lip curled, disgusted. "How can a royal fairy let his power slip away so easily?"

The hedgie witch shook her head. "Thank the moon for simple minds."

Cornsilk flung his arms wide across the rug, trapped in his laughing fit. "I knew I didn't love you!"

"Oh, did you think you would join with little miss perfect Apricot?" Pepper spat the name at him.

Cornsilk shook his head, gasping for breath. "It was *Almond* Nettlesworth, not you!"

Pepper fumbled the gourd full of drugs but caught it before it smashed on the floor. "What did you just say?" she asked him with ice in her voice.

Cornsilk's laughter petered out as his eyelids drooped. He released a heaving yawn.

"He's about to pass out," said the hedgie witch. "Leave him here until tomorrow."

Pepper whirled to face her. "Did you hear what he said?" Her citron eyes bulged. "Did he really say—"

"Almond was meant to be the Fairy Queen," said Cornsilk as he whimpered into deep slumber.

The hedgie witch lumbered from under the foxglove shrub and sat on her haunches, picking at the quills over her left shoulder. Her cottage was already stuffy in the morning heat. She should feel better than this, she decided. Since she struck a bargain with the Fairy Queen—a love potion in exchange for a dried fairy wing—she had grown stronger. The fairy wing vibrated with forbidden magic that infused and invigorated her spells. And it wasn't like she had taken the wing from the fairies. Queen Pepper assured her that it had been shed naturally by an elder.

Its delicate scales did indeed yield stronger results for her magic. There was no harm and no victims. Still...she had been taught that it was wrong. While her conscience was originally easy with the bargain, it now weighed on her quills.

She considered the tiny creatures as she glanced at the twisted black oak tree that camouflaged the Fairy Nook on this side. She had always felt sorry for hive creatures like bees and fairies, with their endless duties and rules. For countless moons she had observed the weary little fairies work in shifts, adding to their overflowing pantry. Instead of celebrating their gorgeous wings and all of the possibilities of flight, they churned and trudged like ants. Not the life for me, she thought. Chuckling to herself, she rubbed her plump belly.

When Pepper first knocked on her cottage door as a pip, offering the desiccated fairy wing in exchange for a love potion, she was inspired. She had told herself that the grasping young fairy was taking a stand against the exploitative system running the Nook. And she had to admit that she'd enjoyed watching from afar as the feisty youngster shocked the Nook by taking over. To her, helping Pepper ensnare her foolish king meant helping another vulnerable creature find her power. She knew what it was like to claw out a space for herself in the wide wood when so many other creatures had better odds. But after witnessing Pepper wielding her new power, the hedgehog had to face the possibility that she had romanticized the Fairy Queen's intentions. Now that Pepper led the Nook, she was a tyrant, not a hero.

And it was the hedgie witch's fault.

Grasses rustled to her right and she stood, patting her quills, checking that she'd remembered everything. The tall grass parted, and a silvery ear swept the ground. Twin fuzzy paws pushed the foliage wider and a cloud-gray rabbit with lop ears emerged. Known as the forest bard, he stared down at her with a disapproving countenance.

"Don't look at me like that, Crispin," said the hedgie witch, waddling to his side.

"I can't help it. You know this is how my face looks," he said, leaning down so that she could scramble onto his back. "Which way are we going?"

"Follow the stream north."

The lop hopped to the bank of Rosepurse Stream with the hedgie witch riding bareback. "Are you sure about this?" he asked. "We've never traveled so far away."

"Trust me. I used the wing to scry our path. It leads to the fairy who left the Nook," she said, settling into the natural saddle of the rabbit's back.

CHAPTER 9

Almond leaned against the trunk of the willow tree, breathing in the estate. Pinecones that she had scrubbed herself lined the tidy clover path leading to the Dollhouse Inn. The path bisected an emerald lawn edged by creeping thyme. Embraced by cascading willow branches, the dollhouse maintained its dignified lines while each room burst with the aesthetics of its occupant. Nutsie's nest was colorful and haphazard, a celebration of life after her oppressive beginnings. Almond's room next door was tidy with nature's tools for organization: nutshell receptacles, taut wall vines for drying flowers, and a small, scrubbed pinecone on which she hung her shift. Her freshly changed sunflower blossom bed's velvety gold petals skimmed the swept floor. Plumped and laundered atop it, artfully arranged bunny fluff pillows waited for her fatigued head. The fatigue felt good here, unlike at the Nook. Here, she believed in what she worked for.

Aksel and Bo had settled into the two smaller rooms next to hers. The nocturnal fireflies kept spare cells, with only rainbow eucalyptus bark mats for sleeping on from sunrise to midday—and rosemary sprigs to hang their swords. Unlike the others, they had fitted bark over the openings of their rooms to keep them dark and insulated from noise while they slept.

They had added the same rainbow bark to the floor in the parlor. Warm and inviting, the room waited for them to gather with its low stone table and scattered cushions. Blunderman's clay figurine of Nutsie stood displayed on the thimble as the common room's focal point. They had kitted out the remaining rooms with simple comforts for any travelers who wished to stay with them: acorn caps for water, small flat stones for tables, and piles of dandelion fluff for resting. Behind the structure, the stone wall created a barrier that protected them from creeping predators. The cascade of fresh green willow branches sheltered the dollhouse from aerial view—they would have to figure out how to achieve similar camouflage in the winter when the tree shed its leaves. Almond made a mental note to bring it up to the others. They would vote on a solution together.

She dragged her eyes from her beloved dollhouse and scanned the property. The bramble frothed with glossy leaves and plump blackberries, shrouding the pool that received a gentle flow of fresh dew dripping from the stones. It tinkled over the edge and watered the bramble. The top of Blunderman's frilly fern yurt poked above the leaves.

Almond covered her pointed ears against a scraping sound that echoed from the pool. Ominous bangs and muttered oaths followed, and she zipped across the lawn. She found the caterpillar attempting to divert water from the ceramic pool to a newly furrowed patch of soil. "Let me help." She shouldered the bowl in his direction, and he propped it with a pebble so that water trickled over freshly laid seed. Almond's chest swelled as she surveyed their blossoming estate, ignoring the tiny voice in her mind wondering if the Fairy Nook remembered her.

She helped him carry a nutshell of water to another patch of seed further away. Almond had never met anyone like the caterpillar, whose sole focus was to promote beauty in various forms. Where she was happy to plant patches of seed, thinking only of the fruit it would yield, Blunderman planted his seeds artfully, creating places for lingering even before the first shoot breached the soil. "It makes it more pleasant to work when the surroundings are nice," he told her. "I come here, I water the soil and speak to the seeds. Sometimes, I take a nap on that divan." He pointed a nub at a hollow of ironbark that perched on the edge of the furrowed soil.

"May I?" At his nod, Almond flopped onto the divan, her body settling into the curve of the inner bark. "This is cozy," she murmured, letting her eyelids droop. Then, she raised one. "But your yurt is ten stems away—why bother to move this chunk of ironbark here when you can do the watering and then relax over there?"

Blunderman undulated his girth to the opposite side of the patch and dribbled dewdrops onto the soil. "Every creature is different, but for me, beautiful surroundings are important. I find joy in perching on the perfect leaf as the breeze spreads the scent of honeysuckle and makes the trees sing."

"You make it all sound lovely," said Almond, arms behind her head.

"There is something beautiful in everything. It's important to learn that—it will keep you sane." He stuck his nub into a patch of sunshine. "Look, Almond! Look what a beautiful shade of green my nub is in the sunlight."

She nodded at his nub. *It is a pretty green,* she thought.

He swept his topmost nubs in the air, encompassing the pool and bramble behind him. "And I find joy in perching where you are, with the ever-giving bramble and the pool, and my nest in the yurt on one side of me, and the invaluable Dollhouse Inn on my other side. It feels like I'm cocooned. Take a look around and tell me how you feel."

Almond stared up at the soothing dome of willow leaves rustling above them. She sat up and glanced at the bramble, heavy with juicy fruit, and swelled with gratitude for the abundance. The metallic nip of lichen on stone filled her nostrils, mingling with the perfumes of roses and violets. She let her gaze fall on the dollhouse. From this angle, the gleaming white side of the structure was at once elegant and solid.

She stilled herself to access the feedback from her body and mind. Pollen-feathered air caressed her skin. The dollhouse reassured her of her safety, as if nothing bad could happen around it. Blunderman hummed under his breath as he soaked the garden. Somewhere behind the wall, rainbow finches called to each other.

"I feel content," she said.

Blunderman doffed his azalea hat and bowed to her. "That, dear Almond, is the ultimate goal."

"Look at this," said Aksel, landing in the yard. He and Bo carried a large, flat, white pod between them.

Nutsie scampered down the pathway and sniffed it. "That's new to me."

Almond flitted from the bramble to join them. "It's a pumpkin seed."

"Pumpkin?" asked Bo.

"It's good to eat, and very big."

"It does smell delicious," said Nutsie, rippling the black and white stripes on her back.

Almond snagged the seed from Aksel and Bo and held it away from Nutsie. "We could eat the seed, or we can plant it and grow a whole pumpkin." She took in the blank stares from her friends.

"Ah, are we having pumpkin seed for lunch?" asked Blunderman, inching toward her.

Almond flew into the air with the seed and scanned the ground for the right spot. At the edge of the willow's leafy canopy, between the tree and the wall, Almond landed and drew an X in the dirt with her toe. She grabbed a sharp stone and dug a hole half as tall as herself, dropped the pumpkin seed in, and covered it up. "Next rain, that seed will sprout. Just wait."

The others shrugged and turned toward the dollhouse for lunch. Nutsie scrambled up her new, stone staircase—the steps already green with a sense of place—and threw down a bushel of succulent dandelion heads. Blunderman plated them while the fireflies set the table.

Almond paused between the tall pinecones lining the front path and surveyed her home. Even the outside was tidy and purposeful. Although she was the only fairy, she felt connected with Nutsie, Aksel, and Bo. They all shared an industrious flair for structure that celebrated individual contributions—so different than the drone mentality prevalent in the Fairy Nook. Even her sweet savior Blunderman, with art swimming through his thoughts, brought order to the forest's chaos. She scanned the sky and took a deep, satisfied breath.

A cold shadow fell over her and obscured the path to the house.

The curls on the back of her neck, alert like an insect's antennae, coiled and pulled her skin taut. Above her, an apparition wheeled through the otherwise peaceful sky. The sun behind it rendered it black and ominous. A voice shrieked through the air, barreling toward her: "You left me to die!"

Almond froze. *Left to die?* There was no time to figure out what the shadow meant. It loomed above her, forcing her to race for shelter. Her wings fluttered faster than her feet could run, and she scooted into the dollhouse like a hound with a tucked tail, barely outrunning a swarm of angry hornets.

"What's wrong?" asked Nutsie. She jumped from her bunny fluff pillow in a cool corner of the parlor and scampered to Almond's side.

"You'll never believe it," Almond panted. "I think it's Boscoe."

Nutsie stiffened.

"The bird who held you prisoner?" asked Aksel.

Chip chip was Nutsie's only answer. Her whiskers vibrated as she stood, frozen.

"Yes," said Almond. "And he said I left him to die. Whatever that means."

"You escaped by having him chase you through a narrow space," said Aksel. "Perhaps he was trapped. Perhaps someone bigger than him came along."

Almond shuddered. "I didn't think about what would happen to him. I just wanted to escape."

They heard a thump on the roof and looked at each other, wide-eyed. The giant bluebird's face appeared, upside down outside of the parlor. Boscoe sat on top of the dollhouse and bent over the eaves to look inside. The feathers on his head were mangy, and some spots were bald and raw, as if they had been roughly plucked.

His eyes were dull buttons. "Hello, Nutsie."

Chuck chuck.

Almond put her arms around her trembling friend, and the fireflies got into formation in front of the terrified chipmunk, bottoms blinking dangerously.

Boscoe screeched with laughter. "Oh, are you going to protect her?" His tone of voice taunted them, but Aksel and Bo didn't flinch when he said: "Give me the chipmunk."

"No," said Aksel. "We are trained for combat. And you have already been bested by this fairy." He nodded to Almond.

She gave him a sharp look for bringing up the trouble between her and the bird but chimed in. "That's right, Boscoe. You can't win, and you can't have Nutsie. She's not yours."

"She is mine! Finders keepers," he screeched.

Nutsie shook her head, slowly at first and then faster. "No. I was just afraid to leave you, Boscoe. Sometimes, I was afraid to leave because I thought you would hurt me. Other times I was afraid to hurt you and leave you alone. But I was never yours. I belong to me."

"You can't survive without me," said Boscoe, his beak twitching. "No one will ever love you as much as I do."

"I might have believed either or both of those statements even a moon ago," said Nutsie. "But they are lies. I am surviving—thriving—without you. As for love, even these fireflies who I've known for four days have shown me more love than you ever have. But, what's really important is that I love myself."

As Nutsie delivered her speech, Almond spotted four squishy nubs struggling to shove the sewing needles over the lip of the dollhouse's ground floor. She edged toward them and peered over to see Blunderman wedged against the base of the house with the remains of the sewing kit.

"You are the best," said Almond, beaming at the caterpillar.

As she slipped her fingers through the eye of a needle, she heard a fury of flapping wings. Boscoe dropped to the ground and struck the parlor floor with his beak. Almond sent up a thanks to the forest that he didn't notice Blunderman. She tossed the sword to Aksel, and snatched the other one, flinging it to Bo. With the fireflies armed, Almond zoomed out of the dollhouse and fled to the ceramic pool.

She grabbed an empty walnut shell as she flew and nearly soaked her wings as she scooped it through the clear water that tinkled in the pool as if nothing was wrong. Almond hauled the shell to the back of the dollhouse, struggling to lift the heavy load to the roof. The delicate, feathery membranes that connected her wings to the rest of her body strained. Please don't tear, she thought. The wings themselves sounded like dry paper as they fought through the heavy air. Her shoulder muscles screamed in time with the midday forest buzz. She shoved the shell to the peak of the roof—careful not to spill the water—and squatted in front of it to hold it from slipping forward.

"Give her to me!" Boscoe demanded from the front of the dollhouse. He sounded like a frustrated pip to Almond, but she knew not to underestimate him.

Her leg muscles shook as she edged the walnut shell down toward the eaves and peeked over. She saw Aksel and Bo repeatedly pierce Boscoe's feathers with their swords as the bird swatted them with his great wings. Pods and shells flew from the parlor, bouncing off of Boscoe's breast. Almond guessed that Nutsie and Blunderman were behind the barrage.

She flinched when she saw Boscoe fling Bo across the yard with a swipe of his wing, bringing his head down to peck Aksel. Almond dove to the side and allowed her walnut shell full of water to careen down the angled roof and land on Boscoe's head before he could devour the firefly. Cold water cascaded across his face, temporarily stunning him, and Aksel drove a sure strike home where Boscoe's wing met his torso.

The bluebird staggered backward, outside of the forest camouflage provided by the willow tree and plopped onto the dirt where Almond had planted the pumpkin seed. He shook the dripping water from his head like a hunting dog emerging from the stream. From her perch on the roof, Almond saw his face recover from shock and darken into rage.

"Nutsie!" He lumbered to his feet, his dirty plumage in stark contrast to the verdant serenity that marked the estate. "I'm coming for you."

Almond shrank back. *Now what?* she thought. Panting, she forced herself to stand on the roof and assess the situation. Boscoe's foot was hurt. He staggered toward the dollhouse. The wing that Aksel stabbed hung low on one side of the bird's body.

They had a chance.

She glanced down at her friends. Nutsie stood tall in front of her home, with Aksel and Bo sentinel on either side. Blunderman stood coiled on one side, and Almond landed to flank them on the other. "We can do this," she said. A warm undercurrent of acceptance ran between them, each prepared to defend the others to the death.

Boscoe charged.

The fireflies surged forward, while Blunderman dug into the ground, armed with a bow and arrow fashioned from reeds and sewing thread. Almond tested first her wings then her legs, determining which had suffered less fatigue, and threw herself into a sprint.

They leapt toward their common foe—this deranged bluebird of unhappiness—ready to defend the new home they had built. Power swelled through Almond's body as she ran. She allowed the outrage that she felt toward Boscoe—toward all the bullies in Rosepurse Wood—to boost her determination and blunt her fear. Lowering her head, she dropped a shoulder and prepared to collide with their enemy.

Rabid, Boscoe growled toward them and then...he was gone.

A red-brown blur obscured everything for a blip, replacing the evilness in their lives with an empty space. Almond staggered forward where she had expected to clash with Boscoe's oily leg plumage. Her knee scraped the ground, and she spread her wings for balance. Craning her neck, she glimpsed a teenage red-tailed hawk soaring above the canopy of leaves. Something blue squirmed in its curved talons.

The hawk dipped under the canopy and perched on a distant pine branch with Boscoe wiggling in its grip. Almond winced as the young raptor shook Boscoe until he went limp. But she couldn't tear her gaze away. He looked impossibly small compared to the fierce monster that he seemed to be just a few moments ago. Without realizing it, she had risen above the ground as if to fly to Boscoe's aid despite all of the suffering he'd caused her friend. But she knew it was too late. She turned away before the first blue feather drifted to the ground.

"He's not coming back," she said to Nutsie, who dropped to her haunches and wept into her paws.

"I know. I'm relieved. I just feel..."

"Overwhelmed?"

Nutsie nodded.

"Come, Nutsie," said Blunderman, carefully looking away from her tears. "A bath is what you need."

Nutsie hopped after the caterpillar leading her to the bramble pool. Aksel and Bo sat on Nutsie's steps cleaning their swords on a bit of dandelion. They spoke to each other in low tones. Almond wandered their estate, careful to keep under the willow boughs. There would be other young hawks eager to stretch their wings. She sank onto a quartz stone that sparkled in the sunlight and cooled the backs of her legs. Her brain told her to be elated—the specter of Boscoe was truly gone. And with the help of their friends, they were able to defend their home. But her heart keened with worry. She knew Nutsie would experience the sorrow of loss that inexplicably presents itself whether the subject is worth grieving or not. She sprang to her feet. They would just have to distract her. *We'll work on building up our defenses,* she thought, turning to the Dollhouse Inn.

CHAPTER 10

Almond shimmied lower into the pool, letting water splash over her shoulders and cool her wilted curls. Midsummer sun beat down on the forest, penetrating layers of foliage and lighting up dark corners. She vibrated her wings, spraying Nutsie's face with mist.

"You're trying to annoy me, but it's cooling me off," said the chipmunk, eyelids lowered and elbows on the rim of the pool.

Almond cupped her hands together, half submerging them in the water. Quickly, she squeezed her palms together, shooting a stream of water out of the opening between her thumbs. It arced in the air and landed on her friend's head, soaking the chipmunk's auburn fur. Almond's laughter echoed through the bramble.

"Teach me how to do that," Nutsie chittered. "Hey, we have guests!" She sprang from the pool and shook water from her fur before scampering down to the pinecone path. Almond turned to see who their visitors were. A medium-sized silver lop hopped onto the lawn while an old hedgehog balanced on his back, her quills slightly fluffed and eyes alert. Nutsie threw her arms wide. "Welcome to the

Dollhouse Inn, travelers! I'm Nutsie, one of the proprietors. There's plenty of room and vegetarian meals are included."

The lop bowed, his nose grazing the grass and Almond caught him taking furtive nibbles before he spoke. "Delicious. I am Crispin the Bard." While his head was low, the hedgehog took tentative steps down his shoulder, but her tiny paws lost their purchase on the smooth fur. She tumbled to the lawn and lay on her back, pink legs wheeling in the air. The rabbit pushed her with his nose, and she flipped right side up.

She stood, legs splayed and quills erect. "Greetings, chipmunk. What is this place?" Her beady gaze locked on Almond, who climbed out of the pool and toweled herself off with a rose petal.

Nutsie offered the newcomers each a capful of water. "The Dollhouse Inn is a safe haven in the forest for tiny creatures." Her eyes sparkled with excitement.

The hedgehog nodded. "I like the sound of that."

"I don't qualify as a tiny creature," said Crispin.

Nutsie eyed him with her paw on her chin. "I disagree, Crispin. I'd say you're on the larger side of small. You'll fit in the parlor after we move out some furniture. Give me a moment." She dashed to the dollhouse and shoved the stone table toward the room's opening, grunting with exertion.

Nutsie's enthusiasm for their mission to provide safety washed over Almond. She swung her hand above her head in an arcing wave. "Welcome!" She fluttered down to the lawn. "I'm Almond. Where are you traveling from?"

The hedgie witch looked up from lapping water from the acorn cap. "You are the fairy who left the Nook." It wasn't a question. Her black gaze bored into Almond, laying her bare.

The curls at the nape of her neck coiled, on alert. "I suppose it depends on who you are."

Crispin hopped to a patch of clover, offering them privacy, and dropped his nose to chew. The hedgehog stared at Almond for another beat before answering. "We've never met, fairy, but I know of you. We are neighbors, although I keep to myself. Your sister sought me out years ago."

Does she mean Pepper? thought Almond, drawing her brows

together. "Why? And what does it have to do with me?"

The hedgie witch sat and scratched an ear with her hind paw. "Young Pepper sought my powers to become the Fairy Queen."

"So that's how she pulled it off," Almond muttered. She eyed the hedgehog. "What was your name, traveler?"

"I'm known as the hedgie witch."

Almond shrugged. "I don't know what kinds of powers you have, madam, but they're clearly effective. However, Pepper and I aren't close. And I don't live at the Fairy Nook anymore—this is my home. Now, can I offer you and Crispin some fresh blackberries?" Before they could answer, she stalked to the bramble on foot, breath shallow. *How did they find me?* Her hands trembled and her sense of security evaporated. She had been living in a bubble with her new friends and their fancy dollhouse, when all along any old hedgehog could easily locate her. Would the Nook fairies be next?

"You're worried that the Fairy Queen will come after you." The hedgie witch followed Almond to the bramble.

She spun around. "How do you know that? How did you find me? I'm not important."

"You're wrong about many things, Almond Nettlesworth," said the hedgie witch. "You're actually quite important. I was wrong, too. I should not have helped Pepper become Fairy Queen. And I should not have—"

Almond waited for her to finish. "Well? What should you have not done?" she asked.

The hedgehog ruffled her quills and sighed. "I took something that I won't give back, even though I should. And I sense a rising doom. You alone can stop what's coming."

Almond felt anger well in her core, tempting her with its power. She tamped down on it, willing reason to slow down her emotions. This strange hedgehog was talking in circles while her rabbit ate all the clover, but she was a guest. And they were probably tired—perhaps deliriously so. It was her's and Nutsie's job as hosts to keep it together. "Please come into the parlor and make yourselves comfortable," she said, forcing a smile. "Then you can tell me whatever it is that you're trying to say." She led the hedgie witch to the dollhouse where Nutsie had laid out a buffet of berries and dandelions. Crispin followed with a series of lazy hops.

Oblivious to the tension between the hedgie witch and Almond, Nutsie buzzed with hospitality. She fluffed a pillow for the hedgehog, settling her near the berries. Crispin climbed inside of the parlor and sank his nose into the dandelions. "You were correct. I do fit in this nest quite nicely," he said between nibbles.

Nutsie's smile stretched across her face and her front teeth gleamed. "Crispin, you introduced yourself as a bard. Once you've had your fill, would you sing us a song?"

The rabbit shook his velvety lop ears, as if coming awake, and looked around the room. "That's why I'm here, of course."

The others waited for him to continue, but he sank his face back into the dandelions.

The hedgie witch smacked her lips on her last bite of blackberry. "You're probably wondering what the two of us are talking about."

"Did you use your magic powers to figure that out?" asked Almond.

The hedgie witch shook her head. "No, it's obvious. We're all rattled so let me start over. Crispin and I have traveled from the grove where the Fairy Nook stands. We live in the same grove. I came to try to right a wrong by warning you that the Nook needs your help, Almond. Crispin came to sing the story of the wicked Fairy Queen, as disseminating news is his calling and duty to Rosepurse Wood." She eyed the rabbit. "Since the Bard is still eating, I'll begin."

Almond and Nutsie sank onto a pouf together, captivated by the hedgehog's sense of drama.

"Pepper Nettlesworth came to me with a plan to become the Fairy Queen while she was still a pip." The hedgehog shook her head. "I thought I saw something in her that wasn't there."

"But how did you make her queen?" asked Almond.

The hedgie witch smoothed her quills. "Love potion. It doesn't matter. Later, she spun tales of her husband's cruel behavior. King Cornsilk was a tyrant, she told me. So, I gave her a potion to keep him insensible. That's when she took complete control of the Fairy Nook."

Almond reeled. Cornsilk was a fool, but he was never cruel. He didn't deserve to be drugged and his crown stolen, no matter how useless he'd been as a king. "I still don't understand what this has to do with me," she said.

"The Nook isn't just suffering under Pepper's rule. Its existence is in danger," said the hedgie witch.

"Allow me to take over," said Crispin as the last of a dandelion stem disappeared into his mouth. The rabbit cleared his throat, lop ears brushing the parlor floor. He lifted his lips, exposing long white buck teeth that made Nutsie's look dainty by comparison.

As he released his first keening note into the room, Almond locked gazes with Nutsie. "What is happening?" she mouthed to her friend. Nutsie shrugged a shoulder and shook her head.

"Shhht!" hissed the hedgie witch.

Crispin's tenor swelled from his fuzzy lips:

> *Free of weeds, we have parsley seeds,*
> *And Rosepurse Stream runs clear.*
> *Alas peace is gone, like the end of my song,*
> *But the queen burns to destroy her sister.*
> *The fairy hive's queen should have been*
> *Kissing the ring of the pixie king.*
> *Alas, oh my, the reason to cry*
> *Is the Fairy Queen lets the treaties die.*

Crispin's last note floated away on the breeze and left them in silence. Nutsie's mouth hung open as she stared at the rabbit.

Was that supposed to make sense? thought Almond.

"I thought it would rhyme," said Nutsie. "It was hard to follow."

Crispin stared down at them, his mouth a triangle of disapproval.

The hedgie witch snorted. "Thank you, Bard of the Wood."

Crispin inclined his head, acknowledging her show of respect.

The hedgie witch turned to Almond. "The song means that your sister the Fairy Queen doesn't know how to rule the Nook. She's not keeping the peace between the Nook and its allies. The Pixie King is urging the Dryads to join forces and attack the fairies."

Almond's face went pale blue. "And Pepper doesn't know?"

"The queen has been warned, but she won't listen to anyone.

Her entire focus is on finding a way to destroy you."

"Me?" Almond squeaked. "That's crazy. I'm no threat to her. She doesn't even think I deserve to live in the Nook."

"The queen's spiteful spirit burns at her core. Come back with us and prove to her that you're not a threat. Only then will she forget about her piphood rivalry with you and focus on the politics at hand."

"I don't think so." Almond crossed her arms and shook her head, curls bouncing.

The hedgie witch's eyes bulged. "What?"

"You heard her," said Nutsie. "It's not Almond's fault that her sister is the Fairy Queen, or that she's crazy. Her home is here." She threw her paw around Almond's shoulders.

Warmth and gratitude flowed over the fairy. "Thank you, Nutsie." She turned to the hedgie witch. "I'm sorry for whatever trouble is coming to your grove, but I don't owe the Nook anything."

"What about us?" asked Crispin, nose wiggling.

"You're welcome to stay here," Nutsie beamed at them.

"You can't run from your destiny, Almond Nettlesworth," said the hedgie witch. "And destiny doesn't care what you want."

"I disagree," said Almond. "I believe that destiny cares very much about what we want as long as we work toward finding it." The hedgie witch's eyes sparkled as she regarded Almond, who squirmed under her scrutiny. "You must be disappointed in me," she said to the hedgehog, including Crispin with a nod.

"I respect you very much, actually," said the hedgie witch. "It takes bravery to say 'no' to me, in particular. And it takes bravery to stand up for your freedom, strike out on your own, and seize control of your destiny."

Almond blushed deep blue. "There was a chickadee involved. But yes, this place and these friends are more important to me than anything."

"I respect that, too," said Crispin.

Almond gave him a deep curtsy. "Thank you, Great Bard, for honoring us with your song."

"Even though it didn't really rhyme," said Nutsie, joining Almond in curtsying to the lop.

He inclined his head.

Almond straightened and squinted at the hedgie witch. "I just realized that you never told us your name."

"I only tell special friends my name," said the hedgehog.

Almond ducked her head. "Sorry, I didn't mean to offend—"

"My name is Frangipani, my friends," said the hedgie witch. "Now, I think both Crispin and I are ready for a nap in this lovely dollhouse."

"Are you sure about going back?" Nutsie asked, worrying her paws together. "You could stay here."

The hedgie witch regarded her from Crispin's back. The rabbit's nose twitched repeatedly above his paws. "What I've seen here of this outpost has renewed my faith in the forest. When different creatures live and cooperate together, only good progress will come," said the hedgehog.

"What about the Pixie King?" asked Almond. A pit of guilt soured her stomach, but she could not imagine going back to the Fairy Nook. It seemed like a grim, faraway dream after all she'd seen across Rosepurse Wood. Her place was here. She just had to make sure that she made it worth it to everyone that she stayed.

"The threat of war is not imminent," said the hedgie witch. "It will take time for the Pixie King to convince the other rulers that the fairies deserve capture. There is still time to reverse the damage that Queen Pepper's negligence has inflicted by eroding those relationships. I feel compelled to return and help if I can."

"And I will return to my warren where there's space to stretch out," said Crispin.

"You must visit us again," said Blunderman, who had joined them for lunch.

"It seems Rosepurse Wood is shrinking," said the hedgie witch, nodding at the caterpillar.

"Or maybe it's becoming more connected," said Almond, petting Crispin's pillow soft shoulder.

"Either way, we will remain in touch," said the hedgie witch. "I have a gift for you before we leave—the gift of foresight. Pay attention. Across

Rosepurse Stream following the sun, at a rusty toy top forgotten on the ground, look straight skyward into the tallest crape myrtle tree and you will see the Royal Beehive of Rosepurse Wood. You must go there and convince the Queen Bee to give you royal jelly. You'll need its healing powers."

Almond froze. Cross Rosepurse Stream? All she wanted to do was nestle into the dollhouse with her friends, and now she had to go on a quest for royal jelly? Unsure how to respond to the hedgie witch's advice, she nodded and forced a smile.

"Goodbye Frangipani," said Nutsie. "Bye Crispin." She swiped the back of her paw across her eyes.

"I will sing of your accomplishments," said Crispin as he wheeled away into the forest, flanked by Aksel and Bo saluting their departure.

They watched his white fluff of tail disappear into the shadows until the fireflies returned to carry on with their day. Almond trailed after the others as they headed for the dollhouse, unable to rid her mind of images of the pixies and sprites invading the Fairy Nook. That would never happen. Would it? Guilt warred with frustrated anger inside of her. Why did the forest want her to be miserable? Why couldn't she just slink off and live her own life? Everyone assumed that the good of the Nook was more important than she was, and it was wrong! But she didn't want anyone to get hurt, either. What could Pepper have already done to anger the other communities?

Nutsie scampered into her nest. "I'm coming with you," said said, yanking bunny fluff from a pillow and stuffing the streamer of violets—now dried—that Almond had woven for her in its place. Next, she ran down the stairs to the storeroom and added a seagrape, then into the parlor for her clay figurine, which she placed in the sack.

"I don't think we'll need any of that," said Almond, eyeing the bulging sack. But Nutsie's enthusiasm for a quest caused a thirst for adventure to rise in her. The hedgie witch knew more than they did— maybe a quest was exactly what they needed. "But we'll need something to trade for the royal jelly. What would the bees want that we have? They're completely self-sufficient creatures."

"We will have to think about it," said Blunderman. He dropped to his belly and loaded a daffodil trumpet full of seeds on his back.

"When I return from planting these strawberry seeds that I've gathered."

"That's it," said Almond, dancing in a circle before she faced Nutsie. "We'll bring seeds to the bees. We'll teach them how to grow their own flowers. Then the drone bees won't have to travel so far from their hive to gather pollen!"

"Do you think they'll give us some royal jelly in exchange?" asked Nutsie.

"They have to!" She threw her arms around the chipmunk and touched her forehead to her friend's. "Our first quest, Nutsie," she whispered. Since she left the Nook, she had been filled with doubt about her place in the forest. Now she knew exactly what she was supposed to do.

And it felt good.

"Are you sure this is the way?" asked Nutsie, picking her way through viscous clay soil.

Almond glanced back, a daffodil trumpet of flower seeds slung over her shoulder. "If you would be quiet, you'd hear the water rushing in the stream. Just be careful where you step and stay away from those craters." She pointed to a deep mud puddle. "That's where Blunderman saved me from being sucked into the mud."

Nutsie shuddered. "I never told you I'm sorry for that. If I didn't push you to stay, you never would have ended up almost dying!"

Almond sidestepped onto a patch of dry grass and faced Nutsie. "It was my own self-centeredness and anger that put me in that situation." She laid a hand on her friend's furry shoulder. "Nothing you did is responsible for that."

Nutsie nodded and pulled Almond into a hug. The fairy slipped on the slick grass and tumbled into Nutsie's arms, who managed to keep them both upright. "I see the end of the marsh ahead," said the chipmunk, settling Almond on her feet.

"I've never been farther than here, but the fireflies said to follow the sounds of the stream. Whatever comes next has to be better than this." She scowled wiping her muddy foot on the dried grass.

"Now you've jinxed us!" Nutsie wailed before dissolving into chittering giggles. "Just kidding—let's go."

As the ground firmed and ferns reclaimed the soil, the marsh bled into a meadow hazy with sage. The rich scent filled Almond's nostrils and a pang in her chest reminded her of her old foraging teammate back at the Nook who was named for the herb. Was Sage still toiling in the pebble pit? Her heart hurt for all of the fairies who were being mistreated by her sister. "She's a bad egg," she muttered.

"What?" Nutsie turned to her where they crouched behind tall grass, scanning the meadow for danger. She picked up the trumpet of seeds. "My turn to carry. Do you see anything?"

Almond shook her head. "Let me fly up and check from above." She zoomed into the sky, relieved to stretch her wings and let her feet rest. She was determined to walk—or at least flutter —alongside Nutsie, who couldn't fly. Frosted with mist, the meadow below languished—a peaceful resting place in the forest. *Like the Dollhouse Inn,* she thought. She spotted a trail leading from the meadow to the stream. *What in the wide wood made that huge pathway?* Almond flew in a circle, scanning the meadow for predators, careful to keep Nutsie in sight below her so they wouldn't be separated.

Then she saw them.

Great furry beasts clustered near the trailhead in the deep shadow of tall trees. Their coats were shaggy, not soft like Nutsie's, and gigantic horns atop their heads brushed the ground as they grazed. Fear of creatures so large instinctively shot through Almond and she zipped to the ground. "There are monsters in the meadow," she panted.

Nutsie's eyes went large, and she ducked deeper behind the grass, cradling the pouch of seeds. "What do they look like?"

"Bigger than any creature I've ever seen. And they have horns sticking out of their heads."

Nutsie clutched the daffodil trumpet tighter, gaze skittering from hiding place to hole. "What do we do?"

"I could see Rosepurse Stream from the air. We're so close—we have to cross the meadow. We'll just have to avoid them."

"We don't know how fast they are." Nutsie dropped the daffodil and ticked off each point on her paw fingers. "We don't know if they'll eat us or suck our blood."

"No, we don't. But there's a lot of tree line facing the stream. We can get there without the monsters even noticing us." She hoped she sounded convincing with her heart hammering in her chest.

Nutsie continued ticking off her points. "We don't know if they have super hearing, or magic."

Almond threw her arms up. "What do you suggest, then? How do we get past them?"

Nutsie cast about, her eyes glittery. Nothing but tall green grass surrounded them. Then one of the grasses moved, all by itself. Almond jumped back, pulling Nutsie with her. Several other green forms detached from the grass, hopping to the ground. Facing the duo, a large grasshopper hummed as he wiped off his antennae. Four other grasshoppers milled behind him, shaking dew from their wings.

"Good morning," said the lead grasshopper, noticing Almond and Nutsie.

"There are monsters in the meadow!" said Nutsie, hopping in place.

The grasshopper clacked his wings together. "Gracious! Are they birds? Let's get out of here," he called to his companions.

"Take us with you," said Nutsie, grabbing the grasshopper's cheeks.

"We need to get to Rosepurse Stream," said Almond. "I can fly but my friend can't. Can you help us?"

The grasshopper scratched his forehead with an antenna, eyeing Nutsie's plump body. "What do you think, fellas? Can we manage it?" Four other grasshoppers grunted their assent. They approached Nutsie.

Backing away, she asked: "Manage what? What are you doing?"

Understanding dawned on Almond. "Hold still, they're trying to help us."

The five grasshoppers gathered around Nutsie, positioning them-selves to distribute her weight between them. Their wings activated, emitting an aggressive buzzing sound as they lifted her off of the ground and balanced her on their little air flotilla. Nutsie clutched the pouch of seeds, fur standing on end.

Almond vibrated her wings and floated behind them across the expanse of meadow. The scent of sage washed over them, and the clouds wafted away, revealing the azure sky.

"I love flying," Nutsie shouted to her.

Almond grinned. Then she spotted the monsters in the shadows. "Shh! They're right over there."

"Where?" asked the lead grasshopper, grunting with Nutsie's shoulder on his forehead.

"There in the shadow of those trees." Almond pointed to the great beasts, who were yet to move.

After a moment of silence, the grasshoppers burst into laughter, causing one to almost drop Nutsie.

"Careful! What's so funny?" asked Nutsie, clutching various antennae within her grasp.

The caravan flew through the maze of tree trunks that marked the meadow's edge and landed on the bank of Rosepurse Stream. Hysterical tears rolled down their cheeks as Nutsie hopped to the ground. The lead grasshopper waited for Almond to land. "Forgive me for not introducing myself, but I feared we were in imminent danger."

"Weren't we?" she asked.

The grasshopper chuckled. "The name's Carver, and these are my fellow travelers." He waved an antenna at his companions, who nodded. "We can't take credit for saving you, because your monsters are harmless."

Almond's mouth dropped open. "How can that be? They're giants!"

"They're called elk—big, for sure, but they only eat grass and leaves, like us." The grasshoppers burst into laughter again and hopped into the underbrush before Almond or Nutsie could reply.

Nutsie faced Rosepurse Stream. "I've never seen so much water before."

A pang rippled in Almond's heart as she thought about her friend who spent her first season held prisoner in a tree. "We should have asked those grasshoppers to take you across." She spun and scanned the grasses and brush for Carver's gang. They were gone or didn't want to be found. Either way, Almond and Nutsie were on their own. "Can you swim?" she asked the chipmunk.

Nutsie eyed the rushing water. "How would I know? Besides, that current looks strong."

"Only right here where it bends. The water backs up and then pours over these stones. But downstream it's calmer. See?" She pointed in the direction of the elk monsters and hoped that Carver was telling the truth about them being harmless. "I'll fly up and make sure." She kicked off the ground and buzzed above the stream. The elk were hidden by the tall trees, and she pushed thoughts of them from her mind.

Where the stream leveled and flowed slower, she spotted a series of flat stones leading across the water. She zipped to Nutsie's side. "I see the perfect place for you to cross. Follow me." She tried not to look in the elks' direction as she led Nutsie downstream. "See? Much less splashy." She pointed to a spot where Rosepurse Stream gurgled past the series of steppingstones.

Nutsie paused and then gave a sharp nod. "Let's go." She marched to the water's edge.

"Wait! We have to assume that you can't swim." Almond rushed to her side and grabbed her arm.

"I'm not planning on swimming." Nutsie yanked her arm, but Almond hung on, pulling backward. Nutsie leaned forward, straining toward the first steppingstone.

Almond clutched the trumpet of seeds in one hand and Nutsie's paw in the other. "Slow down! The stones are slippery."

But Nutsie lunged onto the stone. Her paw slipped out of Almond's grasp and the fairy flew backward with the bundle of seeds. She landed on the stream bank and muffled a scream as one of Nutsie's hind paws slipped off the stone and she wheeled her front paws in the air. As Nutsie lost purchase of the slick rock surface, Almond bolted into the air, still lugging the flower seeds. She flew at top speed, but before she reached the chipmunk, Nutsie landed on her rump, slid into the water, and was swallowed whole by the mild current.

"Nutsie!" Almond screamed. Frantic, she flew back and forth over the water. The auburn tips of Nutsie's ears emerged. She landed on a steppingstone and dropped the trumpet of seeds, careful not to let them fall into the water. Vibrating her wings, she hovered and grabbed Nutsie's ears, pulling hard.

"Ow!" Nutsie yelled as her face popped above the water. "Let go! I can swim!"

Almond released her ears and drew back. Nutsie's plump body bobbed to the surface, her paws paddling in the clear stream.

"This feels wonderful," Nutsie said, panting. "A little scary, but wonderful. First flying and now swimming—what a day!"

Almond retrieved the seeds and flew along with the chipmunk as she paddled to the opposite stream bank. "I thought I lost you!" she shouted, the elk herd forgotten.

Nutsie chittered gleefully. "You're stuck with me, forever!"

They reached the bank and Nutsie shook water from her fur, spraying Almond. "What's next?"

"Now we find a rusty old human toy called a 'top.'"

"You're looking for a rusty old top, you say?"

Almond spun around. "Who said that?"

"Up there," said Nutsie, pointing, while keeping one paw on their seeds.

Almond craned her neck. Red paw toes—much bigger and redder than Nutsie's—dangled on either side of a low tree branch. "Who's there?" she asked.

A fuzzy face peeked over the side of the branch. It wore a mask above its snow-white snoot that was tipped with a wet pink nose.

"What are you?" asked Nutsie. Almond elbowed her.

The creature chuckled. "I'm a red panda. And my name is Hun-Ho, thanks for asking." As if in slow motion, she dug her sharp front claws into the tree bark and slid her hind legs over the side of the branch, dangling. After a moment, she released the branch and thumped to the ground next to Almond and Nutsie.

A longing to caress Hun-Ho's fur overcame Almond—it looked soft as a cloud of dandelion fuzz. But the look in the red panda's eye told her to keep her hands to herself. "Greetings, Hun-Ho. I'm Almond and this is Nutsie."

"Love the name, by the way," said Nutsie, waving. "Do you know where the rusty top is?"

Hun-Ho nodded, examining them as she sauntered in a circle around them. Almond tracked her thickly banded swoop of tail as it dragged across the ground like a giant, fluffy caterpillar.

"Stop spinning to face me," said the red panda. "I want to look at your wings."

Almond blushed indigo. "They're probably filthy. We're on a quest."

Nutsie shook her head. "They're clean and sparkly from the stream splashing you. You look amazing."

Almond smiled at her friend. "You're amazing."

"We're all amazing," said Hun-Ho. "Let's get to it—answer my riddle and I will reveal the way to the rusty top."

Almond smirked at her. "Seriously?"

"You mentioned a quest," said Hun-Ho, sniffing. "This is standard quest stuff."

Almond and Nutsie glanced at each other and nodded. They faced the red panda, waiting.

Hun-Ho cleared her throat and dropped the timbre of her voice. "Name the gift that you can give to yourself but not to others, that you cannot hold in your paws but can in your heart, and someone can take from you, but only if you let them."

"Is the answer to all of that just one thing?" asked Nutsie.

The red panda bobbed her head, then scratched behind her velvet ear, waiting.

Panic shivered up Almond's spine. She couldn't even remember all of the riddle just after she heard it—how would she come up with an answer? "Can you repeat it, please?"

"No," said Hun-Ho, staring at the stream tinkling over rocks.

"I remember it. I've got an excellent memory," said Nutsie. "What's a gift you give only to yourself?" She tapped her paw against her chin.

Almond's thoughts raced through any gift she'd ever given herself—and came up with nothing. She'd never given herself anything. "Let's pivot," she said to Nutsie. "Maybe the gift is what we value the most?"

Nutsie brightened. "Blackberries! No, that doesn't fit. I can give a berry to someone else."

Almond studied the chipmunk. The answer was standing right in front of her. "I know. It's friendship."

"But you can't give friendship to yourself." Nutsie shook her head.

The red panda yawned. "You're on the right track."

Almond put her head in her hands, struggling to think. Other than her friends, she valued her newfound freedom the most. It almost fit the riddle, but she could technically give freedom to someone else, so it didn't work. She vibrated her wings, frustration seeping from her pores with nervous sweat. *What could it be?*

Nutsie sat on her haunches rubbing her paws together. Tears welled in her cinnamon eyes as she gazed at Almond. "For a long time, all I could think about was survival. I never considered what I might want or even deserve. And then I met you and I've learned that I matter." She turned to Hun-Ho. "I know the answer. It's self-worth. I can only give it to myself, and only I could allow anyone to take it from me."

Almond threw her arms around Nutsie. "I love you, sweet friend."

Hun-Ho nodded. "I would have also accepted 'self-respect.'"

Almond pulled back from hugging Nutsie and regarded the red panda. "We answered your riddle. Now tell us where to find the rusty top."

Hun-Ho pointed her nose down a line of crape myrtle trees perpendicular to the stream. There, in the dirt next to the tallest one, they spotted a rusted red object with a blue stripe running around it half sunk in the soil as if it had been there forever.

"Seriously? It was right there the whole time?" Almond spun to face Hun-Ho.

The red panda averted her eyes. "Sorry, I get bored. Please don't be mad. I just proved how clever you are. At least, the chipmunk is."

Almond scowled at her and then tilted her head, thinking. "Do something for us, and we'll forget about it."

The red panda nodded, eagerness gleaming in her orange eyes.

Almond paused at the silliness of what she was about to say and then went for it. "Let us nuzzle our faces in your soft fur."

"Yes, that." Nutsie nodded.

The red panda blinked, gazing at them. Then she rolled to the ground and exposed her snowy belly. "Here is my softest fur. Nuzzle away."

They rushed forward and buried their faces in her thick coat.

Almond luxuriated in the silky cloud against her cheek. Next to her, Nutsie's cheek fuzz stood on end from rubbing it against Hun-Ho's fur.

"That's enough," said the red panda and they jumped back.

"Thank you," said Almond, awkward after the strange encounter.

"Say 'hi' on your way home," said Hun-Ho. She slapped a set of claws into the tree bark and clambered up to her branch, surprising Almond with her speed.

"Thanks for the nuzzle," Nutsie called up to her with the carefree tone of a creature thoroughly enjoying a quest.

Almond shouldered the trumpet of seeds and grinned.

They scampered to the rusty top and peered upward. Nestled against the crape myrtle's trunk squatted the bulbous form of the Royal Beehive of Rosepurse Wood. "It looks like an easy climb," said Almond.

Nutsie twisted her paws together. "I haven't climbed so high in a tree since..."

Almond hadn't considered that climbing to the beehive would trigger Nutsie's trauma from her captivity. How could she have been so thoughtless? But she couldn't leave the chipmunk alone in this strange part of Rosepurse Wood. She wrapped a wing around her friend's shoulders. "It's not safe to stay on the ground by yourself. We don't know who else lives around here." She cut her eyes toward Hun-Ho. "And I'm not sure that I trust that red panda. I promise I'll fly beside you the whole way." The tears in Nutsie's eyes crushed Almond, but the chipmunk swallowed them and nodded that she was ready. Almond leaned her forehead against Nutsie's. "I'm proud of you," she whispered. "And I hope that you're proud of you, too."

Nutsie breathed in the crisp forest air and placed a paw on the crape myrtle's smooth burnished trunk. Almond vibrated her wings, ready to keep level with her friend for as long as it took her to reach the beehive.

"Don't move another paw." The voice sounded like it came from the tree itself.

Almond whipped her head around, searching for its source. From behind the trunk, a platoon of bees swarmed into view, stingers pointed at them.

Almond cleared her throat. "We're here to see your queen."

"Then your wish is about to come true," said the platoon's leader. The bees yanked the pouch of seeds from Almond and marched them up the tree to the beehive. They forced them through a narrow entrance embedded in the honeycomb.

Almond marveled at the honeyed light illuminating the wax structure. She had never been inside of a fully intact beehive, and its beauty and symmetry reminded her of the dollhouse. The workers shoved them into the center of the hive where a larger bee lounged on a throne. Elegant black and yellow stripes ringed her abdomen, enhancing her figure. A golden wax crown perched between her antennae. They stood in the cramped space before her that wasn't constructed of honey-filled hexagonal cells. Almond knelt and bowed her head. "Your majesty." Nutsie scrambled to follow her lead.

"Why are you here?" asked the Queen Bee.

"The hedgie witch told us to find you," said Almond. "We've traveled from our own home in the forest across dread marshes and meadows full of giant beasts. We crossed Rosepurse Stream at our own peril and used our cleverness to humbly bring you these seeds." She pointed to the worker bee who held their pouch.

"We don't trade with fairies," said the Queen Bee. Her antennae clicked together as she regarded them from her amber throne. Sunlight shined through the hive walls and backlit her so that Almond had to squint to look at her. "The Fairy Nook hoards more food than it needs."

"She's not a Nook fairy!" Nutsie cried. "Weren't you listening?"

Almond popped her foot sideways and kicked Nutsie in the rump. The chipmunk jumped but remained silent when she saw Almond shake her head.

"Not from the Nook? How can that be?" asked the Queen Bee. She dipped her languid hand into a cell of honey and pulled out the golden syrup, leaving a sticky trail to her mouth hanging in the air before it fell. "The only other fairies I know of have their Nook in another forest."

Almond reeled. *Another forest? Other* fairies? The thought ripped through her like a bolt of lightning. But now was not the time. She steeled herself and addressed the Queen Bee. "I would very much like to hear about these strange fairies, but first we must discuss the other reason why we're here."

"Here it comes," muttered the Queen Bee.

"We need some royal jelly," Nutsie blurted. Her eyes went large, and she slapped her paw over her mouth.

"I knew it." The Queen Bee threw her arms up and clicked her antennae together. "I told you—we do not trade with fairies. You are greedy creatures."

The accusation flicked Almond's cheeks like a freezing wind. She hung her head. "It's true. I am from the greedy Fairy Nook, but I left and established a new home with my friends. We all have different talents, and we learn from each other. With these seeds, we'd like to share our knowledge with you so that you can grow your own flowers. Your bees would be able to forage less and be here to defend the hive."

The Queen Bee tapped a sticky hand against her marigold cheek. "I like the sound of that. We can always use more defenses."

Hope surged through Almond. If they pulled off this trade, the Dollhouse Inn would be regarded as an established community.

"How much royal jelly are you seeking?" asked the queen.

Nutsie's whiskers fell. "The hedgie witch didn't say. Did she, Almond?"

Heart hammering panic chased away the burgeoning hope that Almond had been nursing. "No. I don't know." *What if we don't get enough?* she thought. Tears welled in her golden eyes.

The Queen Bee blew out a sigh. "How many of you are in your new nook?" she asked.

Almond shook her head, blinking back the tears. "It's not a nook. It's called the Dollhouse Inn, and it's a safe haven in the forest for tiny creatures."

The queen leaned forward on her throne, examining them. "Interesting. What makes it safe?"

Nutsie puffed out her chest. "We do."

Almond nodded. "Yes, we swear to protect any creature under our roof with our lives."

The queen sat back, antennae clicking. The moment dragged and sweat trickled down Almond's back in the close, glowing wax chamber.

"How many of you have taken this oath?" asked the queen.

Nutsie ticked off her paw fingers. "Almond the fairy, me—Nutsie the chipmunk, Blunderman the caterpillar, and two fireflies called Aksel and Bo."

"All of you creatures live together in a dollhouse?" The Queen Bee nodded with pursed lips. "Interesting. Your mission is honorable, and your ideas are sound. One capful of royal jelly."

"Thank you, your majesty!" Nutsie dropped to one knee in an elaborate bow.

Following her lead, Almond curtsied. *Will one capful be enough?* she thought. They'd traveled all this way for very little royal jelly. She pressed her lips together, determined to be as grateful as Nutsie. It would have to do.

"One capful *each*," said the Queen Bee. "Guard, fetch five acorn caps of royal jelly and bundle it all up in a banana leaf for these doll-house creatures." She waved her hand at Almond and Nutsie, who squeezed each other's arms. Almond strained to control her legs that wanted to jump, wings that wanted to vibrate, and smile that wanted to erupt into the room. *We did it,* she thought. *The Dollhouse Inn has arrived!*

The Queen Bee dipped her hand in honey. "Tell me more about these seeds of yours."

The Queen Bee allowed them to spend the night in a luminous chamber of the beehive where they were given wax cups of nourishing honey for their dinner and breakfast. Hun-Ho kindly carried them across the stream the next morning. But with no grasshoppers to transport Nutsie across the meadow, their journey home took longer. They hauled the unwieldy banana leaf pouch of royal jelly between them. "My legs hurt," Nutsie complained as they eased past the dread marsh.

"We're almost there. I'll take the bundle from here and fly it the rest of the way—you run on home and get some sleep," said Almond.

"If you're sure," Nutsie called over her shoulder as she scampered ahead.

Almond hefted the banana leaf bundle, vibrated her wings, and kicked off the ground. She trailed Nutsie scurrying to the dollhouse and landed on the lawn. Dropping the parcel of royal jelly, she stretched her wings and then her legs. Just a little farther and she'd be in her own nest. She barely looked where she stepped as scenes from their quest played in her mind like an exciting dream. *I can't wait to tell the fellas everything that happened,* she thought, scanning the property for Blunderman, Aksel, and Bo.

"You there."

She froze. The timber of voice. The superciliousness. Almond's curls tucked against her neck and trembled.

It was a fairy.

CHAPTER 12

"Almondine Ivy Honeydew Nettlesworth, come with me," said a commanding voice from the shadow of the willow's trunk.

A jolt ran though Almond's torso. She instinctively leaned toward the dollhouse, away from the voice, as if she could escape it. Her snug haven had been infiltrated. But this was worse than any mad bluebird—oppression had swanned past her careful defenses. Wishing she had a sewing needle in her dueling hand, she squinted into the shadow to see the fairy who knew her name.

He stepped out of the gloom.

Almond's breath hitched. The fairy's noble face that emerged from the shadows was handsome, the clover-colored eyes cold. It was the Knight of the Nook. She shrank back. "Beechnut," she breathed, flushing. A confusing thrill mingled with her apprehension. Her body tingled where her shift brushed against it. Her mind screamed at her to flee yet she stood rooted, her gaze locked on his. *He smells like honey,* she thought.

"Did you hear me?" asked Beechnut. "I said come with me." He clapped his powerful hands together twice in quick succession, summoning her like a dragonfly.

Almond pulled a face at him, the spell broken. She'd grown used to the syrupy sweet tones of chipmunks and caterpillars since her adventure began. Fairy arrogance was abrasive, like the scaled stone of the wall tunnel through which she and her friend discovered this place.

I have friends, she thought, lifting her chin. She let her eyelids drop and inhaled sweet willow air. With each breath, she gathered confidence. Opening her eyes, she expected to stand strong and grounded, but another jolt startled her when she looked at him. Her gaze lingered on his tunic stretched across his broad chest.

Beechnut pinned her with his glowing green eyes. His deep purple locks flowed to his shoulders and moved in waves as he strode toward her. "Now." His voice was as impenetrable as the stone wall behind her.

Ignoring his command, she noted his square shoulders and powerful legs. She shook her head and stood tall, squaring her own shoulders to match his stance. "Why should I come with you?"

His full lips curled into question marks that beckoned her. Instinctively, she took two steps toward him. A fearsome growl rumbled in his throat, and she froze. Humidity glistened in the divot between his collar bones. Almond stared, mesmerized, as his heartbeat made the tiny pool of sweat jump. *Is his heart beating faster, too?* She willed herself to run while she still could, but her gaze fell on the hard line of his thigh muscle peeking out from under his tunic. It was his most captivating feature.

"I command every fairy in the Nook, no matter where in Rosepurse Wood we may be," said Beechnut.

Almond gulped. She had been mistaken thinking that her decision to leave the Fairy Nook in her past was confirmed after the incident in the mud puddle. *This is it,* she thought. This was the moment when there would be no going back. Her defection would be real—and final. Maybe she'd been foolish thinking that she could start a new life at the dollhouse. How could she refuse the Knight of the Nook?

There were some fairies who whispered that he was nothing more than a glorified royal bodyguard, but Almond remembered the year that Rosepurse Stream brought a cottonmouth snake to the Nook. The monster ate five fairies—a whole foraging squad—in one morning.

It was a dark time. But Beechnut battled the beast without hesitation, slaying it single-handedly with only a twig and a sharp stone. It had been his first year as knight. Thanks to him, nearly one hundred lives had been saved, and the elders' gourd huts were insulated with snakeskin. She'd heard that the cottonmouth's fangs hung in the throne room. Who was she in comparison? Just a fairy who couldn't seem to do anything right. Heart fluttering in her chest like a gnat, she inclined her head to Beechnut and gave a small curtsy.

He bowed automatically in response to her gesture. Standing erect, he glowered at her. "We should eat before we set off on our journey back. I assume you have provisions."

Almond scratched her elbow and tried not to picture Pepper's furious face. She replaced the image with Nutsie and her big-toothed grin. Her nest sprang to mind—with its tidy receptacles and cozy sunflower bloom bed—and she couldn't stop the words from tumbling out of her mouth: "I've left the Nook. I don't live there anymore."

Beechnut's gaze raked her body. She fought the urge to squirm, digging her slender feet into the land with roots and resolve. She wished he would go away, but also that he would never leave.

His face remained blank, as if staring into space. "I'm ordered to bring you back." He stepped forward in a blur and seized her arm with his thick fingers.

Startled, a thrill ran up her spine at his touch. But she couldn't allow herself to be pushed around like this. "Why?" She yanked her arm free and danced away from him, enjoying the surprise on his face that she broke out of his grasp. But there was no way he would let her get away with that move twice.

Beechnut pressed his full lips together. "You will be made into an example for the other fairies, to warn them against disobedience and defection."

Almond gaped at him, her arms breaking out into aphidbumps. Made into an example? That sounded painful. Her dislike for her sister spread like damp mildew. "Pepper." The word slipped from her forlorn lips. She plopped onto a smooth rock and put her chin in her hands. Beechnut loomed over her, but she felt too sorry for herself to care. Thankfully, he remained silent.

She peeked up at him. His perfect lips were twisted in disgust—either for her, or for Pepper. *There's no way he likes serving that nit,* she thought. *Maybe I can use that to my advantage.* Sitting up, she forced a sunny grin. "You've had a long journey. Do you think one more day to return to the Fairy Nook will matter? I hope to say a proper goodbye to my new friends—before I never see them again." She made her eyes large and dewy.

Beechnut pulled an exasperated face and put his hands on his hips. For the first time, he didn't look like a soldier. Heaving a sigh, he said: "It has been a long and treacherous journey. We'll stay here tonight and set off for the Fairy Nook tomorrow." His gaze hardened. "And if you try to flee, these friends of yours—you wouldn't want me to force them to say where you went."

A chill ripped down Almond's spine at his threat.

He strode toward the dollhouse, nodding to Blunderman as he passed the bramble.

Nutsie scampered down the path to meet him. "A new guest at the Dollhouse Inn! Welcome!"

Beechnut was used to fairies getting out of his way—back at the Nook, he was second only to the royal legacy. But Nutsie didn't know that, and Almond chuckled at the confusion on his face when he nearly bumped into the jabbering chipmunk before him.

"A room for the night." He jerked his thumb back at Almond. "And one for my prisoner."

Nutsie gasped. "Nonsense," she sputtered and drew herself up, her stripes bristling. "Almond is no prisoner of yours."

Beechnut sneered and stood on tiptoe to look Nutsie in the eye. "Almondine Ivy Honeydew Nettlesworth is under my sovereignty and my protection until I return her to her queen."

Nutsie gave Almond a questioning look. "Almondine?"

Almond shrugged and kicked the dirt. She sighed inwardly. *There was no leaving that name behind.*

"But she lives here!" Nutsie's whiskers vibrated at the knight.

"It's okay, Nutsie," said Almond, peeking around Beechnut. She gave the chipmunk an oversized wink.

Nutsie saw it and her eyes went wide in understanding before she recovered herself. "Of course, Mister..."

"Beechnut. Knight of the Nook." He strode past her and into the parlor, where he flopped onto a bunny fluff pillow and helped himself to a handful of seeds. Eyeing a nearby walnut shell full of blackberries, he plunged his strong hands into a berry's ripe pillows of juice. "Do not try to run while I rest, Nettlesworth. There is no place in the forest where you can hide from me," he called, juice dribbling down his chin.

"What in the forest, Almond?" Nutsie rounded on the fairy for answers, but Almond's attention was fixed on Beechnut licking blackberry juice off his fingers. She couldn't tear her gaze away from his wide tongue lapping up the liquid. Heat blossomed in her chest and her skin tingled.

Nutsie waved her paw in front of Almond's face. "Tell me what is going on."

Almond fanned her face with her hand. "I don't know. I'm having the strangest feelings. Like, I know I should be afraid—I'm in big trouble here—but I feel sort of floaty...and hot. Why is it so hot?"

Nutsie patted herself down. "I'm not hot. Almond, what does the big guy eating our blackberries mean about you being under his 'sovereignty protection' and you being returned to the queen? Is that your kid sister?"

Almond stared at Beechnut stretching his brawny arms and legs across the entire parlor floor. *Such long, strong legs.* "What? Oh, yes. This is Pepper's knight come to bring me home."

Chip chip. Nutsie's fur stood on end. "Almond, you are home! What are you saying?"

Almond forced her attention from Beechnut and faced her friend. "Beechnut is legend. He's the fiercest knight the Fairy Nook has ever had. And he's right—how could I escape him? And don't say run away because I want to stay right here where we're building the Dollhouse Inn, so that's out."

"Just hide somewhere for a little while?" Nutsie bent and rested her forehead against Almond's.

Almond shook out her wings. "Like he said, he would find me. He once tracked a pond snail to a lilypad floating next to a rotting fish carcass, just to prove his skill." She tapped her chin. "Maybe we can find a way to delay our departure."

"Ah, it's good to have a full belly. This seat is most comfortable," Beechnut muttered. "I haven't properly slept in a waxing moon."

Nutsie eyed the great fairy in their parlor and turned back to Almond. "What do you mean, delay your departure? Like hide his scabbard?"

Almond clapped her hands, her wings fluttering and iridescent in the sunlight. "Exactly!" She glanced at Beechnut, who took up the entire parlor floor as he drifted to sleep, grumbling. Without thinking, she entered the room and pattered toward his prone body, inspecting the eminent hero. He was broad and sculpted. His nose traveled from a stern brow—even in slumber—down his face to point toward greatness. She reached out to touch a lock of his silken plum hair with her fingertips.

"What are you doing?" Nutsie and the fireflies peeked over the plinth of the dollhouse, mooning at Almond and the newcomer.

"Good specimen," said Bo.

"Looks good to fight," said Aksel.

Nutsie squished her body into the parlor and grabbed Almond's hand before it made contact with Beechnut. "Leave this fairy alone. You said that you're already in enough trouble. Why are you antagonizing him?"

Almond shook her head, as if coming out of a trance. "I don't know what's come over me. I must be in awe of him—he's quite famous in the Fairy Nook. I'll go have a rest." She fluttered to the second floor and nestled in her sunflower bed.

Nutsie plopped from the dollhouse onto the ground and walked to the bramble. The fireflies drifted next to her. "Do you think Boscoe pecked her in the head?" she asked them.

Aksel and Bo giggled and made faces at each other.

Nutsie huffed. "Are you making fun of me?"

The fireflies burst into riotous laughter.

She made quieting motions in the air with her paws. "Don't wake up that angry fairy."

"You are only one season old?" asked Aksel. When Nutsie nodded, he continued: "Almond is ready for nesting."

"Yes, she built her nest upstairs, remember?" she said.

"Not by herself. Nesting with another," said Bo.

"Yes, she nests with us. What are you two getting at?" Nutsie stopped walking to face them.

"You'll understand next season, probably," said Aksel. He and Bo flew, chuckling, into the leafy gloaming.

"Where are you going?" Nutsie called after the retreating fireflies in a loud whisper. Their rumps winked in unison with honeyed light. "We have to come up with a plan to get Almond safely away from this fairy knight."

Aksel turned back, still chuckling. "No matter what we do, Nutsie, nothing will get her away from the fairy warrior." He made a lazy arc in the air and rejoined Bo to meander and glow.

Nutsie gazed after them, twisting her paws together. She looked over her shoulder at the dollhouse and saw Almond curled in her sunflower upstairs. Beechnut sprawled in the parlor. He wouldn't nap forever—knights had to be ready for action.

If she didn't act now, they might lose their chance to delay Almond's journey and figure out a plan. *Just act casually,* she told herself. She sauntered toward the parlor and rested her elbow on the dollhouse's plinth. Beechnut lay motionless. She had to admit that he was a good-looking creature. A ray of sunshine flooded his sleeping profile, washing out the sternness. Almond sure seemed distracted by him.

Whiskers twitching, Nutsie crept into the room and approached him. Wound around his waist was a utility belt that included a dagger sheath—dagger missing—as well as various loops and compartments for survival essentials. A split twig cinched the belt.

It was the best thing to hide to sabotage their departure— how could he journey through the deadly forest without supplies? She reached to unfasten the belt, but her rump brushed against Blunderman's sculpture of her. Time stood still as the figurine teetered on its thimble pedestal. Nutsie scrambled to catch it before it fell and shattered, but she fumbled, and it slipped out of her grasp.

She batted it up with an elbow, juggling to keep it from falling to the floor. It bounced and flipped in the air, teasing her with the promise of chaos. She gave it a firm push up with the tip of her claw, and it hung in the air before gravity pulled it toward the floor. Magically, the figurine fell into her paws, resting like a baby, and she cradled it before replacing it on the thimble. She blew out a sigh. Freezing, she let her whiskers detect any breath of movement.

The fairy knight remained asleep.

She let out a shaky breath and angled herself away from anything that she could knock over. Leaning over Beechnut's belt fastener, she ignored her panicked thoughts about what he would do to her if he woke and caught her stealing from him. The possibilities were too terrifying.

There, she thought. She had the split stick fastener in her grasp and pulled it off the belt. It slipped loose, as if waiting for this chance all its life.

Beechnut let out a snort, the kind of sound only produced in deep slumber. Before Nutsie could react, he rolled over onto his side, pinning her paw under his bulk. Even though she was bigger than him, his solid muscles weighed as much as a fallen branch. Her delicate paw bones crushed together. She tugged her arm, trying not to wake him. It was no use—she was trapped.

Sweat trickled down her fur. The urge to *chip chip* was nearly overwhelming and she lost control of her breathing, sucking in mouthfuls of air that never reached her lungs.

Nutsie pulled her arm until she lost feeling in her paw. There was nothing within reach that she could use to free herself. She cast her gaze to the ceiling, willing Almond in the room above to wake up and help her, but the dollhouse remained silent.

A chill crept up her back. She was certain she was being watched. Checking Beechnut's face, she held her breath, making sure that his eyes remained closed. Under his eyelids, they danced and skittered. He was clearly dreaming of knightly adventures.

Keeping her body as still as possible, Nutsie turned her head to look behind her. There it was. The peak of Blunderman's ruby red azalea hat poked up above the lip of the house.

Nutsie almost heaved a giant sigh but remembered in time that she was still in trouble. "Pssst. Pssst." She hissed as loud as she dared without waking Beechnut, who continued to snort and mutter as he cuddled her trapped arm.

Blunderman lifted his body so that his head gradually rose above the floor. "Here I am." He undulated into the parlor and made his way to her side.

"Help me, my paw is stuck under him."

"These things happen," said Blunderman.

"First, we need to get his belt off and hide it," she said, whispering.

Blunderman dipped his front nubs under his hat and pulled out a dagger clasped precariously between them.

"Is that his dagger?" Nutsies eyes bulged. "You stole it?"

"It seems we had the same plan to keep the fairy knight here." He stuck the knife in his mouth and lumbered toward Nutsie, squishing his nubs under Beechnut's body to remove the belt.

"Quickly, hide them well," said Nutsie, breathless.

He undulated in a circle, casting about for a hiding spot before rushing to the open side of the room. After tossing the belt and dagger into a shrub, he made his way back to Nutsie's side, spent from the excitement.

"I'm still stuck," said Nutsie in a near-hysterical hiss.

Blunderman doffed his azalea hat and used the petals to tickle behind Beechnut's ear. The knight swatted at it and snorted in his sleep. Nutsie, fur standing on end, pulled and yanked away from the prone form.

The flower petals teased Beechnut's ear again, and this time he rolled over onto his back. Nutsie flew backward, surprised by her liberation. She scooped Blunderman into her arms and dove over the brim of the room into the shrubbery.

They scrabbled until they located Beechnut's gear and Nutsie ran for the bramble, lugging Blunderman with her.

"Stop!"

At Beechnut's command, Nutsie felt Blunderman stiffen in her arm. She skidded to a halt and glanced down, seeing that the belt was mostly hidden behind the caterpillar's squishy girth. His leg nubs wheeling helplessly in the air. Nutsie turned in slow motion to face the dollhouse where Beechnut sat in the parlor, rubbing sleep from his eyes.

She squeaked. "Did you want dinner? It's included in the price of the room."

"I was exhausted," Beechnut muttered to himself. He squinted at the cagey chipmunk clutching a caterpillar. "Just so we're clear, I'm not paying to stay here."

Shoulders stiff and heart pounding, Nutsie gave a sharp nod and began to turn toward the bramble.

"Stop, I said," growled Beechnut, lurching to his feet.

Nutsie froze and Blunderman trembled in her arms like a young leaf buffered in a storm. "Yes, sir?"

"Where is my prisoner, Almondine Nettlesworth?" He fluttered above the floor and hovered, his sneer menacing.

Nutsie's gaze darted to the second floor where Almond napped. Beechnut saw the flicker and zipped out of the parlor, hovering outside of Almond's room. Blunderman and Nutsie clutched each other as they stared up at the imposing fairy spying on their friend while she slept.

"What are you doing?" Almond's voice screeched from the depths of her room.

"I...I..." Beechnut's topaz cheeks flushed golden, and he coughed.

Before he could say anything further, Almond flew from her room holding handfuls of sunflower seeds. She raised her arms and flung a flurry of seeds at him, peppering his face and shoulders. Beechnut raised his muscled arms to protect his wings as he stared at her in disbelief.

"Go away!" Almond folded her arms and raised her nose to the sky as she retreated to her chamber. On the ground, Nutsie stuffed her paws in her mouth to keep from cheering.

CHAPTER 13

As she hurled seeds at him, Almond admired that Beechnut's wings shimmered deep metallic purple in the waning sunlight.

"How dare you?" Beechnut's voice thundered as he swatted seeds out of his hair.

A blackberry flew out of Almond's room and splatted across the front of his tunic, the juice mixing with the garment's dried mud.

"Stop that!" Beechnut flew into the room and grabbed for her arms.

She floundered around her sunflower bed, kicking and screeching until he backed away. Out on the lawn, she saw Nutsie cringe, holding Blunderman, who hid his face in her fur. "This is our house," Almond screamed. "You don't get to tell me what to do until we leave tomorrow!"

Beechnut hovered in the air and stared at her, stunned. A cloud gathered across his face. "No one can ever tell you what to do!" he shouted at her. "You couldn't just slink off into the forest, could you? You had to make a show of defying your sister at the dawn of her reign."

"I was carried off by a chick-a-dee." She spat each syllable.

"There's always some excuse, Almondine."

"It's Almond."

"It's true that you think you're too good for the Nook. You who doesn't do her share of the work. You who is lazy," he said.

"I'm not lazy!"

"All the fairies think so." Beechnut nodded as he spoke.

Almond flushed deep blue. "I am too good for the Nook!"

Shock rolled across his face in waves, followed by confusion, and then disgust. "Ungrateful fairy! The Nook raised you and made you strong. Show some respect."

She took a deep breath, forcing herself to match Beechnut's gaze without swooning, and bellowed as loudly as she could. "I, Almondine Ivy Honeydew Nettlesworth, am not meant to do forced labor for the Fairy Nook forever. I did my share of work there; now I choose to work hard here, in my home and with my friends."

"Woohoo!" Nutsie, still holding Blunderman, danced around on the front path, cheering for Almond.

Careful not to let her gaze linger on Beechnut's heaving chest, she settled back on her bed, emboldened by her friends' showing of solidarity. She smirked at him, exaggerating each movement, languidly crossing her legs at the ankle and her arms behind her head.

"You deserve whatever the Fairy Queen—where is my belt?" Beechnut broke off, patting his waist. He spun around and zipped down to the parlor where he'd slept. "Where's my dagger?"

Almond heard crashing below her, the sounds of furniture being upended. Thunderclouds gathered in her breast, and she allowed the anger to build and spread, filling her body. "Stop messing up our house," she bellowed. She rushed to the open front of her room and hung her head over the edge.

Beechnut reappeared on the lawn and stormed up to Nutsie.

"Where is it?" he asked, extending an open palm. His voice was forced, clearly struggling to remain calm.

Nutsie and Blunderman exchanged a look and then stared at him, mute.

Almond knelt at the edge of her room, peering at Beechnut's broad, angry back and clenched buttocks, like two pistachios nestled together. His handsome profile swung into her view at a sound—

a keening shriek, followed by grunting. She flew out over the dollhouse to survey the wall behind it.

Peeking over the top of the stones, she saw a streak of burnt orange. A monstrous fox striped from tree to tree on padded paws, approaching their stone fortress. Finally, it stopped with its black nose to the wall, panting, then searched left and right along its rigid line.

Below her, the keening grew louder, and Almond rushed to the hole in the wall through which she and Nutsie had squeezed to arrive on this side. As she suspected, a fluff of peach-colored fur filled the tunnel, vibrating and grunting. Almond reached in and grasped two downy handfuls, pulling as hard as she could.

"Ow!" squealed the fluff.

"Push yourself through," said Almond through gritted teeth as she pulled the fur.

With a whoosh, the teddy bear hamster tumbled from the hole and landed at Almond's feet. He sat up and cast about with wild, black bead eyes. "Help! A fox is after me!"

Almond crossed her arms. "I did just help."

The hamster sprang to his paws, his luxurious cloud of fur whisping to and fro with every movement. "Help more, please! He's going to eat me." He ran in a circle and stopped in front of her, imploring her with eye sparkles.

She grabbed his paw and hauled him to the dollhouse. "Don't worry. We have a plan for this." She marched him to the lawn in front of the Dollhouse Inn, where Beechnut faced them with Nutsie struggling in his iron grasp.

He hadn't noticed her holding his gear behind her back. Blunderman had dropped to the ground and socked his nubs into Beechnut's legs as the fairy shook him off, dragging Nutsie by her nape, and stormed toward Almond. "Who is this? And where is my belt and dagger?"

Almond stepped up to him, gripping the hamster's paw. "There is a fox hunting for, er..."

"Mr. Pickles," said the hamster, wringing his free paw.

"A fox is just beyond the stone wall hunting Mr. Pickles. You must cease your bellowing and allow us to initiate the Dollhouse Inn's predator protocol," she said. "Put the chipmunk down."

Nutsie sat trapped by the nape of her neck in Beechnut's fist. "Welcome to the Dollhouse Inn, Mr. Pickles," she said to the hamster. "Vegetarian meals only."

The hamster inclined his head. "My pleasure."

"Fox, you say?" asked Beechnut. "Where is my blasted dagger?" He dropped Nutsie's nape, and she scampered to the base of the willow tree.

"Like I just told you, we have a protocol," said Almond, gritting her teeth. "You and Mr. Pickles, please hide in the dollhouse and find something to cover your noses. Try the storeroom."

"In there?" Beechnut pointed to the structure where each room stood exposed to the forest on its front side. "Put ourselves on display for a fox buffet? I don't think so."

Almond shoved him toward the dollhouse, but he didn't budge. "Trust me!" she said.

Mr. Pickles scampered for the house and flung himself behind Nutsie's steppingstone staircase. He grabbed a handful of lilac blossoms and rubbed them across his swaths of fluff, concealing his scent.

"Remember to cover your nose!" Nutsie called to him.

The hamster draped the blossoms across his snoot.

Ignoring Beechnut, Almond scooped up Blunderman and raced after Nutsie to the willow tree where the chipmunk kicked and slapped a thick mat of weeds. Blunderman rolled out of Almond's arms and bounced onto the mat.

"Wake up! Wake up!" he cried, cavorting in the tangle of thistles and burrs.

Almond threw herself at the edge of the weeds and heaved the mat into the air with trembling arms. "Code Red, friends!"

Nutsie reached underneath and clapped her paws against the warmed dirt. A triangular, gray stone trundled from the darkness and faced them. "It is time?" she asked.

Chuck chuck. "It's time!" screeched Nutsie.

The stink bug raised two leathery wings and clacked them together thrice. A wave of her kin surged out of the weed patch, knocking Almond to the side, and scuttled to the perimeter of the willow's weeping branches—the whole of the Dollhouse Inn's estate. As one, the little insects unleashed a miasma of odor like a pungent cilantro salad.

It hung in the air around the dollhouse while everyone inside of its gaseous atoll—stink bugs included—raced for cover. Almond and Nutsie hauled Blunderman with them up the trunk of the willow tree. The only one who remained exposed was Beechnut, whose jaw hung open in the middle of the lawn.

Almond spotted fiery fur in the distance—on their side of the wall. The fox slunk along the stone structure, sinister and laser focused. Beechnut stood right in the predator's line of sight, still stunned and presumably processing the finely choreographed military performance delivered by the denizens of the Dollhouse Inn.

Almond couldn't risk calling out to him to move his pistachio buns—she didn't want to draw attention to Nutsie and Blunderman in the willow. But she couldn't let the fox eat Beechnut—even though he drove her crazy. Maybe because he drove her crazy. She flexed her wings and rocketed into the larger fairy's back, pushing him toward the doll-house. He flapped his wings in unison to hers, lifting off the ground, and they crashed into Almond's sunflower bed, huddling out of sight.

The fox nosed closer. Almond crouched behind Beechnut, arms wound around his torso, her fingers splayed against his hard chest. Shivering, she hugged her body into his, drinking in his warmth. In that moment, with death so near, she allowed herself to melt into him. He was solid as an oak. A tiny current seemed to roll through her. She rested her cheek against his back, eyelids squeezed tight.

Panting, full of tongue and drool, the fox approached. A paw knuckle touched the ground where the farthest willow branch hung. The next paw descended, then paused midair. The dry, black nose came down and then jerked back. The fox's paw continued to hang in the air, deciding their fate.

"It's working. The fox doesn't like the stinkbug odor," said Beechnut in an awed whisper. "We may not need to fight."

His warm hand braced against hers, holding them to his chest. She pressed closer to his back and held on. He pushed his bottom out to fit into the concave of her belly. Energy surged between them, and she wanted to do loop-de-loops over the dollhouse. But they still had a fox to deal with.

She held her breath. The paw disappeared and the white tip of the fox's bushy tail flashed as it wheeled around and raced away from the troubling smell. Almond released her breath and rolled her forehead against Beechnut's back.

They continued to crouch together until he lifted his hand off hers and turned his face her. "I think it's gone," he said.

Almond floated in the gooey warmth. "Of course it's gone. Everything went according to plan," she said dreamily.

He circled her wrists with his fingers and pulled her hands from his chest.

Her face flushed ultramarine. Grateful he couldn't see it, she repelled from him and bounced off the back wall of her room. Her wings bruised against the hard surface. She kicked off of it and flew forward, searching for her friends from the room's opening.

Nutsie and Blunderman waved willow leaves at her from the tree and the stink bugs whooped and celebrated from beneath their mat of weeds. Beechnut followed Almond to the pinecone path where they all congregated.

"That was the most impressive bit of regimentation that I've ever witnessed—much better than anything the young battle fairies have managed lately," said Beechnut. He surveyed the odd group of allies. "Well done, troops."

Almond cleared her throat. "Thank you. It just takes teamwork."

He nodded, seeming to approve of her attitude, and scanned the area with new interest sparkling in his eyes. "What other defensive measures have you taken?"

Almond tapped her chin. "Let's see, we had a recent invasion from...an old enemy."

Beechnut's eyes turned jade and snapped back to her face, eyebrows quirked in question. "Already? You haven't been gone from the Nook for long."

She lifted one shoulder and offered a strained smile. "In that situation," she said, hurrying on, "we poured a walnut shell full of water on our invader. It offered a decent distraction."

Beechnut continued to nod. "Swamping," he murmured.

"Bless you," she said.

"No, I didn't sneeze. I'd call what you just described 'swamping.' It's a clever tactic."

She blushed sapphire. "Thank you."

"When we go back to the Fairy Nook tomorrow, I think that you have a future in the knighthood." He beamed down at her.

Almond's face fell. "I forgot all about leaving."

Nutsie gasped. "But wait! What if the fox comes back? We need Almond to protect us."

"I just observed you protect yourselves superbly," said Beechnut.

Nutsie held up Blunderman for Beechnut to see. "Without Almond, we're just a chipmunk and a caterpillar."

"You'll be fine," said Beechnut. "Now, I just need to find my belt and dagger."

Nutsie shook Blunderman under Beechnut's nose, the caterpillar dangling amiably from her paws. "Without Almond's wings we can't carry out our plans. Do you think the two of us can fly?" asked Nutsie.

"Not yet," said Blunderman.

Mr. Pickles crept from beneath the staircase. "That was magnificent. You're like forest superheroes. Thank you for saving me." He bowed, the fluff on his head sweeping the ground.

Almond grinned at the hamster, pointedly ignoring Beechnut. "Here at the Dollhouse Inn, we offer our guests a safe haven in the forest."

CHAPTER 14

"I was born in a pet store in Rosepurse Village—that's where the humans live," said Mr. Pickles, leaning against the lip of the bramble pool. He spread his arms over the sides of the bowl and closed his eyes, luxuriating in the water. His fur floated like kelp. "It wasn't so bad at the store, but I always knew that outside of that picture window was a world full of adventure. And that I had to see it."

"How did you get here?" asked Almond, watching for the fireflies under the twinkling stars.

"I saw some kids looking in our habitat at the pet store and ran out in front of my kin, fluffed my fur, and did a little dance number that I had put together for just such an occasion. Of course, they bought me, but I immediately learned that they were shrill and terrible children. They prodded me in my cage and made me afraid."

Nutsie's doe eyes glistened. "What did you do?"

Mr. Pickles leveled his gaze at her.

Almond grinned at the bolt of electricity that seemed to shoot between the two creatures across the pool. She glanced at Beechnut, who was facing the other way as if on guard. He clearly wasn't listening.

Mr. Pickles continued: "We were in the backseat of the family's car."

What's a car? Almond wondered, trying and failing to catch Nutsie's eye. Her friend was enchanted by the newcomer's tale.

"I cowered in the corner of my cage. One of the kids opened the top to reach in and taunt me with a cheesy crisp. She poked it at me and then yanked it away when I tried to take a bite," said Mr. Pickles.

"Very mean," said Blunderman, lounging on the lip of the bowl next to the hamster.

Mr. Pickles nodded. "And I was so hungry! Finally, the car stopped at a gas station and the father got out of the car. The other child jumped out of the backseat to follow him, and I saw that he left the door open. That's when I bit the taunting child's thumb as hard as I could and held onto it so that she pulled me out of the cage along with her hand. I leaped out of the car and ran across the street into the forest. I thought I was safe until that fox caught my scent and chased me all the way here."

Beechnut twisted around to face him and stared in awe along with Almond, Nutsie, and Blunderman. "What's a gas station?" he asked.

Nutsie scowled at the knight, and turned back to Mr. Pickles. "You just experienced all of this today? Are you exhausted? You must be. We hope you know that you are welcome to stay at the Dollhouse Inn for as long as you like."

The hamster gazed deeply into her eyes and smiled. "I may never leave," he said in a breathy voice.

Almond wasn't sure why she felt uncomfortable watching Mr. Pickles flirt with her friend or why it was worse that Beechnut was there, too. She was hyper-aware of his presence—fascinated by the sight of his thick fingers trailing through the trickle of water that fed the pool as if they could play music over her body.

"I have to tend to the bramble," said Blunderman, interrupting her thoughts. He rolled off of the pool's brim, plopped onto the ground, and scooted into the tangle of berries.

Beechnut's head snapped to the side like a hare anticipating danger. Moments later, Almond heard rustling behind the dollhouse and the damp curls tied at her neck coiled. The night was as black as oil. Beechnut shot out of the water and fluttered his wings like a hummingbird to hurry the drying process. He gestured for silence and beckoned the others with two fingers. Almond climbed to the lip of the bowl and dried her own wings while Nutsie took Mr. Pickles's paw and dragged him into the bramble. Safely under the tangled leaves, they shook water from their fur, making the berries tremble.

Beechnut hovered next to Almond and whispered: "Who else lives here?"

"You already met Aksel and Bo, but they're not here. They go out every evening." She glimpsed a ripple in the darkness, like two shadows slipping around the corner. Just as quickly, they melted into the landscape. Almond strained her fairy sight to find them. All she saw were two boulders on the ground in grayscale. *Wait. Where did those boulders come from?*

Next to her, Beechnut sprang into the air but something in the darkness snagged his ankle and held him tethered like a balloon. Almond reached for his caught foot. "Hold still," she whispered. "Don't kick me." She ran her fingers over his ankle, searching for whatever anchored him, while scanning the shadows for the boulders.

They were gone.

Almond scrabbled to find whatever gripped Beechnut as he struggled to free himself. Her fingertips danced over a lasso of grass fibers encircled his ankle. Beechnut pulled and yanked, trying to fight his tether with brute force. Almond grabbed for his foot but ducked when it swung at her face. "By the sky above, hold still."

He stopped struggling and she quickly bit through the lasso with her sharp fairy teeth. Beechnut surged into the sky with a silent roar that Almond felt rather than heard. She teetered and stumbled backward, landing on her rump on a boulder. He spun in every direction above her, seeking the intruders with eyes that glowed a poisonous green. Then, his face blanched. "Almond! Run!"

Almond stared at him from where she sat, trying to get her balance and work out what he was saying. Her palm stroked the smooth surface of the boulder underneath her—and then froze. *There are no boulders in the bramble, either!* She hopped to her feet as Beechnut swooped above her head and grabbed her arm, pulling her to the other side of the pool. He landed and steadied her next to him as she yanked her arm out of his grasp. "Stop grabbing me!"

Beechnut ignored her, fixated on the darkness. "Who's there?" His deep voice echoed into the gloom.

Almond heard scuttling and then the night stilled. The fairies found each other's hands, listening intently. "Is it the fox?" she asked. She looked up at his strong brow, creased with worry.

He shook his head. His night vision shifted from poison green to the hue of a meadow after the rain.

"Who then?" she asked. It hadn't been fairies. The only one in the air had been Beechnut.

For a moment his gaze intensified, and then he gave a frustrated snort. "I don't know. You're sticking with me tonight, just in case."

"In case of what?"

"All I know is we better get back to the Nook tomorrow."

Gripping Almond's hand more gently, he led her to the dollhouse and fluttered them up to her room. Settling onto her sunflower bed, she pulled her hand away gently, embarrassed that she liked the way his fingers warmed hers.

Stumbling back a few steps, Beechnut slumped against the wall. He brought his palms to his face and covered his chiseled features. "By the great wings, I am tired." He spread his fingers, peeking at Almond, and quickly pulled them closed again. "You are exhausting."

She scowled. "Then go back to the Fairy Nook without me and keep being Queen Pepper's beetle." The spiteful words burst off her tongue without warning, surprising even her.

He pounded his fist on the wall, causing reverberations throughout the dollhouse. Then, he seemed to get control of himself through a series of muscle flexes, which Almond found fascinating. He stalked to the edge of the room and peered into the darkness.

She admired his great shoulders heaving up and down with his jagged breathing. "I'm sorry I said that...about you being Pepper's beetle. It was disrespectful."

He stood silent for so long that Almond held her breath, terror growing in her throat that she would be punished for the insult. She scooted back through the soft disk flowers of her sunflower, ready to spring into the air and fly for safety, when he spoke.

"I haven't treated you with respect, Nettlesworth—none of you here at this strange place have been treated kindly by me."

Stunned, Almond stammered, unsure what to say. "I...please, call me Almond."

He nodded, still facing the open night.

"You may call me Beechnut."

"Really?" This was an honor for an unremarkable fairy like her. "But why?"

He faced her, scanning her body from toes to wingtips. Meeting her gaze, he said: "As a sign of my respect for you, Almond." He hesitated. "Just for while we're out here in the wild. Back at the Nook, things will be different, I'm sorry to say."

Fear ripped through her, shaking her focus from the gorgeous fairy in her nest. She had been so distracted by him that she almost forgot her sister intended to punish her for leaving the Nook—never mind that it hadn't been her choice. Worse, she was certain that it was to get back at her for all the times she picked on Pepper at Fairy School. She couldn't go back to the Nook—not now. But Beechnut said that he respected her. If she could build on that, maybe she could convince him to let her go. She inched closer to the edge of her bed, approaching him. "What's it like to serve Queen Pepper?" she asked.

Beechnut stood, stoic, but she caught the slight eye roll that he gave the ceiling.

He doesn't like her as his queen. Her heart fluttered with hope.

"What is it like to have a queen for a sister?" he asked.

Almond shrugged. "I have a lot of siblings just like any fairy. But Pepper was with me at Fairy School for one year before I graduated."

"I didn't go to Fairy School," he said.

She nodded. "Your legacy has always been to protect the Nook."

"Did you enjoy it?" he asked.

"My life was better at school than after it, when I constantly had to perform duties to the Nook. Foraging, cleaning, patrolling, feeding the elders—nothing was ever fun after I graduated." She stared at the impossibly smooth, white floor of her beautiful nest. Not one speck of dirt marred it. Even the air was fresh and clear of pollen.

"Nothing in my life has ever been fun, except for sitting around the puddle with my family when I was a pip," said Beechnut. "I loved listening to my elders tell stories of the Great Possum Battle while we feasted on dried moss together. But that stopped when I left for training camp."

Even though he was Knight of the Nook, with every advantage, Almond pitied him. His life was lonely.

"Tell me about Fairy School," he said. As a knight, he had no idea what school was like for the rest of the fairies.

She patted the edge of her sunflower and scooted over to make room for him. "As you know, we start school when we're still pips, so it's fun at first. Lots of games that I now understand taught us how to forage and care for a nest. But at the time, it felt like playtime."

"But it becomes more difficult as you progress?" asked Beechnut.

Almond considered this. "Not more difficult, just less fun. You begin to accept that you are just a small piece of a system for the greater good."

He nodded. "That is honorable."

"But it also leaves no place for a fairy like me to be happy," she said. Her cheeks flamed and she picked at the disk flowers cradling her. Somehow, she felt guilty for needing more than the Nook had to offer. Who was she to demand more than any other fairy? But she'd failed at joining the army, she detested forced labor, and she had no interest in laying eggs. There were no other options for her in the fairy community.

"Why can't you be happy?" he asked.

She shrugged. "I don't get to do anything I like. I hate my duties. No one asks me if I want different ones. And I never see my friends because they've all chosen to lay eggs."

Beechnut squinted. "You do seem a little old for foraging duty. Why haven't you laid eggs of your own?"

Almond's neck flared violet. "Because sitting on a pile of eggs all day sounds even more boring than anything else in my life. At least I get to fly around and stretch my wings."

"You really don't want to go back to the Fairy Nook, do you?"

She felt his gaze on her. When she met it with her own, there was respect there.

"Here at this Dollhouse Inn, you must still forage and work hard. What is it about this place that is different?" he asked.

"Freedom. It's my choice to work hard here, not my sister's or anyone else's." She looked away. "Not even yours," she whispered.

His stony face didn't change but his gaze darted around the tidy nest she had created, taking in the blossom curtains and carefully arranged nutshell bins. The room was as organized as a barracks, but warm with whimsy.

"You said Queen Pepper was at school with you. What was she like then?" His question almost sounded shy, as if he was asking for a secret that he shouldn't have.

Almond laughed. "Not so different than she is today. Mostly because it wasn't very long ago. She has always been annoying, brash, taking up more air than was hers to take."

"You dislike your sister," he said, watching her.

Shame washed over her. "I suppose so. It was my last year of school. All I had to do to graduate by then was show up and flit around with my friends. We had as much fun as we could manage before our adult responsibilities began. Laughing all the time, pulling lots of pranks. Unfortunately, Pepper was the fairy we pranked the most." She peeked through her curls to gauge his reaction to her youthful misbehavior.

He said nothing, gazing into the night.

Admitting that she was mean to Pepper made her stomach sour like eating a rotten berry. Almond hurried to continue her story—get it over with. "She was such an easy target because she always followed us around like a beetle. And her reactions were so big. It was quite entertaining."

"Do you regret treating her so?" He stared into the night, keeping watch. Or maybe he couldn't look at her.

She groaned. "Now that she's the Fairy Queen? You bet I have regrets!" She hung her head. "Yes, I am sorry for being unkind to my little sister. I wasn't fair to her. I embarrassed her and snubbed her. And now, I'm going to pay dearly for what I did." Desperate to forget her shame, she threw herself back on the bed.

Her gaze lingered on his striking aubergine wings and a current of desire for him to lay across her and kiss her neck shocked her. Staring at the ceiling, she squeezed her thighs together and made herself still, willing him to get closer. Just one hot hand on her breast. *What is wrong with me?* She put her face in her hands. Here she was, about to be arrested and delivered to Pepper like a sacrificial cricket, and all she could concentrate on was the tingle that coursed through her body when she drank in the heat from his honeyed sweat.

Beechnut turned to her and raked her body with his green opal gaze. Almond's breath hitched and she scooted back, inexperienced and nervous. *This is it.* She wasn't sure what 'it' was, but she wanted it. There was no question that she ached for it.

His arm, roped with hard muscle, reached for her across the bed. On her back, she held her breath, taut stomach trembling. He raised up on his knees, gaze locked on her and leaned over her body. Charged energy rolled between them. Reaching for her hair, he stretched his arm past her head and grabbed a rabbit fluff pillow from the pile behind her, and turned away. "I'll sleep on the floor."

"No!" Almond shouted without meaning to. She panted, controlling her breath. "Sleep here in the sunflower with me," she said more softly. "Just in case."

He stopped short, back to her, still as a clay statue. She willed him to say yes, not caring about what the next day would bring. If her life was over, she might as well share her nest with the Knight of the Nook for an evening. "I'm scared," she breathed, swallowing her laughter at pretending to need his protection. He nodded and fell into the bed, enveloping them both in his wings. "There is much danger here," he said.

"That's why I need to stay and help settle the Dollhouse Inn," she whispered into his wings.

He was quiet and Almond thought that he fell asleep. "I can't leave you here. Something bad might happen to you," he said, his voice low and tired.

Almond's face pinched. "Something bad is going to happen to me back at the Nook. At least I have a chance here."

Again, he was quiet. Then his voice drifted. "I will speak to the Fairy Queen on your behalf."

Almond's heart fluttered as if it was the blessed night of the Berry Moon. *Does he really care what happens to me?* The thought was warm and snug in her chest. Her body relaxed out of the thrall it had been under into sleep.

Outside, two ladybugs materialized on the pinecone path, their black spots melting into the night. They stood, invisible, observing the fairies settle into Almond's nest.

"Shall we disable them?" asked the larger ladybug.

"No. Let them become complacent. Our orders are to report back to Queen Pepper as soon as we found them. Let's go."

As dawn licked gray fog from the land, Almond stared at the ceiling of her nest with a stone in her stomach. Beechnut hadn't found his gear yet, but how long could they stall him? More importantly, how long could she linger in his arms before he growled to life? Warm and strong, they wrapped around her body while he slept.

Fingers of rose and tangerine streaked the sky as Aksel and Bo droned by on their way to their nests, next door to hers. They glanced in and tittered seeing her wrapped in Beechnut's wings. Rolling her eyes, she snuggled deeper into his embrace, inhaling his scent on his chiseled forearm—honey and lilac mixed with metallic sweat.

"Good morning, Dollhouse Innkeepers!" Mr. Pickles's voice sang from downstairs.

Beechnut stirred at the gleeful greeting. Almond gritted her teeth. *Be quiet, fluffball!* She aimed her thoughts downstairs at the exuberant hamster, unready for this cuddle to be over—or for whatever the day would bring.

"Breakfast is served!" boomed Mr. Pickles.

Beechnut sat up, yanking his wings off Almond in the process. Where the morning had been impossibly cozy, she now felt chilly and exposed. He rubbed his eyes. "Good morning."

She sighed and sat up, rubbing her cold shoulders. Peeking over the edge of the room, she saw Mr. Pickles heave an armload of blackberries into the parlor. Nutsie trailed behind him with Blunderman in his azalea cap draped over her shoulders like a boa. The bark covering remained over the fireflies' nests.

"Aksel and Bo must have had a long night cavorting in the forest," said Almond. She fluttered to the ground and stacked berries onto the table while Mr. Pickles scampered to the bramble for more.

Nutsie dropped Blunderman into Beechnut's arms as soon as he landed and sauntered past him. Beechnut cradled Blunderman like a baby and leveled his gaze at him. "Have you seen my belt and dagger?"

Blunderman gulped. "Perhaps amongst the pinecones?"

Beechnut dropped the caterpillar—who righted himself midair to land on his nubs—and stalked to the pinecone path. "Say your good-byes," he said over his shoulder to Almond.

She frowned. He wasn't quite so dreamy in the morning light. She waited until he wasn't looking and stuck her tongue out at him. Turning to Nutsie, she looked her friend over. Sunlight gave her shiny auburn fur a halo and Almond smiled, happy to have had such a good companion—even for a short while.

Soon, Beechnut, a honed tracker, would locate where they hid his things and that would be the end of Almond's life at the Dollhouse Inn. She drank in the room that she helped decorate. Closing her eyes, she replayed the laughter and cheer she had shared here with Nutsie, Blunderman, Aksel, and Bo—even Beechnut. Somehow, having another fairy here made this alternate life with all its adventures seem more real.

But it would have to be enough to carry that happiness with her in a memory. She glared at Beechnut grumbling in the pinecones. Apparently, a gruff voyage back to the Fairy Nook loomed. She accidentally squeezed a blackberry so hard that it burst in her hand.

"Keep it together," said Nutsie. "He'll never find his gear." Her eyes twinkled.

"Did you sleep in the bramble last night?" asked Almond, noticing that her fur was freshly washed.

Nutsie's smile crept across her face. "Yes."

"And Mr. Pickles? Where did he sleep?"

"What was that rustling last night by the pool?" Nutsie changed the subject and crouched to wipe up the spilled berry juice. "I assume we would have known if we'd had unexpected visitors." Nutsie's voice climbed, more high-pitched than normal.

Almond scowled at a berry that refused to remain at the top of her stack. She grabbed it before it rolled to the floor and snugged it in place. "I don't know what it was. There was a boulder by the pool, and then it was gone."

"What kind of boulder?" Nutsie's fur bristled.

"It was dark, I don't know. But Beechnut became nervous and... stayed in my nest, just in case."

Nutsie squeaked. "In case of what?" *Chip chip.*

Almond's face heated and she thought her cheeks would burst. "Intruders? I'm not sure. Did Blunderman put a boulder by the pool yesterday?"

"I didn't notice." Nutsie shrugged and closed her eyes, swaying from paw to paw.

"What are you doing?" asked Almond.

Nutsie opened her eyes. "Hmm? Oh, just dancing." She pirouetted across the room.

Dancing? Almond shook her head and turned to call the others to the table. She smacked into Beechnut's chest and bounced off of him, knocking over her careful pile of blackberries. "Why are you standing there?" She scowled up at his silhouette, a black shadow with the sun behind him.

He took a step into the room and his face became visible. It was dark and frightening as a summer squall. He pinned her with glowing clover eyes, taking another step. The edge of the table dug into the backs of her legs, and she felt his heat as he pressed against her. She arched her back to meet his gaze. He silently searched her face, her soft ringlets and graceful neck, squinting at her chest, as if looking for his belt and dagger on her body.

"I don't know where your gear is," said Almond, crossing her fingers behind her back.

"I'm staying," said Beechnut, his glistening topaz skin electric against hers.

Staying? Here? Did that mean she was staying, too? *It had to!* Almond's mind swiveled in every direction—elation rushing through her at the prospect of remaining with her friends, apprehension about the why and how of Beechnut's announcement to stay, and a tickling, tingling, warm flutter up her spine that his sojourn in her life would continue.

She swallowed, not wanting to spook him. "Very well," she said. "We...you can make a nest in any unoccupied room of your choice."

He shook his head.

She hurried to fill the silence. "Vegetarian meals are included."

Beechnut reached past her and picked up a berry. He jerked his thumb toward the willow tree flanking the front lawn. "I'll camp in the crux of that willow. It will do until I build something more permanent." As quickly as he had pinned her against the table, he turned away, scanning the estate.

Almond gulped. "Did something happen?"

Beechnut lifted the berry in his hand above his head and drained its juice into his open mouth. He strode past her and grabbed another one. "The intruders last night—"

"So, there were intruders! You said it was nothing."

"I said I didn't know what, or who, it was. I do now." He pulled a shred of cloth from his tunic and held it out for her to see. "Do you know what this is?"

Almond peered closer. The cloth was mostly red. Where it was torn, there was a portion of a black circle. "Is that from a Royal Ladybug Brigade sash?"

The corners of Beechnut's mouth turned up slightly as he nodded. "Your sister dared to send ladybugs to spy on me. Me. The Knight of the Nook."

"Maybe she sent them to find me," said Almond. She cringed inwardly at her big mouth. *Be quiet, you fool,* she thought. *There's a chance that he'll stay here forever—don't ruin it.*

Beechnut paced the parlor. "She sent me to find you. She sent them to make sure I did so. As if the Knight of the Nook cannot be trusted. It is beyond disrespect. I will not serve her."

Almond was agog. She didn't know any fairy to defect from the Nook, especially not its knight. Sure, technically she defected—but not by choice. It didn't count if you were carried off in your sleep by a chickadee. She stood in his path, interrupting his pacing, and lay a hand on his forearm. "Are you sure? Or are you upset?"

"I am upset." He paused, searching her face again. "But this is the final outrage. Pepper is a tyrant. Cornsilk was a fool to become caught up with her." He slumped against a wall. "And I like it here. Everyone is kind and honorable."

Almond's neck flamed. "We like having you here." It came out in an awkward squeak and she flinched, willing herself to breathe. When she mastered her voice, she said: "We could use your fortitude and wisdom to make the Dollhouse Inn a real haven in the forest for tiny creatures."

He stared at her, confusion playing across his face. Then he turned and marched to the willow tree. Dizzy with the sudden shifts in her situation, Almond distracted herself by staring at the muscles rippling across his retreating back.

Pepper luxuriated in the warm sunshine bathing the balcony as the nettle and rose hip face mask settled into her skin. She'd been tense lately, with so many aspects of her plan in motion. Cornsilk had to remain incapacitated—with help from the hedgie witch's foxglove tincture. She had to haul that nasty sister of hers back here and make sure that the entire Nook witnessed her punishment. Her lips turned up at the corners. After hearing Cornsilk's drugged admission that he had meant to join to Almond until Pepper tricked him with a love potion, she had a special plan for her. It involved having her wings plucked and using her for a living foot stool.

Then, no fairy would challenge her power again.

The thorn she didn't know how to dull was the unexpected defection of the Knight of the Nook. She never saw it coming. Beechnut was so steadfastly loyal, and generally mute, that she never questioned his fealty if not to her, then to the royal Frost legacy that she had joined. His betrayal made her look weak. If fairies questioned her absolute rule because Almond left, then no one would obey her unless she found a way to haul him back, too. But no fairy nor beast had ever bested him.

What she needed was an army—an elite army within the fairy soldiers who answered only to her. But where to find such fairies? Who could she trust? More importantly, who could she command? She gazed out over the meadow where the young cadets trained. Most flew in formations at the command of their superior officers. Those officers were loyal to Cornsilk's father, and Pepper saw the way they cut their eyes at her when they thought she wasn't looking. They had no respect for her.

"Over here!" A swashing voice carried to the balcony where she lounged.

Pepper sat up from her rose petal chaise longue, scanning the meadow for the source of the voice. It was deep and boyish at the same time—the kind of voice other fairies would follow. She spotted a group of cadets tossing a red peppercorn near the edge of the meadow. The voice she'd heard belonged to a fairy called Cloudforce—an up-and-coming soldier with excellent tracking skills and no respect for authority. She had heard it said that he could just as easily end up an officer or toiling in the pebble pit.

Perfect, thought Pepper, watching how the three other cadets in the game obeyed his command and tossed him the ball without hesitation. He caught it in his powerful hands and zoomed to the goal, spiking it to victory.

Pepper grabbed a rose petal and toweled off her face mask, pinching her cheeks until they glowed pine green. Straightening her peacock featherlette around her neck, she flitted from the balcony toward the cadets squatting on a low branch, finished with their game and chortling over the older soldiers doing drills.

Pepper paused in the air, centering herself with a deep breath. It would be best if the fairy officers didn't see her consorting with their cadets. She approached from behind so that they shielded her from view. From the leaves she said: "You there. Cloudforce."

Cloudforce turned his sea-moss face toward her, quirking an eyebrow. He sprang to his feet on the branch when he saw her royal featherlette, coral tresses flying. Focusing on the middle distance, he stood at attention, waiting for her to speak.

Good, she thought. *He knows to respect the royal legacy more than the army.* "Flutter with me," she said to him, ignoring the other cadets.

They had followed Cloudforce's lead and stood shoulder to shoulder, avoiding her gaze with tight lips. Cloudforce zipped to her side.

"You're a natural leader," she said, her voice oozing with praise as she led him to the shadow of a wild peony.

He gulped, remaining silent.

"What the Nook needs is a special group of officers, trained for unique missions," she continued.

His gaze darted to her face and scuttled away. "My queen, I'm just a cadet. This is my second season of training."

She flapped her hand at him. "Cloudforce, you and your friends can remain cadets—or you can serve me directly in a place of honor that those withered officers who order you around could only dream of." She examined her nails. "The choice is yours."

A gleam of desire lit his eyes. She smiled, understanding his yearning for power.

"And I would lead the others?" he asked.

"You already do," she purred. "I'm assuming you accept my offer. Now, your first mission is to raid the meadow armory tonight. Take the most powerful weapons and bring them to my throne room. Then go to the stables and bring the fastest birds to the palace. Make sure you bring my own steed, Nectar. Can you do that?"

"You want us to steal—"

"No!" She hovered and chuffed him on the back of his head. "It's not stealing—it's taking what's mine as the Fairy Queen. Do you understand?"

A smirk played around Cloudforce's mouth. "Absolutely, my queen. Consider it done."

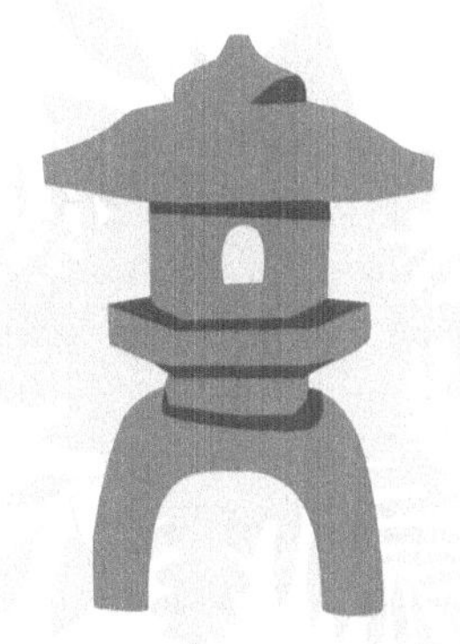

CHAPTER 15

A symphony of chirping crickets filled the velvety night. Almond landed where the willow branches marked the edge of the estate and let their sacred songs wash over her. Violet light filtered through the trees despite the late hour. It streamed from the high moon—usually silver but tonight, a deep berry purple. It was the blessed night of the Berry Moon. Back at the Nook, fairies were enjoying their celebration privileges—dancing, feasting, and merriment long after curfew. It was the only fun night of the year. But it had always seemed strange to her to join in revelry with fairies whom she normally didn't interact with.

Almond had always felt a deeper connection to the purple orb. The blessed night was her chance to search inside of herself for answers. Why was she unhappy in the Nook? Why couldn't she accept her role in the fairy community? As a pip, she had instinctively fluttered to the top of the hawthorn tree during the Berry Moon. While most fairies used the drop of freedom to run amok, celebrating, she spent the night soaking up the shimmering ultraviolet light. She learned that selecting meditation privileges meant unsupervised time in the Nook temple while the Berry Moon shone upon them. So when it was time for her to choose her privilege, she chose meditation rather than celebration.

It was another reason she had grown apart from her school friends—they didn't understand.

Constructed from river stone, the fairy temple perched above the fallen stone waterfall, its entrance usually locked against all fairies except for the most powerful legacies. As Knight of the Nook, Beechnut had access to the cool, stone pagoda any time he wanted to visit the rowan wood altar to the Tree of Life. Unlike Almond, on any day that he wished, he could offer a sprig of night-blooming jasmine for the Tree of Sorrow joined with a splinter of hawthorn for the Tree of Hope. These were the sacred pillars of the Nook fairies, but Almond's only chance to kneel before the altar—water trickling through the stones below the temple—was on the blessed night of the Berry Moon.

There was no fairy-built temple here at the dollhouse, so Almond knelt in a patch of fragrant thyme where the berry-tinted moonlight broke through the willow boughs. She imagined the smooth temple stones under her knees as she bowed her head and placed her palms on the ground. There was no fall of water murmuring under the sacred rowan staff to soothe her restless spirit. But the same moonlight fell on her crown and shoulders, deepening her curls to fuchsia, and she hoped that the violet wisdom seeped into her skin.

She was surprised to experience the same feelings of peace out in the open that she turned to while in the stone temple with the altar. Relief washed over her. She could still honor the Berry Moon outside of the Nook. Her spirit wasn't tethered to that place—she carried it within her. Any tatters of doubt that she was in the right place evaporated. She lost nothing of herself by being at the Dollhouse Inn. Inhaling the scent of thyme mingled with wild jasmine—its presence the reason she chose this spot—Almond accepted as truth that she only gained and improved by living here.

She had crept from her nest and fluttered to this spot, unsure why she kept the special occasion from her friends. Other creatures didn't seem to celebrate the Berry Moon and Beechnut hadn't mentioned it all day. She assumed that he abstained from the festivities—someone had to be in charge while the fairies of Rosepurse Wood went crazy for a night. Her curls slid in front of her face as she bowed her head, and she turned over the various pieces of her adventure in her mind. Everything made sense since she came to the Dollhouse Inn.

Except for Beechnut.

He'd seen that she wasn't as lazy and terrible as her sister accused her of being. He'd become used to her, it seemed, but he still sometimes treated her like mildew, as if he'd suddenly remembered that she was someone distasteful. *And no matter what he does, I still like him,* she thought with disgust. Prostrate, she opened herself up to the moon, desperate for answers about how to deal with her overwhelming feelings for him. Her crush was manageable—it was the physical cravings that were new and terrifying. There was nothing else that she could do. She had to kneel here, offering herself to the moonlight, until an answer appeared.

"May I join you?"

Almond went rigid. *I'm asleep. This has to be a nightmare.*

But he was there. Vulnerable on her hands and knees, she recognized his heat behind her. "What are you doing here?" she asked without turning her head from the moonlight. She sensed Beechnut kneel beside her but refused to look at him.

"I didn't know where to kneel outside of the Nook temple," he said in a hushed voice.

She clamped her lips together and hunched her shoulders. Of course, he never knew the frustration of being barred from the temple. The Nook gave the best of everything to its knight.

When she didn't reply, he continued: "I went to the bowl in the bramble, but it seemed wrong to touch something made with human hands under the Berry Moon. Then I saw you flit from your nest and followed you here. I'm sorry for intruding, but I don't want to kneel alone."

He sounded so lost that the irritation melted from her shoulders. Tonight was the night to lead with an open heart. She had gleaned that wisdom from precious snatches of contemplation in the temple. The heat from his body leaned into her. She couldn't stand it— peeking to the side, she saw his knees cradled in the thyme, and his strong thigh awash in violet light. She felt completely exposed. She knew she couldn't sit up without seeming like she was doing so for him. Which she wasn't. She just didn't want him staring at her bottom.

Or did she?

With a wrenching groan, she sat up.

He drew back with a look of surprise. "I didn't mean to bother you. It's just that I, too, celebrate the blessed night of the Berry Moon with meditation. It's refreshing to meet another fairy who doesn't use the night for debauchery."

Almond agreed with him, but who were they to judge? "Fairies don't have much else to be excited about in their lives," she said.

Beechnut scowled. "I disagree. The Nook cares for every fairy."

"How would you know?" Her voice was sharp. She clapped her hand over her mouth and her wings drooped. "I'm sorry. I should keep my temper tonight of all nights."

He remained silent.

She sank back into her thoughts, trying to empty her mind as glowing ultraviolet rays washed across her skin. But his deep breathing intruded upon her meditation. Did she hate the sound or love it? It was distracting yet assured her that he remained nearby. How did two such powerful feelings war over something so trivial? She clamped down on her thoughts.

"I'm sorry, too." Beechnut's voice was rich with feeling. "I know what you're thinking—that I don't know what life is like for the average fairy. And you're right. What I should have said was that the Nook cares for me. And I've chosen to believe that everyone else has the same opportunities."

Almond peeked at him. He stared up at the Berry Moon. A silver tear rolled from the corner of his eye, down his jaw, and splashed onto his shoulder. He was completely vulnerable. How could she be so guarded and angry in this moment? She scooted closer so that they knelt side-by-side, elbows touching. Keeping her eyelids lowered and her face raised to the sky, she reached out and hooked his pinky finger with hers, holding it lightly.

He didn't pull away.

As the light of the Berry Moon faded, Almond shivered. An early morning chill replaced the ferocious warmth of the night. Where the moonlight had caressed her skin, aphidbumps now covered her arms.

Beechnut eyed them. "Follow me inside," he said. "I want to tell you something."

She rose and trailed after him to the empty parlor. Floating onto a pouf, she remained silent, content to trace his full lips and long lashes with her gaze. He leaned against the wall, preening under her attention. But his brow was drawn. Instead of ruining the effect of his chiseled features, it shadowed him with depth and intrigue. *How can one fairy be so perfect?* she thought. After kneeling with him under the moon, he seemed stripped of menace, if not of danger. She was intoxicated that such a fierce warrior was tender with her. It gave her a strange sense of pride that she refused to acknowledge.

He pushed off of the wall and held his hand out to her, open palmed.

She stared at it, not understanding. Then she eased her hand on top of his, hoping he wouldn't crush it with his brute strength.

He closed his fingers, wrapping her hand in his solid warmth. Searching out her gaze, he locked onto it with his. "When I finish building my permanent nest, I will ask you to join with me."

Almond blinked. "Permanent?" Blood rushed from her head and the world spun.

He bent and pinned her lips with his, pulling her to him by the small of her back and cradling her head in his palm. The thrill that traveled down her spine earlier rushed right back up and exploded into the place where their lips met. Just as quickly as he'd kissed her, he turned and marched out of the parlor, down the pinecone path, toward the willow tree.

Her knees buckled and she caught the edge of the table, stopping herself from tumbling to the ground. She touched her fingertips to her lips where Beechnut had just crushed them with a magical explosion of excitement. A kiss could make a fairy reckless. The thought sobered her, and she considered Beechnut's parting words. *Permanent?*

Almond's life had finally begun—she belonged somewhere doing something meaningful. She and Nutsie had never felt safe until they found the dollhouse. It was vital to both of them that other power-less creatures feel secure at the Dollhouse Inn. Would she be able to make that happen if she nested with Beechnut? Would he think he could boss her around? Would he want her to lay *eggs*? Her stomach flipped at the thought. 'Permanent' sounded so...permanent—like she didn't have a choice in the matter. Just like back at the Nook. In a way, Almond supposed she had no choice if she wanted to stay at the doll-house. If she refused, Beechnut might decide to drag her back to the Fairy Nook after all.

She plopped on a pouf and stilled her thoughts. What had she planned to do if Beechnut carried out his orders? If he went through with arresting her? Her friends couldn't hide his gear forever. At some point, she would have had to—what? Escape from him on the journey back? And then what? She wouldn't be able to return to the Dollhouse Inn. It would be the first place he'd look. But she couldn't actually give herself up to Pepper for whatever torture the Fairy Queen had planned for her. She picked the problem apart in her mind, turning it over like a spool of spider silk, looking for any loose end that could lead to an answer. Her wings went rigid. *That's it.* There was no answer. Whether Almond's goal was to avoid being Beechnut's prisoner or his nestmate, she had to stand up to him and fight with everything she had.

He might have been the Knight of the Nook, but now he was part of the Dollhouse Inn family—even if he nested in the willow tree. Somehow, she had to find the strength to confront him and make him understand that he no longer had sovereignty over her. If she could get herself under control. Despite what her heart and mind wanted, her body—from her toes to her wingtips—was doing everything in its power to push her straight into his arms.

Exposed tree roots arched overhead, marking the entrance to Fairy School. The roots buttressed a foyer that opened to the campus. Sunlight lit the translucent leaf walls of the school's grand corridor with a soft glow. Along the wide passageway, columns of fiddlehead ferns marked the entrances to the classrooms where Almond and her gang of friends reigned as Seniors.

Professors bustled to lectures and students rushed to drills on a brisk morning at the beginning of the school year. Almond and her friends squeezed together at a side table in the dining hall, surveying the teeming courtyard through the rose window. She scowled. Not one fairy glanced their way.

"Let's make a pact," she said, turning to her friends. "Let's get everyone's attention."

"What are you talking about?" asked Paprika, rustling through her satchel.

Almond's wingtips vibrated. "It's our last year together at Fairy School." She looked pointedly at Paprika, whose fate everyone knew. "Maybe the rest of us don't know where our lives will go, but let's leave this part of it having as much fun as we can." She stuck her hand out, waiting. Paprika edged her hand on top of hers, followed by Amaryllis, Cherry, and Apricot. They perched with their outstretched hands at the nucleus of their friendship, warmth flowing between their fingertips and up their arms.

"Let's make this school year epic!" said Almond, her grin spreading to each of her friends' faces.

Their first epic act had been charming the faculty into letting them paper their classroom windows with flower petals so that sunshine filtered through, lighting them with flattering pink hues as they lounged at their desks. They found excuses to pull the entire Senior class out of lessons to cheer on Amaryllis, aerialist team captain, as she led practices. And Paprika had convinced Chancellor Tweed, Head of Fairy School, to designate the toadstool at the center of the dining hall as their private table.

Unlike Almond and the rest of her friends who would move from the school dorms to the ivy in six moons, Paprika prepared for her life to shrink into the inside of a musty gourd. There, she'd memorize the Fairy Nook's many laws. When she was ready, she would step into her inherited title—the Voice of the Nook—and judge disputes between fairies on behalf of the royal legacy.

Almond's wings had drooped for Paprika. Just because of where and when she hatched, she had no control over her future. She'd miss all the fun at the ivy where foraging duty would mean adventure. But she was grateful that Chancellor Tweed wanted the future Voice as an ally and granted them their special table. Having all eyes on them as she sat with her friends in the center of the hall had felt like a warm meadow breeze.

But nothing they accomplished that year had compared to their fashion show.

Cherry popped her head out from under the driftwood runway they had erected in the school courtyard. "Are you sure Professor Ember agreed to all of this?" she asked.

Almond glanced at her frazzled friend as she straightened the grass bow on Apricot's skirt. "There's nothing for you to worry about besides your look, Cherry. The rest of us are ready." She fluffed the bunches of Lily of the Valley blossoms that formed her own skirt.

For their Senior project in foraging class, Almond had convinced Professor Ember to let them throw a fashion show. They would model outfits that they created from objects they found on the outskirts of the Nook. After working all semester, they'd created garments through trial and error that Almond was proud of. And thanks to Cherry's aunt, a temple keeper, they had a sturdy length of driftwood on loan from the temple garden to use for a runway. Fairies streamed into the courtyard, their chattering and vibrating wingtips echoing throughout the space.

With her friends in place in their forage-crafted outfits, Almond peeked out at the crowd. "Are we ready?" she asked without turning around.

"I was hatched ready," said Apricot in a breathy whisper.

Cherry smoothed her woven pine needle kilt. "As long as Pom-Pom is watching," she said, referring to her boyfriend.

"Let's go!" said Amaryllis, clapping her hands.

"You first, Almond," said Paprika. "This was your idea."

Almond flashed her a smile and strutted down the runway to wild cheers, letting her swinging arms ruffle her skirt blossoms as she walked. Willowy Apricot followed her, and the audience surged to their feet. Almond looked back to see Professor Ember hover above the crowd with a rapt expression as he took in the delicate grass knots and bows covering Apricot's shift. Athletic Amaryllis sprang after her into an aerialist routine, spinning end-over-end so that the iris petals of her skirt swirled like a dancing butterfly's wings. Finally, Paprika's billowing heather gown accentuated Cherry's streamlined kilt as they sashayed along the driftwood, arm in arm.

Tears teased the corners of Almond's golden eyes as she gazed at her beautiful friends captivating the school. Faculty and students of all ages crowded for a closer look at their unique clothes. Almond spotted Pom-Pom fluttering his wings at Cherry. Professor Swift, the riding instructor, noticed and suppressed a smile. Her annoying little sister, Pepper, elbowed her way to the front of the crowd. *Typical,* Almond thought.

She turned her musings to the future. The ivy would be just as fun as school, at least until Apricot went nesting. They all knew that the prettiest fairy would be the first to get joined to a mate. Almond scowled. No one would ever force her to join with another fairy and sit around on an egg while everyone else had fun. Her thoughts drifted to leaving Paprika behind, but she pushed them away. Nothing would ruin this moment.

Squaring her shoulders, she rejoined her best friends on the runway, soaking in the attention of every fairy she knew. She scanned the crowd, making sure that her Lily of the Valley blossom skirt was fluffed and bouncing.

Life had always been easy for her. Why wouldn't it stay that way?

Almond needed to get away from the dollhouse. She knew that she needed to talk her feelings through with Nutsie, but not just yet. First, she had to clear her head and shake off the rising flood of tears in her throat. She wanted Beechnut. But all he wanted was to rip away the scrap of freedom that she'd caught hold of—freedom she craved. She needed to feel it again the way that she needed dew drops to quench her thirst and berry juice to fill her belly. And she needed to feel it immediately.

Her wings vibrated on their own, lifting her high into the treetops. While painful thoughts crashed through her mind, she let her body strain upward. The azure patches of sky between the leaves spread and rendered until she perched on the highest branches of the highest tree and the forest canopy receded into a pixelated green.

Fairies can't fly during the day, she thought angrily, tears springing to her golden eyes as she remembered the lies she'd been taught in Fairy School. *Fairies can't fly above the treetops. All I'm told is that I can't.* She stamped her foot on the tree branch. Taking a calming breath, she tested her wings, waiting for the perfect moment. *I'm sick of hearing that I can't do what I want.* She bent her knees, ready. *They say that my wings will tear if I fly too high? Watch me!* Timing her jump, she leapt onto the back of an oblivious nuthatch that soared from her nest in the tree. Almond tucked her legs around the bird's neck, enjoying the wind sweeping her shoulders.

The nuthatch gave three rapid wing beats to dislodge the pest on her back, but Almond held onto her feathers. Her wild steed swooped high into the air current. Almond peeked over the side and scanned her domain from the clouds. Between the puffs of foliage, she spotted the line of stone wall that led past the Dollhouse Inn toward the silver vein of Rosepurse Stream.

Was that lighter green spot the willow that embraced her home? Was the tidy white dollhouse nestled beneath, full of Nutsie's chittering laughter? She pictured Blunderman just to the side in his blackberry bramble, dreaming up beauty and fun for them to enjoy. Were the fireflies napping after whatever it was that they got up to at night? And was the willow shielding Beechnut, who demanded that she make an impossible choice because he'd never thought for himself—just like most Nook fairies?

But she needed him to think. She needed him to understand—no, agree that she deserved to make her own decisions, even if he didn't agree with her choices. Because she needed him. She didn't understand why, but it was a yearning that was useless to ignore.

She strained to see the Fairy Nook, but it was too well-hidden. Scanning the streamline, she searched for Blunderman's meadow, where the caterpillar architects erected vast monuments to their ingenuity. She longed to see his village someday. After discovering the dollhouse—so different than the natural structures in which fairies dwelled—experiencing the many ways to live in Rosepurse Wood sounded exciting.

She scowled, wind buffeting her cheeks. *That won't be possible if I'm sitting on eggs.*

Swinging her head in the opposite direction, she wondered where the tree bark nest that incubated Aksel and Bo lay. They had become like big brothers to her and Nutsie, steadfastly loyal for no good reason other than they were friends. That was enough for the dashing creatures. Would she ever travel to a grove so thick with the coded glow of fireflies that darkness slipped from the night as if from a sieve? Did they dance together in complex choreography, derrieres flashing, commanding the attention of larger creatures who knew enough not to eat them? The thought was thrilling—to fly confidently as a tiny being, carefree as neither predator nor prey. Just free.

She squinted to see the great trail Mr. Pickles had called a 'road' that led from Rosepurse Village. The hamster's tale of escaping from a human contraption and scampering across the road and into the forest had sounded like an impossible quest. She still couldn't imagine such a trail, or even the human village. Almond had never seen a human, although evidence of the creatures lay throughout the forest—from the chipped teacup in the Nook's hawthorn tree, to the stone wall that protected their estate, to the dollhouse itself. *That would be quite an adventure—a quest to see human dwellings and watch the giants go about their immense lives,* she thought. Would their buildings look like gigantic versions of the dollhouse? Her mental map of the world expanded further, encompassing places she might never see, but would forever know were there.

The first time she had been this high in the sky—a stowaway on a chickadee's own quest to build her nest—her world had been so insignificant that she hadn't even known it. The Nook had been her nucleus, hemmed in by an old oak tree on one side and Rosepurse Stream on the other, with a spray of fern fronds overhead. After gaining the wisdom of time and travel, she understood that for every fairy drama in the Nook, scores of other dramas rippled across the forest, in hundreds of communities. And each one was pivotal to each creature involved.

Her own conflict—whether to join Beechnut or risk losing her new life at the dollhouse—was a perfect example. Either outcome had no impact on oodles of creatures throughout the forest, and yet either way, Almond would lose her freedom. There was one consolation. Rosepurse Wood was still vast, but no matter what happened to her, she now had landmarks that webbed the forest together through lines of friendship.

As the nuthatch crested the air current, Almond slipped off her back. "Thank you," she called over her shoulder to the bird, tucking her wings and aiming her face toward the earth. She soared toward Rosepurse Wood at top speed, arranging her arms and legs to steer her body through the rushing air. Before dropping too low, she curved her body to the side and spiraled through the silky atmosphere until her equilibrium faltered and then allowed herself to tumble in a free fall, arms and legs akimbo.

The soft hills of foliage forming the treetops sharpened into thousands of individual leaves within sight before she unfurled her wings to catch the air. She slowed and then revved her wings, aiming and shooting through the tree canopy, soaring in loop-de-loops, and weaving at top speed through the surrounding groves. One thing was certain—whether she ended up in Beechnut's nest, in her own in the dollhouse, or in the pebble pit back at the Fairy Nook, no one would ever convince her that she couldn't fly high again.

CHAPTER 16

"Does this mean you're moving out of the Dollhouse Inn?" asked Nutsie. She swept the floor of the room under her stone staircase, currently a storeroom, while Almond stuffed found bunny fluff into pods for cushions.

She had just told her friend about Beechnut's announcement to woo her. "I don't want to," she said, burying her face in fluff and thinking of her own nest that she had built in the dollhouse. She'd carefully gathered precious things from the estate to decorate it and make it special. It was hers and she loved it. She wasn't ready to give it up and move to the willow tree.

Even if Beechnut did make her wings tingle—and other places. "What about Mr. Pickles?" she asked.

"Pickles..." Nutsie breathed the name like a petal riding the breeze and twirled around, hugging her dandelion broom to her chest.

Almond paused, fluffing the cushions, before asking: "Does thinking about Mr. Pickles make the space between your legs tingle?"

"Like when you climb a tree root and have to scoot halfway over to propel yourself to the other side?" asked the chipmunk.

Almond scratched her temple. "I typically flutter over tree roots, but I think we're talking about the same thing. Where pee comes out."

Nutsie nodded. "Oh yes, when I'm around Pickles, I feel like I need to pee. But then, I don't end up having to."

"I wonder what that is," said Almond.

"Excitement, I suppose," said Nutsie. "Do you want to join with Beechnut?" She kept her gaze on the floor where she swept. "I can tell that he makes you feel energized."

Almond flushed. What was so important about nesting with Beechnut? She wouldn't feel any more energized by him than she already did if she moved nests, would she? What was the point? Then she replayed that first morning in her mind, lingering on the memory of the chills that ran up her arms when Beechnut's wings had brushed her shoulders. She sensed them now, as if he were caressing her in person. Perhaps it would be worth giving up her nest to begin each day with that sensation. She sighed. "Everything keeps changing so quickly."

Nutsie chittered. "Every time you talk about the Fairy Nook, you say how boring and gross it is. Now, things are fast-paced and exciting. Isn't that what you want?"

"I just want a moon or two to absorb it all," said Almond, shrugging. She eyed Nutsie, a question on her tongue, but hesitated, afraid to hear the answer. Would this be like her friends leaving the ivy after school all over again? "I suppose you and Mr. Pickles will nest together?"

Nutsie stopped twirling. "Certainly not. We've only just met. That's why we're turning this into a nesting space. It's for him—conveniently downstairs from mine!"

A wave of relief washed away Almond's anxiety. "Your own nests! I love that." If Nutsie didn't have to give up her space in order to spend time with Mr. Pickles, then it must be okay for Almond to keep her own nest, too. Beechnut had to understand. She blew out a huge sigh. "I thought there might be something wrong with me."

"Why?" asked Nutsie.

Almond looked up at the chipmunk through her lashes. "I want my own place, too."

Nutsie hugged her, squishing their cheeks together. "You can keep your adorable nest and become closer friends with Beechnut in your own time."

She hugged Nutsie back. "Oh, thank the forest for that. I'm going to tell him right now." Before she lost her nerve, she marched down the pinecone path toward the willow tree. Looking back over her shoulder, she saw Nutsie stare after her for a beat before resuming her sweeping. Almond faltered. What was that look? She shrugged and squared her shoulders, facing the tree. The gentle breeze swayed a nearby willow tendril.

There are three outcomes, she thought. *Ideally, he'll be completely okay with having a relationship with me while we keep separate nests. Unlikely. It's more likely that he'll be offended and never talk to me again. Worse, never* kiss *me again. Or he could freak out and arrest me—again.* No matter what, she had to do this. She had to know. Because not knowing would be just one more thing that controlled her life and made her worry.

Fluttering through the willow branches, she found Beechnut's camp where an adolescent bough forked into two. A stick propped a drape of fern moss for shelter. Hovering in place, he struggled to tighten the ends of the moss to the tree with some thread from the sewing kit.

"This would be easier if I had my dagger," he said through clenched teeth.

She rushed to help him, grabbing one end of the thread. Together they secured the moss with a tidy knot.

He straightened and took her hand, rubbing his thumb across her knuckles. "Now that I'm staying, you don't have to hide my things anymore."

Almond avoided his gaze. *He knows we hid his stuff.* Her face flamed. *Just act natural,* she told herself, flicking her curls over her shoulder. "I'm not sure what you mean."

Beechnut sighed, staring down at her as if contemplating a variety of mushrooms that he didn't recognize. "Maybe they can just turn up in the parlor soon?" He flung his arm in a wide arc as master of the tree. "What sort of nest would you like? Two levels? Three? I can start building it tomorrow."

Almond gently pulled her hand from his and perched on a bark whorl. She patted the seat next to her and he took it. Taking a moment to indulge in a deep gaze into those opalescent clover irises, she forced herself to remain calm. It was important that she worded this just right so that he understood her need for a little time to process her emotions—but also that she still wanted him. He especially needed to understand that part. She didn't want to lose her chance to be with the Knight of the Nook. It just had to be on her terms.

"Respectfully, it feels like one moment you were my captor, and the next you're my suitor. My feelings are all mixed up," she said.

He laughed. "I know you felt what I felt. It didn't need to be said."

"That's not true."

His face blanched and he leaned away from her, studying her from a new angle. "You don't feel the same way for me?"

Almond hid her smile at his shock. The Knight of the Nook assumed that whoever he chose would be honored and ecstatic to join with him before the next moon.

He wasn't wrong.

"I do feel what you feel, of course," she said. "But it's not true that it didn't need to be said. Things need to be said."

"What things?" His brow stitched.

She considered the muscles glistening down his body as he rested his elbows on his knees. Her resolve wavered. *Would it be so bad to cuddle up to this gorgeous fairy at night?* She shook herself, struggling to think clearly despite the sweat rolling off him smelling like hot lilacs. "Most things need to be said, Beechnut. For instance, how was I to know that you felt it, too, or if I was just dazzled by the Great Knight?"

At her use of his provincial title, Beechnut grinned. He caught up her hand and held it to his heart with both of his. "Almondine Ivy Honeydew Nettlesworth, you captivate me. Your spirit is freer than I have ever been. I want your generous heart near me always. When I complete this nest for us, join with me."

Her chest swelled with syrupy light that poured throughout her body, and she struggled not to flutter into his muscled arms. She didn't even care that he called her 'Almondine.'

"I can't wait," he said. He turned away from her, leaving her staring at his back, confused, while he rummaged in a satchel on his hip. Her skin prickled. What was going on? This normally stoic, dignified fairy was flailing about, making declarations and hunching over secrets. He faced her and her gaze traced the lines of his muscled arms to his hands, which he held out to her. A glossy pied feather tipped in crimson lay curled in his palms.

She sucked in her breath. *Is that what I think it is?*

"I have no claim on a peacock feather, but I want you to wear this," he said.

If he placed the delicate turkey featherlette that he held around her neck, they would be joined. She would be bound to kit out their nest, lay an egg—which sounded like agony—and sit on it for seventeen long moons. Doing nothing else. An unbearable tang filled her mouth, and she ground her teeth. Her underarms flooded with sweat. It was too fast. She dragged her gaze from the treasure and searched his eyes. They were deep green and tipped up at the edges, rimmed in thick aubergine lashes, and gave off the slightest glow as he waited for her answer.

His bottom lip hung ripe, full of hot blood that stained it cinnamon against his glistening topaz skin. She wanted to reach up and nibble it. Every fiber in her body screamed to mate with the great hero of the Nook. She had once thought that she would feel badly about herself if she joined with a fairy to whom she was attracted. Their beauty would make her look dull and disheveled by comparison. She was too thin— all elbows and knees—and her wings hardly ever glimmered as magically as other fairies'. But rather than making her insecure, Beechnut's physical perfection elevated her self-image so that in her mind's eye, she was a prime example of fairy beauty, grace, and strength. Her tangled lavender curls became flowing, silky tresses. Her sweaty periwinkle skin glowed; her recalcitrant personality was, in fact, effervescent. She liked herself more under the glare of his desire for her.

How had she forgotten what it was like to be carefree? Next to him, it all came back to her—confidence, self-worth, a feeling of control over her destiny, the exuberance for life of a school pip. She wanted to melt into him and watch his smile light up as he fixed the featherlette collar around her neck...like a noose. Her heart fluttered so that she clutched her chest. She struggled to control her breathing, drawing slow, deep breaths through her nose. Taking her time, she exhaled. No, she never wanted to join—never wanted to lay eggs.

She knew this about herself as surely as she knew that she loved cloudberries and hated getting her wings dirty. These were truths about herself that had no reason to change. Changing her mind now would not be an achievement, but the first step on a long road to sorrow.

But then she noticed the silkiness of the featherlette. She imagined how it would feel caressing her neck. So soothing...and to wear such treasure—would it be like an added layer of protection? Like another defense against enemies both known and unknown? Its crimson tip drew her gaze, at once so impossibly deep and vibrant. Pulled closer, she lost herself in the hue reserved for berries, birds, and danger.

Almond shook herself. Her nose nearly touched the featherlette in Beechnut's hands. He continued to hold the offering out to her, seeming to instinctively know not to interrupt her mind as it absorbed the possibility of treasure. *I don't need this,* she thought, scowling. *I have treasure—Nutsie, all my friends, a home. Why would I give all that up for a status symbol? No matter how rare and valuable it is. It's not going to impress anyone I care about, anyway. What do chipmunks know about feathers?*

The thought of showing Nutsie the ornament and then explaining what it meant snapped her out of the spell that it cast on her. Her friend would laugh at the idea of exchanging her freedom for a feather and probably find a scrap of goose down to replace it. And she would be right. No matter how gorgeous or impressive Beechnut was, he was not worth giving up what she and her friends had built with their own tenacity. And they had so much more to do. What was Almond going to say to them as they toiled to build out the dollhouse's defenses and expand its possibilities? That she couldn't help? How would it feel to tell them that she couldn't participate in the projects because she had to sit on her egg?

And then what would happen when that egg hatched? With no Fairy School, no cohorts, and danger everywhere, how could she bring a pip into the forest? No. She couldn't do it. Taking a deep breath, she closed her eyes and doused her desire by picturing herself picking ticks out of Nutsie's fur. "I can be near you always—from over there." She pointed to the dollhouse.

Beechnut dropped his hands. "Are you refusing my turkey feather?"

She placed her hand back on his heart. "Beechnut, it's taken me a lot of time and hard work to figure out where I want to be. And how to make it happen. I'm not going to give that up for some knight."

He jerked away as if struck and pushed the featherlette back into his satchel.

She wished that she could stuff her careless words back into her face. "I didn't mean to say, 'some knight' as if you are not a great champion," she said hurriedly. "I am supremely honored by your attention. I just like my own tidy nest and to be around my friends. Can't we have a bond without sharing a nest or joining?" She reached out and stroked his arm.

"Even if I build a two-level foxhole?" he asked.

Almond's lavender curls bounced as she shook her head. "I hope that you still want to spend time with me since I'm staying in my own nest—maybe forever." She dragged her big toe in a circle and turned toward the dollhouse, hoping he'd wrap his arms around her and murmur that she could do anything she wanted. She hovered off his branch, still waiting. Would he call out to her—beg her to come back? Fluttering toward the Dollhouse Inn, she desperately wanted to hear him say that she was worth it.

He didn't stop her from flying away.

Pepper picked at the luxe peacock featherlettes surrounding her throat. She needed to break this new habit of worrying the delicate under-feathers—they had already lost some luster and looked mangy. But her best spies had brought disappointing news. No, infuriating news. The thought of Almond frolicking free in the forest made Pepper want to rip the feathers from her throat. She forced her hand to her side. "Saddle up Nectar," she said to Cloudforce, her new general. "I'm going after Almond myself."

General Cloudforce's wings twitched. "Perhaps we should ride together to do reconnaissance."

The queen bared her sharp teeth. "This isn't a reconnaissance mission, Cloudforce. It's war."

Cloudforce stiffened. His eyes darted around the throne room, taking in the great snake fangs hanging in a place of honor; the over-turned toadstool table that the queen had kicked in a rage. Tugging at his new general's tunic, he switched his hardwood spear to his other shoulder. "The troopers can follow behind us along Rosepurse Stream and be ready for your orders."

Pepper rounded on him, her royal blue tresses swinging in a tangled sheet. "I can handle my sister."

Cloudforce bowed his acquiescence, careful not to meet her gaze. "Of that I am certain, Queen Pepper. I only remind you that the defector has somehow taken control of Beechnut's senses and turned the Knight of the Nook into a traitor. Best not to take chances?"

Pepper tilted her head. Sunlight streamed through the spaces where the leaf walls met, illuminating orange threads of exhaustion in the whites of her eyes. "That fool knight. Yes, let's all go. A show of force is what the Fairy Nook must witness."

Cloudforce bowed and walked backward out of the throne room. As he went, he spied her picking at her royal featherlettes and winced.

The pointed tips of Almond's ears burned. Her curls drooped down the nape of her neck in the soupy air. She had wanted Beechnut to tell her that he respected and admired her need for independence. But he'd remained silent. She beat her wings, flying just above the ground to Nutsie, who pretended to sweep the pinecone path. The chipmunk threw down her dandelion broom when she saw Almond's face. Gathering her in her fluff, she held Almond, letting her cry.

Almond soaked her friend's fur with tears. "I'm sorry," she said pulling away and wiping her nose on her wingtip.

Nutsie waved her paw. "Never mind the fur. I bathe four times a day. Speaking of baths, what you need is a soak and—" She shifted her gaze around the estate, as if the lawn was teeming with eavesdropping creatures rather than one fairy, one chipmunk, a caterpillar sunning himself on the lip of a pool, and seven stinkbugs on their way to a late lunch.

"And what?" asked Almond.

Nutsie grinned, displaying her impressive front teeth. "And Blunderman says some of the blackberries dropped from the bramble and rolled into a niche, where they fermented."

"What does that mean?"

Nutsie hesitated. "I'm not sure. But he said if we squeeze the juice and drink it, we'll feel wonderful!"

Almond shook her head. "Juice is wonderful, but it can't help me right now. If I don't keep moving, the confusing feelings scratching at the inside of my chest are going to fill up my throat."

Nutsie's eyes went wide and the stripes down her back bristled.

Almond paced tiny footprints into the pinecone path. "The only way I'm going to distract myself is with hard work." She raked her fingers through her hair. "That's about the only wisdom I've carried with me from the Fairy Nook."

Nutsie twisted her paws together. "I feel like you should be with your friends. If you don't want to come drink fermented juice, how about I join you?"

Almond shook her head and revved her wings. "No, let me just do a turn around the perimeter, and then I'll meet you at the pool. I promise." Before Nutsie could protest, she kicked off the ground and zipped behind the dollhouse.

Bending to peek through the tunnel in the stone wall, Almond saw a bit of fluff left from Mr. Pickles when he ran from the fox. It was a reminder that they could not be too careful. For all their preparations, the denizens of the Dollhouse Inn were alive mostly out of luck. She decided to scout on the other side of the wall for trouble. Tucking her iridescent wings close to her body, she squeezed through the tunnel. She could fly over the wall, but they had all agreed that checking on any ingress to the dollhouse was vital.

Safely through, she scanned the underbrush for any signs of predators. Fallen branches and sticks littered the ground, reminding her of how wild this patch of Rosepurse Wood was when she and Nutsie first found it. They had cleared and organized the land around the dollhouse on their side of the stone wall. But on this side, discarded nut casings hugged the soil, never sinking below the surface for a chance at life.

No scat or paw prints marred the ground and Almond relaxed her muscles. She hadn't realized that she'd flexed them while scanning for enemies, ready to defend her home. Her wings drooped. They needed to rest, so she set off down the line of the wall toward Rosepurse Stream on foot, determined to keep watch to the end of their grove and back. And then she would patrol in the other direction—without thinking too much about Beechnut.

CHAPTER 17

Almond's legs swung over the edge of the wall as she gazed at the tree that used to be Nutsie's prison. It had been less than a moon since they escaped and found the dollhouse, and yet their lives had changed completely. She had already reached the section of the wall where Rosepurse Stream's sloshing grew loud. That, along with a violent splotch of lichen on one of the wall's supporting stones, marked the end of their territory. Without stopping to rest, she'd spun in the opposite direction and marched here, where memories were unforgiving. Perhaps one day they could visit this spot without the specter of Boscoe haunting their dreams.

He's gone, she thought. But jagged memories of Boscoe's fury unleashed a burst of adrenaline that chased her back to the tunnel in the wall. She'd encountered no interlopers in either direction. A long slog, but worth the certainty that the Dollhouse Inn was safe for the moment. She opened herself up to the fatigue.

At the mouth of the tunnel to her own side of the wall, she hesitated. What would she walk into? Would Beechnut shun her?

Threaten to arrest her? Back at the Nook, bad things happened to fairies who refused a joining.

She slid her back down the great stones, finding a comfortable spot in the grass. *I'll just stay here,* she thought. Her tongue was gluey in her mouth. *I can ignore my thirst—it's better than facing him.*

She dug the bottoms of her feet into the earth, pressing down into the sedge with her palms. Her heart raced alarmingly. She focused on a torn leaf that waved at the end of a branch, swallowing buckets of saliva that flooded her mouth.

Breathe, breathe, breathe. She repeated the thought again and again.

The torn leaf waved.

Breathe.

Her brow cooled. The nausea subsided and her heart settled back into its cavity. As Almond regained control of her senses, she realized how exposed she was. Her prey instinct activated deep in her primal brain, and she dove into the tunnel headfirst, streamlining her wings as an afterthought. She yanked her feet inside, waves of fear rolling over her. Forcing herself to slow down, she placed her trembling hands on the floor and crawled on her knees. Halfway through, a squeal cracked the silence and Almond's head snapped up. She waited, motionless, but nothing followed. Stretching a hand in front of her, she increased her pace to reach the circle of daylight and grass beyond. *Almost there,* she thought. *Just keep it together.*

Her head jerked back.

Something held her hair. She tugged as hard as she dared but couldn't move. Panting, she fluttered her fingertips up the tunnel wall beside her. Nothing protruded. She swiped her hand across the wall in a slow arc. Her wrist bumped against the lock of her hair stretching to the wall like a tight rope. She scrabbled to find what held her and something scraped her finger. A sliver in the stone had caught her curls and held tight, trapping her in the middle of the tunnel. She had been so concerned about protecting her wings that she let her hair become caught. Jerking to free herself, her skin burned where several strands ripped from her scalp. She had to stop.

"Nutsie!" she called, squirming as the tunnel seemed to shrink around her. Surely Nutsie would hear her. The dollhouse was right there, a pebble's toss from the tunnel. "Nutsie!" Listening to the burble of fresh water tinkling into the pool, she heard the murmur of voices nearby mingling with the watery sounds—probably Mr. Pickles and Blunderman.

"Help!" she cried.

No one came. *Where's Beechnut, the big hero?* she thought sourly. He was all the way in the willow tree, building his nest. Her shoulder chafed against the stone. Aksel and Bo were still sleeping off a long session of lighting up the night—she knew there was no point in calling to them. *Stay calm. Someone will look for you soon,* she thought. But would they? She'd asked for time to think. On the other hand, she'd been gone for a quarter of the sun's journey across the sky. That was reason to search for her, right?

Breathe, breathe, breathe.

She leaned her head against the tunnel wall, relaxing her weight into it to ease the pulling at her scalp. She couldn't lay down, but the curve of the tunnel cradled her enough. The cold stone soothed her cheek. *There's a way out of this,* she thought. *This situation is too ridiculous to be real.* She slid her hand up the wall to the sliver that held her hair.

There weren't just a few strands caught. She had no problem ripping a few hairs. Somehow, an entire lavender ringlet had slid into the slim slice of stone that she had never spotted in the tunnel. She tugged at the lock. It was wedged in and held fast by natural serrations in the sliver. Pressing one hand against her scalp to dampen the pain from tugging, she grasped the end of her caught lock with the other. Gently, she bobbed her head to run the hairs back and forth across the serrations. How had this formed, anyway? Perhaps moisture had seeped into the stone, separating a jagged scale of rock from the wall. It didn't matter. She stopped sawing.

I'm really trapped.

She rested her cheek against the wall again. Life never stopped offering up situations that she could never imagine. For example, how could she know that she'd be carried off by a chickadee? *You shouldn't have taken a nap outside of the Fairy Nook,* a voice deep within her scolded. How could she foresee the wall of a tunnel snatching up her hair? *You were careless rushing through,* said the voice.

These wild events had appeared like they were happening to her.

But Almond had to admit that her own impulsive actions led to the adventures—both good and bad. It had been her own ill temper that almost got her swallowed up by a deadly mud puddle. It had been her own careless words that had stung Beechnut so that he probably didn't hear what she was trying to tell him. Her words had also hurt her friend, Nutsie, in the past. She had to change that about herself.

At the same time, she couldn't berate herself endlessly for youthful mistakes. After all, if it weren't for the chickadee, she wouldn't have met Nutsie and saved her from Boscoe. And they wouldn't have found the dollhouse. And if not for the mud puddle, they wouldn't have sweet Blunderman to make things fun and beautiful. *Yes, good can come with the bad,* she thought. But maybe it was time to think things through a bit more carefully and be thoughtful with her words. Her emotions settled. She would start with her relationship with Beechnut.

From her cold stone pillow, she spotted a crescent of lawn between the willow's trunk and the bramble. Peachy afternoon light tinted the area. *At least I'm trapped with a pretty view,* she thought.

And then ice crept down her spine.

She watched a needle's tip pierce the space that marked the beginning of the estate. *It can't be,* she thought wildly. It was a nightmare worse than a snarling raccoon—the needle revealed itself to be a hummingbird's beak.

And not just any hummingbird.

Nectar! Panic clutched Almond at the sight of her sister's bird. She struggled to breathe, fighting against the snag that held her. Her forehead scraped stone, burned cold, and then wet blood seeped from the abraded skin. The pain shocked her out of her panic, and she willed herself still, huffing air but no longer thrashing out of control.

Pepper was here.

Like a dark dream, Pepper sat astride her thoroughbred hummingbird, back erect, surveying the gleaming dollhouse. Her gaze glowed magenta as it raked the pinecone-lined path and river stone steps. Trapped in the tunnel, Almond marveled at her little sister's face. The younger fairy's once haughty exuberance had morphed into brittle disgust that made her look twice her age. There was weariness there, as well—possibly the badge of a disappointing joining. How had she completely transformed so quickly?

Despite Pepper's worn appearance, she had the bearing of a fairy with backup. Almond didn't have to see past her to know that she wasn't alone. She was sure that her sister had led her officers here, gliding over the pebbled banks and puckered mosses of Rosepurse Wood on the backs of their swift birds. The ladybug spies must have given her detailed directions to the Dollhouse Inn.

Pepper was so young and brimming with newfound power. If Almond had only considered what her sister was capable of. She had a plan for foxes, floods, and fires. Why didn't she have a plan in place to halt any aggression from the Fairy Queen? The answer was that it had never occurred to her that Pepper would actually venture here—even after she'd sent Beechnut and the Royal Ladybug Brigade. But she knew that it was too late to stop her sister. By the time she saw Nectar's beak breach her sanctuary, Pepper's eyes glowed with the hunt.

Almond didn't hear the Nook's troopers buzzing behind their new queen. Hummingbirds flew eight times faster than fairies. But the soldiers were probably less than a day behind the aerial reconnaissance. Even without her full army, it was clear that Pepper intended to strike immediately. Almond strained to see the dollhouse, which must have looked unprotected to her sister.

Where was Nutsie? How could she alert her friends? Sweat inched from her brow to the corners of her eyes, stinging them with salt. Chittering floated to her ears from the front of the dollhouse, just out of her line of sight. Almond closed her eyes and sagged, picturing Nutsie scolding Pepper and her officers—the silly chipmunk. She could only see her sister, but Pepper's expression dripped contempt and malice. The Fairy Queen raised a signaling finger.

Almond sucked in her breath. From behind Pepper, arrows arced across the sky and rained upon the dollhouse. "Nutsie!" she screamed from the tunnel. The chittering ceased and Almond held her breath, staining to hear anything. Pepper must not have heard her scream because her gaze remained laser focused on the lawn, outside of Almond's field of vision.

A low keening cry increased in volume like a slowly boiling teapot. Almond yanked at her trapped hair, feeling it slip loose and then catch again on the stony teeth. The keening rose, nipping at Almond's threshold of pain. Then she saw a red-brown blur barrel toward Nectar.

Chuck chuck!

A lesser bird would have reared, but he stood at attention. The chipmunk raced toward him, and he brought his needle beak down in an arc, pinning Nutsie's paw to the dirt.

Almond struggled to hold in a scream when her best friend's keening battle-cry erupted into a shriek. Nutsie sobbed and pulled at her pinned paw, causing blood to spray across Nectar's beak. Almond stared at the macabre scene, shocked. Then an image of the scars that laced Nutsie's neck and shoulders—inflicted by Boscoe's beak—flashed into her mind.

She grabbed the lock of hair that was trapped in the stone and yanked again and again. Ripping and pulling in a frenzy, she tore her hair free. She had to get to Nutsie before that bird took off her paw. Hair pulled from her scalp and a trickle of blood washed her temple. She groaned and gave one last yank, leaving a length of lavender curls to decorate the tunnel's wall. Almond zoomed out of the hole, wings vibrating with rage, and aimed for Nectar.

Pepper saw her coming.

At her signal, Pepper's officers let loose a spray of arrows, grabbing the next deadly shaft as soon as they let one fly. There was no escaping—there were too many. Almond didn't notice the searing pain in her wing-tip until after the arrow pierced it. Her wing collapsed and she spiraled to the lawn, landing hard.

"Stay down!" Pepper warned her, eyes glittering.

Blood rushed in Almond's ears and Nutsie's screams melted into the thud of her own heartbeat. She saw the excruciating pain on her friend's face. Sucking in air, she tried to catch the breath that was smacked out of her when she hit the turf. Mentally, she examined each section of her body for broken bones. *There.* The inside of her left kneecap swelled under her fingertips. It was just a sprain.

She had to free Nutsie.

Don't you tell me to 'stay down,' she thought, glaring at Pepper through outraged tears. Sitting up, she pushed herself off the ground with her hands, testing her weight on the sprain. It was nothing she couldn't push through. She lowered her chin and faced her sister astride Nectar. Pepper stroked his shimmering neck feathers as he held Nutsie fast to the ground for all to see. Almond took a step toward her and then cried out as she fell to the ground like a dead branch. The pain in her leg sang in her ears, stealing focus from anything else except for Pepper's cackling glee.

"Look at us now," said Pepper, grinning down at her as if she weren't battered and broken. "You, below me, in the dirt where you belong."

Almond gripped her knee and rolled her head to face Pepper. "Release the chipmunk! Why are you doing this?"

Pepper ignored her question. "Maybe you didn't hear me the first time, sister, when I told you that I am the Fairy Queen. *Not* you."

"Of course I'm not queen," said Almond. *What in the forest is she talking about?* "And I wouldn't want to be. Congratulations, Pepper. You are finally relevant."

Waves of heat emanated from Pepper's body and Nectar shifted under her, unsettled. "You don't deserve to be queen! I'll make sure that you will never be anything except a cautionary tale passed from every parent to every pip in the Fairy Nook, warning all to obey me."

Again, Almond was shocked by her sister's hatred. What had she done to foster these dark feelings in her? Just because she gave her a hard time in school? Back then, it never occurred to her that Pepper was anything but self-satisfied and pampered. The entire freshman class did her bidding, and Almond wasn't willing to let her take over the senior class, as well. Pepper had to pay her dues like every other fairy at school.

Maybe her friends took some pranks too far, but Pepper never seemed bothered. She was the one who kept coming back for more. Almond shook her head. She couldn't justify her behavior—even to herself. If her behavior had been okay, Pepper wouldn't be inflicting this evil upon them. She had to take responsibility for causing this pain.

"My Queen," she called, keeping her gaze lowered. She pressed her willowy limbs into the ground, making herself as lowly as possible. "I surrender. Please take me to do with as you wish and leave this place in peace. Fairy business doesn't concern any other creature on this estate."

Pepper jolted forward on her mount. "They aided you! Every

creature here is guilty of harboring a fugitive. No one can be allowed to get away with that. And I didn't fly this far from the Nook without returning with the spoils of war." She licked her lips.

That last statement chilled Almond's wings. *Spoils of war? She can't mean*—her thought was interrupted when another blur of fur, this time peach and white, streaked by. Mr. Pickles raced from the bramble toward Nutsie, his eyes glittering beads. He skidded next to her and wrapped the sturdy bones of his jaw around Nectar's sleek beak.

Nectar's neck feathers flared, and Pepper struggled to stay upright as her steed shook the hamster back and forth. Mr. Pickles's paws lost contact with the ground and his fluffy hindquarters waved in the air. Nectar beat his feathers and scrabbled through a patch of loamy soil. With two rapid jerks, he pulled his beak out of the ground, releasing Nutsie, who fell back, clutching her mangled paw. Mr. Pickles hung from Nectar's beak and the proud hummingbird flung him into the trunk of the willow tree, where he slid to the ground in a limp ball of fur.

Almond stared in horror. *Don't be dead,* she thought, gripping her swollen knee. The fur ball stirred, and she let out her breath. But then Pepper's officers boxed in the hamster and hauled him to his paws. They shoved him inside a cage woven from strips of young bark. Mr. Pickles tumbled inside the cage and lay still. Nutsie kept up a low keening, cradling her mangled paw, as they marched her to the cage and pushed her in after him.

They were captured.

And it happened in an instant. From the ground, Almond's nightmare came to life. Her closest companions were injured, under attack, terrified in their own home. But the mortification was nothing compared to seeing the mask of hate that gripped Pepper's face. They had never been close. She took the blame for that. But the fact that her own sister loathed her this much—to hurt innocent creatures just to hurt her, to destroy and terrorize. It was wrong.

And it was especially wrong to let it happen on such a pretty day, with a breeze so gentle that its caress went unnoticed. Nothing good happened today. Beechnut's exasperation with her sense of independence flashed through her mind, mingling with all the other pain. Almond stiffened. *Beechnut!* Where was he? If ever the Dollhouse Inn needed a hero, it was now. She scanned the tableau. The former Knight of the Nook was nowhere to be seen. She wondered, throat burning, if he had returned to serving the Nook now that the Fairy Queen was here.

Queen Pepper forced Nectar to hover in place, an acting throne from which she surveyed her chaos, and screeched orders at her officers. "Cage any creature you find!" Her eyes glowed deep magenta.

Almond would have pitied the hummingbird whose wings and beak must be screaming, had he not just maimed her best friend. She cast about for anything that she could use to stand and spotted a pile of sticks. Her shift shredded beneath her bottom as she scooted toward them and grabbed the stoutest. She hauled herself to her good foot and hobbled behind low-hanging willow boughs, looking first at the cage holding Nutsie and Mr. Pickles, and then at Pepper—who appeared oblivious to Almond's movements as she yanked Nectar's reigns.

Almond froze with indecision. What should she do?

If she could stop Pepper, make her call off her officers, this horror could end. But no one guarded the cage. The officers ransacked the dollhouse, tossing furniture out of the open face. The violet streamer that she wove for Nutsie's nest floated to the tops of the pinecones and snagged there, like the tears caught in her eyelashes. Blunderman's clay chipmunk figurine that he sculpted for Nutsie arced from the parlor, hanging in the air as if looking for answers, and then smashed on the river stone steps. Almond sucked in shallow breaths. She had to free her friends and get them to safety before the situation worsened.

Starting toward the cage, she stopped mid-step at a high-pitched war cry. Her mouth dropped open. Blunderman's oblong green body swiveled through the air and landed with an oof on Nectar's head.

It's not over, Almond thought.

The harassed hummingbird finally reared but the caterpillar, face-to-face with Pepper, managed to hold his seat on Nectar's slippery, mother-of-pearl crown feathers. Blunderman's apple-red azalea hat tipped rakishly over one eye, and he quivered under the Fairy Queen's furious glare.

"Where did you come from?" Pepper glanced up and saw that her steed had shifted them under a branch. "Get off, worm!" She swiped at him with the back of her hand, but he flattened himself into a scoop of jelly and clung as Nectar whipped his head back and forth.

Blunderman bounced up and leaped at Pepper. Almond's stare widened at his agility. He clung with his nubs to Pepper's hair. With every grab she made for him above her head, he shivered his gelatinous body away from her grasp.

"Let my friends go," he cried.

"Who?" Pepper screeched and tried to shake him off, but he held fast. "You're pulling my hair!"

Forgetting the cage, Almond skipped and hobbled toward them on the walking stick. Panic that Pepper would hurt Blunderman fueled her to push through the pain. She didn't hear the whirring sound that increased in volume as two stones, each on opposite ends of a thin vine, hurled toward her, wrapping around her legs and walking stick on impact. One of the stones smashed into her hurt knee, and she cried out as she fell. Her face hit the ground, and her lower lip split like the skin of an overripe berry.

She hadn't helped anyone.

Through her tangled hair, she saw the smug jawline of Cloudforce astride a hummingbird, twirling another bola aimed for her. Did Pepper want her dead? She lay face down in the dirt with blue snot running onto her forearm. Her knee and pierced wing throbbed out of sync, forming one continuous beat of pain. She wasn't meant to be a fighter, slashing through this foliage of violence. Almond had prided herself on defending the Dollhouse Inn, but that was pip's play compared to the mayhem that Pepper unleashed on the forest. She was no match for her.

Cloudforce still *whirred* the weapon in the air, but his attention was focused on Blunderman, who clung to Queen Pepper's head. The ransacking had ceased, and Almond scanned the air, spotting two of the other officers circling Nectar on their birds as Pepper pulled at Blunderman's nubs.

No one bothered to look Almond's way. She could still save Nutsie and Mr. Pickles. Unwinding the bola from her legs, she dragged her good leg under her, knee to chest, pushing from the ground. She stood, keeping her weight off her hyperextended knee, and used the stick to counterbalance her torn wing.

With her head still ringing where it struck the ground, she eased toward the cage, taking care not to move too quickly and draw attention. The stick slid through the dirt. She was sure that one of Pepper's lackeys would send another projectile her way at any moment.

The plaited cage rattled as her friends struggled to free themselves. *Hang on. I'm almost there,* she thought, willing them to be quiet.

Steps from the cage, she looked over her shoulder at Cloudforce flinging his weapon at Blunderman. Pepper saw the bola coming, eyes like acorn caps. She ducked in time for it to missed her—as well as the caterpillar on her head—but Almond instinctively cried out.

She dove into a clump of daisies before anyone saw her, landing hard. An officer wheeled her bird around and tracked the area around the cage. Almond crouched as she prodded her hummingbird toward them, scanning the sponge of dark green moss and twisted tree roots clawing up from the earth.

"Be still," Almond whispered to Nutsie and Mr. Pickles. The cage stopped rattling, and dry sniffles emanated from the gloomy interior. Almond held her breath, careful not to sway the daisies above her head. Her pierced wing trembled, and she pressed her hand against the wound to restrain it.

The fairy officer finished her surveillance but stayed close. Almond couldn't make a move without being caught.

CHAPTER 18

Beechnut emerged from the deep, cool hollow in the willow tree that would serve as his emergency bunker. He chose it for its knotted bark walls that were so thick he wouldn't hear any Dollhouse Inn shenanigans. Which would be handy when the Innkeepers—as he'd begun to think of Almond, Nutsie, Blunderman, Aksel, Bo, and Mr. Pickles—hosted late-night pool parties. Perhaps he'd want a sanctuary away from the celebrating. He was still getting used to having time for relaxation and socializing.

As the Knight of the Nook, his sole purpose was being strong. Physically, mentally, and emotionally. The only fairies he ever witnessed having fun were royals. And he wasn't one of them. He attended their events as muscle—there, but not. More like a menacing ghost. He had never allowed himself to consider what it felt like to be one of them— to recline on the softest toadstools, or sip the freshest berry juice, or even admire the trophies of his own conquests. He understood being a regular fairy even less. He had been bred and groomed for a life that he never chose. And before now, he had never questioned it.

As he squeezed out of the hole, he spotted Almond falling at the hands of Cloudforce, a low-level cadet who was inexplicably wearing an officer's tunic and escorting the queen. He bit back a shout when Almond's gorgeous ringlets hit the dirt, her long legs entangled in a bola. Rage bubbled in his gut. *Why in the everlasting sun is my chosen fairy being attacked?*

His training took over.

Flitting between leaves, he moved downwind before dropping to the ground. He didn't know how these cadets had jockeyed into escorting the queen as officers, but he knew that Cloudforce was a formidable tracker. Beechnut had to assume that they knew he was there. *A hedgie witch hex on the Ladybug Brigade,* he thought sourly of the royal spies. He crept through the tenacious switchgrass and crouched, hidden, to assess the situation.

His wings went rigid as he witnessed Blunderman drop from a branch onto Nectar's head and then launch himself at Queen Pepper. He shook his head at the unpredictable caterpillar. *Brave and true,* he thought, impressed. He retreated to the farthest fall of willow leaves and scooped a wad of clay mud from a soft spot in the ground. Smearing the sticky red soil in slashes along his cheeks and down his limbs, he camouflaged his scent and faded further into the surrounding vegetation.

Beechnut compressed his rage at seeing Almond attacked into a cold stone of fury that he tucked away for later. He couldn't help her now. As much as it broke his heart, he needed to remain focused and alert—or he'd never survive. He couldn't ever be captured. There would be no grace offered to a runaway knight. Every fairy's focus was on the caterpillar berating their shrieking queen. No one noticed him skirt the edge of the property behind the hummingbird squad and race for the bramble—except for Almond.

From her hiding place under the snowy daisy petals, Almond witnessed Beechnut running for the bramble. She shook her head, confused. *Why would he run away?* she asked herself. *There's no one left—unless he's saving himself from the wrath of Pepper.*

Cloying disappointment and despair coated her heart as she contemplated his betrayal. It was barely discernible from the horror that surged through her at her friends' abuse. Her thoughts spun—haggard and defeated.

Nutsie, her best friend in all of Rosepurse Wood, sat suffering with a severe paw wound—possibly crippling. Would she even survive this macabre invasion? And poor, innocent Mr. Pickles had escaped one cage just to end up in a more brutal one. Blunderman bravely launched himself into the fray when he could have easily slipped away unnoticed... just like she saw Beechnut do. But the caterpillar who had once saved her life at the sticky marsh would never run away.

With a shriek of triumph, Pepper flung Blunderman into the shadows. Almond watched him sail through the air, his body wriggling in a spiral as he went. With dread, she scanned his airborne height and gauged his velocity. Surviving that fall would be a miracle. She twitched her injured wing. *Maybe I can get to him in time.* She strained the muscle that controlled it, hunching her shoulder and gnashing her teeth, willing it to unfurl and catch air. The wing hung limply, throwing her off balance.

She swiped the tears that trickled down her cheeks and surveyed the fairy officer guarding Nutsie and Mr. Pickles. Pepper barked orders at the squad and the officer urged her hummingbird closer to the queen—away from the cage. Almond's pulse charged with hope. She waited a beat in case the guard came right back but her luck held. Crawling on her hands and one good knee from behind the daisies, she pulled her hurt leg behind her.

I don't care about being down in the dirt, she thought. *I just need to free my friends.*

The grasses rustled as she crawled through, but there was nothing she could do about it. Pepper or one of her Nook fairies would look her way any second. She just had to get to the cage door before that happened. Bolts of pain shot up her sprained knee as she dragged it over vegetation and pebbles that littered the area. Orange smears of blood slicked her palms from scraping against rough ground cover and she dug her elbows into the turf, pulling herself toward her friends. Her good wing fluttered helplessly. *Nearly there,* she thought.

"You there! What are you doing?" Cloudforce shouted.

Almond ignored him. She reached for the latch on the cage door.

Laying on his taut stomach, Beechnut pulled himself under the bramble with his elbows, doing his best not to rustle its leaves. Captivity was not an option. Reaching the tangle of thorns forming a cell that Blunderman used for storage, he rummaged until he dislodged a length of rope woven from spiderwebs.

He tucked the rope into his belt and continued to pull himself under the purple-hued bramble, avoiding pools of sticky blackberry juice. Closing his eyes against the thorns, he groped his way to the back of the tangle, toward a hidden exit. The few story sessions he's spent in the bramble with Blunderman, Aksel, and Bo were paying off. He knew his way around.

Where were the fireflies? As he wormed along, he thought back to when he saw them last. Was it this morning that they lazed into their nests after their typical nocturnal carousing? Or was that yesterday? The days had been running together as he worked on the estate with his newfound neighbors. Wherever they were, he hoped that Aksel and Bo were someplace far from here and the wrath of the Fairy Queen.

From what he had just witnessed, Pepper, unchecked, had become crazed with power. How could Cornsilk let this happen? Beechnut scowled at the answer—foxglove. Cornsilk likely didn't know about this invasion. Growing up, Prince Cornsilk had been the closest fairy that he had to a friend. He protected the young prince as part of his knight training. Although their lives had been headed in opposite directions, both were uniquely lonely as part of their stations. Neither a prince nor a knight-in-training were allowed to play and roughhouse with the other fairy pips. They spent many evenings whispering about Nook gossip and dreaming of adventures.

Something in Beechnut had broken watching Cornsilk descend into a foxglove habit. Secretly, he blamed the new queen and the pressure she applied to get her way. But his loyalty to the young king was why he had tolerated serving Pepper. Watching her now, he knew that she was here for one thing only—destruction. There was no point in sticking around to try and talk it out.

Beechnut reached the back opening of the bramble and peered into the dusky forest. Whatever lay out there, it had to be better than facing an unhinged fairy queen. He pulled himself out of the opening and threw a glance over his shoulder at the terrible scene behind him—someone's blood in the soil; what might be a scrap of Almond's beautiful wing discarded like refuse. He shuddered and pushed the sadness away. It would do him no good here.

All he had to do was fly up the backside of the bramble to the lip of the bathing pool. None of the fairy officers had approached it yet, and no one looked his way. Safely behind the ceramic bowl that formed the pool, he reached out from where he hid in the bramble and wrapped his iron fingers over the brim, hanging his body down the side. It was slippery, and he struggled to keep his hands edging along its perimeter.

Found it, he thought, pressing his lips together. In the gloom, his palm slid over the rough spot where the bowl had once chipped in a long ago fall. An isthmus of steadfast pottery poking up in the chip was enough to secure the spiderweb rope before he rappelled to the front of the bramble. He bent his knees, grounding himself, and tested the rope.

It held.

As Pepper screeched at her cronies to find Almond's body and collect the cage full of new work animals, Beechnut heaved himself into a squat, throwing his considerable strength into pulling the rope with him. The bowl shifted. He squatted again and flung his body forward, wings buzzing. This time, the bowl edged forward. Sweat poured into his eyes, but he didn't let go of the rope to clear them. *There's not enough time,* he thought. His wings sagged into futile flapping.

Still, he strained forward.

A pair of green dots flashed in his peripheral vision. Aksel and Bo, looking refreshed from their deep rest, posed next to him with stances wide and fully armed with new fox bone swords.

"Looks like we woke up in time for a little sabotage," said Bo.

"Grab the rope and pull," said Beechnut, grunting.

They dropped their swords and fell into line behind him, pulling with their buggy super strength. Again, Beechnut flung himself to the ground with the spiderweb rope pulled over his shoulder, this time with the fireflies yanking behind him. The bowl rocked and then scraped along the stone.

Almond and Pepper's gazes found each other across the lawn as they both understood what was coming. They'd heard the bowl scrape. Time seemed to hover in the air, and then water sloshed over the pool's lip and splashed onto the ground in front of the bramble.

Her heart surged—Beechnut hadn't run away as it had seemed. He was trying to save them! *And he's using my tactic,* she thought, chuckling through her pain. He was swamping the battlefield through brute strength—just like she'd swamped old Boscoe, although she had only lifted a nutshell of water. *That pool must weigh as much as a lead pinecone.* Riveted, she strained her body, beaming strength at Beechnut. She focused everything she had on willing each of his pulls of the rope to overturn the bowl.

Aksel and Bo strove behind him, helping it forward.

Queen Pepper didn't have time to warn her squad before the bowl slipped off its plinth, slowly, like a tortoise righting itself after a poor experience. She kicked her hummingbird's flank, causing him to levitate angrily. He hovered above the ground, bucking wildly as a chaos of water crashed below, splashing Cloudforce's bird from the air and sweeping him into the forest. The rest of the officers and their birds floated after him, past the sticky marsh, toward the stream and their marching troopers.

With a gasp, Almond scrambled backward despite her injuries and perched on a low-hanging leaf. *They did it!* she thought. A wave of warmth toward Beechnut crashed over her as the tsunami of spring water flooded the lawn. With Pepper's goons removed, the playing field was leveled. Before Almond could let out a whoop of relief, her mouth went slack. In slow motion, the cage holding Nutsie and Mr. Pickles floated away in the deluge. She threw herself into the air after them, but the wound refused to let her injured wing unfurl and she crashed back to her bed of golden daisy pistils.

Her best friend drifted beyond the willow tree on the flood tide.

The dollhouse swam before her, out of focus and distant. She gazed at Beechnut, steadfast, as he came into her line of sight around the curve of the overturned bowl. The last thing she saw before thunderclouds of dizziness crowded her vision was a stray fairy arrow arc against the under-leaves of the willow tree—released just as the water swept the invaders away—and bury itself in his chest.

CHAPTER 19

A tangle of daisy stems held Almond's limbs where she fell. They restrained her from being swept away by the deluge as the flood petered out. But as her eyelids fluttered open at the sound of her sister's shriek, all she knew was that she couldn't move. Her gaze found Pepper, who hovered above the sodden lawn on Nectar. Was any of this real? Strangely, in this moment, she felt closer to her than ever before. Why had she never been nice to her? Her sister was still a pip. But she never did her duty in the ivy—never experienced much of anything having to do with Nook life. She had just fast forwarded to greatness. She didn't look happy to Almond. The skin around her dull eyes was tight with hatred.

Almond was too tired to care. Her entire body was one huge bruise, and she shook with loss. Beechnut couldn't have survived that shot to the chest. He lay in front of the overturned bowl with the arrow sticking out of him. It looked unnatural—because it was. How could something so tiny ruin everything? The arrow was slim, barely a shadow hovering over her favorite fairy.

He is *my favorite,* she thought in a fog of grief too vast to penetrate her tear ducts. As it probed for an opening into her soul, she was yet to feel it shatter her. She inhaled the memory of his lilac scent. Despite Beechnut's bluster, she loved that he was exceedingly patient with the Innkeepers. And that he looked like a king but was built like a hero—her hero, who she needed. She couldn't fly with her wing wound and her knee was swollen like a tree nut; she couldn't fight; she could barely move. Nutsie and Mr. Pickles were gone. How could she save them now? Blunderman was gone. It was over.

They had lost.

It was time to surrender to her sister and leave this place—let it heal. Perhaps someone else would find the dollhouse. Maybe even carry on the work that they started by turning it into a haven in the forest for tiny creatures. The fantasy gave her a small reprieve to her grief. She even smiled through the pain.

The shadow of a cloud scudded across the forest floor until it reached the dollhouse, where is sucked the color from everything it touched, matching Almond's bleak and broken spirit. Maybe she deserved a joyless, lonely Nook life. She never realized how much she hated that place until she was lucky enough to be swept up in adventure. Where she came from, the forest was a scary, filthy prison. Here at the Dollhouse Inn, she found companionship, purpose, and the freedom to be herself. Rosepurse Wood opened up to her and became a marvelous world with space to explore. During her short time here, rather than fear the forest, she had learned to love it.

Now, thanks to Pepper, her world would once again become shriveled to a blanched raisin of existence, with nothing to fall back on and nothing to look forward to. She had dared to consider herself powerful but here she was, broken at Pepper's feet, with everything she and her friends had built gone like the fuzz of a new dandelion on a brisk day.

Almond pulled herself upright, leaning on her walking stick, and pushed through the daisy stems toward Pepper. *It was always going to end up like this,* she thought. *Even if I never got swept away by a chickadee, Pepper would have made me suffer.* There was no empathy for teenaged mistakes—no mercy for immature behavior. Whatever her little sister had wanted from her on her first day of Fairy School, Almond had not been capable of giving to her. Nor on the second day, or the third, all the way through to the end of the school year—Almond's last and Pepper's first.

Honestly, Almond hadn't thought much about her at all. They had dozens of siblings—technically—but fairies didn't operate like that, with a nuclear family taking precedence. Their mother sat on their eggs and kept them warm, but she wasn't even there on the day that they hatched. Every hatchling went their own way, teaching themselves to fly and seeking food, which was usually laid out for them on a buffet next to the nest—the fairy equivalent of maternal love.

When Pepper approached her group of friends on her first day of school, Almond had thought it was a joke. That wasn't how they did things—every fairy was on their own. Clearly, Almond had gotten it all wrong—the fairy who once craved her attention was now in the ultimate power position and burned with a yearning to end her.

Without realizing it, Almond had made enemies with the Fairy Queen.

A flash of light in the dusk caught her attention. Twin glowing streaks zoomed from the bramble toward her, and she ducked. Aksel and Bo settled next to her, wielding their fox bone swords.

"We missed the fracas," said Aksel.

"But here we are," said Bo.

"Everyone's gone." Almond sagged against her stick.

The fireflies raised their swords above their heads and glared at Pepper. "Then we are here to back you up," said Aksel.

Almond shook her head. "It's too late." She pointed her chin at Pepper, who peered at them with feverish eyes. "My sister has won."

The fireflies shifted their attention to Pepper, scanning her and her bird before turning back to Almond.

"There is one of her," said Aksel.

"Two if you count the hummingbird, which we should," said Bo.

"There are three of us," said Aksel.

"And our sword tips are dipped in poison," whispered Bo. "Hemlock."

Aksel's rump pulsed with light as he gravely met her gaze. "We cannot allow our friends to have fallen without fighting to the end."

Almond raised her head and peered at her sister with new eyes. She wasn't wounded, but she wasn't in sound shape, either. Her gaze flicked to Beechnut's prone body lying in the ruined bramble and her heart stumbled. He deserved better than this. She smiled weakly at her friends and nodded, the ember of ire sparking and reigniting deep in her wing roots.

Galvanized, she hopped in a half circle to face her sister, the armed fireflies flanking her, grim and deadly. "Queen Pepper of the Nook," cried Almond. The words snagged in her throat like burrs before flying into the air between them. It was the first time she had addressed her sister with her new title. Hopefully, it would also be the last. She threw back her shoulders. "I command you to surrender."

"No." Pepper's face was triumphant as she sat aloft Nectar, looking down on Almond. The thoroughbred's wings whizzed with force and his glossy, emerald chest heaved, ready for revenge for the bite marks in his beak. "Where are your strange little friends, anyway? I don't see them." Pepper looked around in an exaggerated way, as if searching for the scattered and beaten Innkeepers. "I'm taking your resources and bringing you home for punishment."

"Why, Pepper?" Almond stared up at her little sister. Once again, she realized that she didn't recognize the fairy glaring down at her.

"This is what happens to anyone who defects from my Fairy Nook," said Pepper, sneering. "From where I sit, it looks like you're building your own competing nook. I cannot allow that. Nor can I risk looking weak to my subjects. So, your animals are now mine, and I'm having your spring poisoned. This place will be uninhabitable. It's time you surrender to me, big sister, not the other way around."

"This is no fairy nook, Pepper." Almond flung her free arm toward the Dollhouse Inn, spraying muddy water in an arc. For the first time in her life, she didn't care that her entire body was filthy with muck. This was her muck, and this little dollhouse in the forest had nothing to do with Pepper and her annex of power. "We're just a group of creatures providing a safe place to rest in the forest. We take no resources from you. We have no designs on what's yours. Just leave us in peace."

Pepper opened her mouth as if to fling an insult at Almond's head when it abruptly snapped shut and she paled.

Aksel and Bo hovered on either side of Almond with their swords raised, but Pepper wasn't looking at them. She glanced behind her. The ground undulated, entirely covered in a carpet of hard, brown-grey shells like tiny crabs. There were hundreds of stink bugs, standing at attention to follow her into battle. In the middle of the army stood Beechnut, statuesque and vital, even with an arrow sticking out of his chest. He had a fresh arrow fitted into a bow and, squinting one eye shut, aimed it at Pepper's head.

Almond's body was suddenly alive, tingling and light. She wanted to skip into his arms, but they were full of arrow-tipped malice.

Pepper's eyes widened at Beechnut. "Traitor! I am your queen—you serve my Nook! How dare you?"

Beechnut didn't break his aim. "It's not your Nook. And neither is this. You are outnumbered and have five dew drips to retreat, or you will die."

The Fairy Queen's face twisted, as dark as a tree once struck by lightning. She yanked at Nectar's reigns, and Almond saw exasperation flash in the great bird's eye.

"Traitors!" Pepper spat again.

"You're the traitor, Pepper," said Almond, waving her hand in a rude gesture. "The other fairies are not your personal play army. You don't deserve to rule the Nook."

"And Cornsilk will hear about what you've done, be sure of it," said Beechnut.

A small, sinister smile tickled Pepper's lips that Almond could not understand. Her eyes glowed red like a revenant and she flicked her gaze to Beechnut, whose arms remained iron-straight on his bow. She spat again and wheeled Nectar to point toward the stream. Her scarlet eyes flashed when she looked back over her shoulder. "This isn't over," she said before zooming into the gloom of Rosepurse Wood.

"Promises, promises," Bo called after her. He turned to the others as the stink bugs wandered back to their bunker. "Aksel and I will follow to make sure she goes back to where she came from."

As Nectar's tail feathers disappeared through the trees in a crimson blur, Almond lowered herself to the sodden ground, at one with the muck, and lay back, looking at Beechnut upside down. "You're alive."

He lowered his weapon and lay on his back, positioning himself so that his body lay in the opposite direction, with their heads cheek-to-cheek. "You are alive, too. I hoped that you were."

Nothing more needed to be said just then as the fireflies followed Pepper toward the stream, ensuring her departure. Despite her wing that now screamed like a chased rabbit and her aching head, Beechnut's nearness warmed Almond. She barely acknowledged a passing curiosity about why being around this fairy—this not particularly amiable fairy—eased her mind more than any other relationship did. Even more so than her friendship with Nutsie.

Nutsie.

Sorrow pooled in her chest. She had a wild urge to turn over in a cartwheel and dump it out through the top of her head. Instead, she reached over and traced Beechnut's cheekbone, running her thumb over the ridge above the valley of his cheek. Overhead, the cloud that shadowed the Dollhouse Inn moved along, revealing a sky as blue and pure as a rain-washed morning.

Aksel and Bo tracked Pepper to the stream, where they later reported witnessing her foot soldiers reverse at her command. They marched away as if they had just passed by on their way to a berry picking party. The duo retraced their flight back to the Dollhouse Inn, wings heavy with regret.

"How could we have slept through the battle?" asked Aksel. "All we got to do was help Beechnut flood the combat zone."

Bo slashed his sword through the air. "It is shameful. We must find a way to recover our honor. Perhaps—did you hear that?"

Aksel drew back when Bo zipped away from their path and disappeared into a thicket of sweet peas. "It's not time to explore," he called after him, watching the gloom swallow Bo's flashing pattern. "We must return and help the fairies clean up the Dollhouse Inn." Bo didn't answer. The forest fell silent, as if awaiting his next move. Then, it erupted into its usual buzzing and birdsong. He sighed. "Very well, here I come."

Before he could follow, Bo was back at his side. "I hear something. Perhaps the sounds of grief." He aimed his sword toward where Blunderman had once saved Almond from drowning in mud. "I think it's coming from that swampy area."

Chip chip.

The fireflies held their deadly fox bone swords aloft and zoomed into the low growth that skirted the sticky marsh. Aksel went left while Bo went right, and together they flew in opposite directions, tracing concentric circles until they spotted the source of the noise laying on its side in a low spot of muck—a cage woven from reeds. Muffled voices and wails floated from its interior, and with every movement, the cage sunk deeper into the slime.

"Be still!" Aksel flew to the woven fairy cage. "Pickles, is that you? Is Nutsie in there with you? Whoever you are, be still. The opening is sinking into the marsh."

The cage stopped shimmying, and a tense silence emanated from inside. "It's Pickles and Nutsie," said a voice from within. "She's badly hurt."

Aksel poked the portion of the door that was above the sucking, slurping mire with the tip of his sword. The cage jiggled and sank a bit more. "The latch is already under. If I try to cut it open, the whole thing will sink."

"What will we do?" asked Mr. Pickles.

Aksel shook his head and sheathed his sword.

Bo flitted around the circumference of the mud hole. "I have an idea. The rest of the surface is unbroken. Mr. Pickles, can Nutsie walk?"

"Yes, it's my front paw that's wrecked." Nutsie's voice was thin and weak.

Bo nodded. "As one, the two of you face to your right, follow the sound of my voice. Are you both facing toward me?"

"Yes," said Mr. Pickles.

"Slowly, as one, like I said, walk forward."

The round cage rocked and then shivered lower in the mud.

"We're sinking!" Mr. Pickles's voice rose in pitch.

"Don't stop," said Bo. "Trust me."

The cage shivered once again and then bit into the edge of the fresh skin of slime. As the animals within took careful steps, it rolled onto the slightly more stable patch of mud. As its sunken corner emerged, the mud sucked, but did not draw it back in.

"That's it," said Bo, conducting them from the air with his legs. "Just a bit farther and the latch to the door will emerge."

The captives took another step in tandem, rolling the cage onto the next patch of firm mud.

"One more of those and you'll be delivered straight to solid ground, I think," said Aksel, slapping Bo on the back.

The cage shuddered and sank like a pebble dropping into the stream.

"My paw," wailed Nutsie.

"Nutsie!" said Mr. Pickles. "She fell down," he called to the fireflies.

"I spoke too soon!" Aksel flew in anxious loops.

Bo turned to him. "We have to open the cage up where it is."

The cage lay in the center of the mud hole, but the latch to the door, thick with clay, faced the sun. As the fireflies slashed the lock with their swords, the clay hardened under the sun's heat, sealing the door shut.

"It's no use." Aksel grunted.

"Don't you dare give up," Nutsie growled from the darkened cage. "Keep smacking it. Pickles, help me down so that I'm on my back." She and Mr. Pickles kicked the door from the inside as the fireflies slashed at the caked mud. The cage shivered into its mucky nest, threatening to sink at any moment.

"Just...one...more," Nutsie heaved. The fireflies backed away as the door flew open. No one emerged and they zipped to the doorway. Peering into the dim opening, they gasped in unison when they saw Nutsie bleeding from the gaping hole in her paw. A delicate bone that shot through the appendage was cracked and pushed to the side when Nectar's needle beak pierced her fur.

"She can't climb out," said Mr. Pickles. "That final kick to open the door took the last of her strength."

"At least we didn't drown," said Nutsie, her breath hitching from the depths of the cage.

Aksel and Bo cast about for anything to tie to the cage or its captives to pull them out but saw nothing. The glen was barren except for the greedy divots of mud that dotted the swampy earth.

"We need something to lay across and form a walkway," said Aksel.

"What about this?" Bo dropped from a tree holding a flat, waxy leaf.

Aksel considered it. "I suppose that could work, if they are swift and lucky."

"No," said Mr. Pickles, poking his head out of the opening. His fur stood on end where it wasn't plastered with slime. "If it breaks, you have no way of pulling us out of the mud."

"If you stay in there, you will sink anyway," said Aksel.

Bo positioned himself to drop the leaf onto the surface of the mud as soon as they were ready to step out of the cage. "Can you get Nutsie out of there?"

Mr. Pickles dropped his head into the cage and the fireflies heard murmuring. The cage rustled and shifted, and Nutsie appeared through the opening, her eyes dull. She folded in on her wounded paw and levered herself onto the cage's exposed surface with her elbows.

Pressing an unsteady hind paw forward, she leaned back against Mr. Pickles, who followed her out of the hole. Blinking into the weak sunlight, Nutsie allowed Mr. Pickles to guide her to the edge of the cage opposite to where Bo hovered over the bank. He edged forward, careful not to drag the tip of the leaf through the mud.

With the tip poised at Nutsie's paws, Bo set the rest of the leaf down, one section at a time, so that it quivered on top of the skim of slime.

"Be as quick as you can," said Aksel. "Don't touch it more than you need to."

Mr. Pickles moved to hand Nutsie off of the cage and onto the leaf.

"Wait!" Bo zipped into a tree and returned with a second leaf. "Let's lay this on top of the first for extra support."

"I don't know, Bo," said Aksel. "Is it worth the risk of breaking the surface of the mire?"

"The surface will break as her paw steps on the leaf, Aksel."

"Yes, but it could be the previous breaking that steals our chance of success."

"She has to go now," said Mr. Pickles, his voice cracking. Nutsie's gaze was unfocused, and she swayed dangerously where she stood on the overturned cage.

"Keep your tread light," said Aksel.

"Think light thoughts," said Bo.

Mr. Pickles grasped her elbows. "You can do this," he whispered into her delicate ear.

Nutsie nodded but stumbled on her first step down from the cage. The leaf buckled so that her hind paws were under the mud where she stood.

Before she lost her momentum, Mr. Pickles gave her a tremendous shove that sent her sprawling on the leaf as it skidded toward the bank of the hole. She caught the lip of solid ground with her good front paw and the fireflies hauled the leaf ashore. "The mud feels good on my paw wound," she said, her cheek on the ground. She lay on her side, lethargic, her fur slick with fear and spiked at the ends. Her nose was dry and her beautiful doe eyes held no twinkle indicating her zest for merriment.

"Did she make it?" Mr. Pickles's black eyes gleamed with panic, and he flailed his arms, sinking deeper in the mud where he had tumbled, shoving Nutsie ashore.

"Be still," said Bo. He and Aksel circled the hamster, but they couldn't pull him from the sucking mud. He was in too deep.

"Pickles!" The wail came from Nutsie, crawling back toward the hole with her wounded paw clutched to her chest.

"He just saved you," said Aksel, pulling at her hind paw. "Don't let his sacrifice be a waste."

Nutsie sobbed into the crushed grass beneath her as Mr. Pickles shimmied lower into the gelatinous slime. *Chip chip.*

Bo zipped back and forth across the hole, searching for a way to save him, seeing nothing, and hovered near the hamster's head in misery.

"At least I got out of the pet shop," said Mr. Pickles, gasping. "The world seems to want me in a cage. It's not so bad dying out here in the open, a free hamster."

Bo nodded. "I understand."

The forest was silent except for Nutsie's muffled sobs, as if paying respect to death as it came calling.

"It seems as if I am forever saving my friends from this marsh," said a cheerful voice. A large butterfly swooped out of the sky and grabbed Mr. Pickles by his cheek pouches. The butterfly was clearly Blunderman, except that he now had a set of glorious, rippling, golden and burnt orange wings carrying him aloft. He gave two great beats of his wings and pulled Mr. Pickles free so that they both tumbled into the knot of bedraggled friends.

"Sorry I had to leave the party early," said the butterfly. "Nature called me home."

"Nice wings." Nutsie grinned up at him.

"Quickly," Aksel said to Blunderman. "Can you carry Nutsie to the Dollhouse Inn? Her wound must be tended immediately."

"I have a capful of royal jelly," she said, rasping.

Aksel and Bo clicked their sword tips together and hauled Mr. Pickles to his feet as they marveled at the butterfly's fresh wings testing themselves against the weight of a well-fed chipmunk. The fireflies filled their chests with hope to help buoy their friends on their short journey home.

CHAPTER 20

As Blunderman fluttered Nutsie to her nest, Almond lay on the other side of the willow tree, unwitting of the rescue mission that had just been pulled off despite a thistle down's chance of succeeding. The swell of hope that had warmed her moments ago had been replaced by hard, cold despair. Her fingers—elegant despite their film of grime—continued to trace her beloved's strong brow.

It was icy.

Tears streamed from the corners of her eyes and dripped into her ears, filling the pointed tips before cascading into the clover. Beechnut had been with her—finally, and in a way that she'd never questioned— and then, in a breath, he left his body behind for her to keep as a souvenir of her heartbreak.

Grief gutted her and prevented her from standing. Her fingers wrapped around something silky and she pulled, plucking a tidy flower a shade darker than her own periwinkle hand. She put the blossom to her cheek, letting her tears gloss its blue petals. Slowly, she pulled it from her face and reached across to lay it over Beechnut's closed eyes. The petals covered the pallor of death, giving him the dignity that he deserved.

"Forget-me-not," she whispered in his ear, naming the flower.

Almond sat up and surveyed the tumbled mud that was left of her lawn—numb from trauma and exposure. They had fought hard, but she knew that the battle wasn't over. Pepper would be back with more of her fairy army. She couldn't let herself sink into grief over losing Beechnut, Nutsie, Blunderman, and Mr. Pickles. The fireflies were still with her, and the Dollhouse Inn would have to be ready to protect any creature who sought shelter on its estate. Crafting the beginning of a plan, she would talk to Aksel and Bo about setting up a real perimeter, with patrols and more clever defenses. Pepper would never get so close to the Dollhouse Inn again, Almond promised herself. Time was on their side—for now.

"Almond!" A deep voice drifted from the dollhouse.

Almond's head whipped to face the structure, gaze darting for the source. Outside of Nutsie's nest, a magnificent butterfly with buttercup yellow wings hovered outside of Nutsie's nest as if gathering pollen. She squinted, activating her fairy sight, and zoomed in on the butterfly waving at her.

She pushed off the ground to fly, but her wing hung uselessly. Gaze locked on the butterfly, she slogged through the mud toward the dollhouse. Every step she took away from Beechnut's body wrenched her. But she had to see what this creature wanted. It might need her help, although she didn't know what she had left to give. She reached the river stone steps that led up to Nutsie's room and stopped, peering up at the great yellow wings. They spanned at least three times wider than her own and rippled like sunshine. "Do you need shelter?" she called up to the butterfly.

Peering into Nutsie's nest, the creature swung around to face Almond, and she gasped, taking in the familiar features now rearranged on a whole new body. "Blunderman! You're magnificent," she cried. A wave of relief at recovering a friend crashed over her and fresh tears soaked her cheeks, the curls around her neck sopping.

He swooped down and wrapped her in his buttery wings, rocking her like a baby while she cried. Holding her until her shoulders no longer shook, he pulled back to examine her face. After a moment, he tut-tutted. "I have never seen you quite so filthy."

A guffaw burst from her lips at his surprising comment considering the circumstances. "That's a lie."

Blunderman nodded. "It is. Come, Nutsie needs your help."

"*Nutsie?*" Almond skipped back, tripping over a quartz pebble. She hobbled up the steps to the nest. The chipmunk shivered in a ball of matted auburn fur while clutching an acorn cap of royal jelly. Almond froze for a moment, trying to understand how Nutsie could have possibly survived the swamping—and how she was now snug in her nest. Then she threw herself at her best friend, hugging her fiercely.

"Ow!" Nutsie complained, but she squeezed the fairy back with tears in her eyes. "Help me fix up this paw. I think we can still save it."

Snuffling, Almond nodded, too emotional to speak. *Nutsie's alive!* The thought plucked her heart from her toes and let it rise to her chest. She dropped to her knees, packing the wound with royal jelly and wrapping her paw in clean wads of cotton.

"I will head back to the marsh and help the fireflies carry Mr. Pickles," Blunderman called from the air.

Almond's gaze met Nutsie's, wide-eyed. "Pickles? You're all okay?" She choked back tears as her face split into a radiant smile.

Nutsie grinned back. "I don't know about being 'okay' but we're all alive."

Almond's face fell. "Not all of us."

Gravely, Nutsie laid her good paw on Almond's shoulder. It was as heavy as a full-grown toad. "Are you saying that Beechnut is gone?" asked the chipmunk.

Almond nodded, misery straining her features. "To the Spirit Meadow." She pointed toward the willow tree where she had left him in the clover, a forget-me-not shrouding his face.

Chip chip. Nutsie stared at the tree, its long leaves cascading like tears to match Almond's and her own.

As the willow tree's ballerina boughs lightened from iguana to canary, sunlight filtered through them to bathe the dollhouse in a golden patina. Almond stood in the parlor and surveyed the finishing touches of the repairs to the property after the Great Battle. The ground had dried out from Beechnut's torrent, and the pinecone path leading to the Dollhouse Inn was rebuilt.

Since the other fairies had arrived, the rebuild had become a robust community project, although she hated that the estate was littered with cowslip bells and the spent husks of blackberries. She was tired of tripping over them. But the upside of so many new fairy hands was a bridge built between the roof of the dollhouse and the bramble, as well as a spiral staircase leading down each floor.

She scanned the estate, taking in the newly built fairy nests dotting crevices in the stone wall, attached to thorns in the rose bush, and clustered on the shadowy side of the plinth that supported the pool. Thankfully, the ceramic bowl survived the battle, and the pool was open to gather fresh spring water and add a recreation amenity to the inn. Almond waved to her old foraging squadmate, Sage Thornsmith, as he and his mate polished the bowl's exterior. He had escaped from the pebble pit, and they had arrived at the Dollhouse Inn just last moon.

Nutsie joined her in the parlor and gave the scene a satisfied smile. "The new addition triples the size of the inn, which we need since so many fairies fled the Nook. But I think we should still leave some nests in the dollhouse for weary travelers."

"I agree. That was our original idea, and we should stick to it." Almond gave her friend a sly smile. "I noticed you opened up an extra nest, in fact, by moving Mr. Pickles into yours."

Nutsie preened. "Since I'm the managing partner of the Dollhouse Inn, it's up to me to set an example. Besides, I am a morning person, and Pickles is nocturnal. Night watch is perfect for him, and I still get time to myself."

"I hope it works," said Almond. "I already miss Aksel, that old rascal."

"A quest to the other side of Rosepurse Wood," Nutsie whispered, awed. The leaves above the dollhouse rustled, dappling the lawn with flitting shadows.

"Bo said that they've made the trip twice already, so not to worry. I'm glad he stayed—thanks to that charming stink bug he met after the Great Battle." At least her friends had found love. Almond remembered her helplessness as Beechnut's life force drained away under her fingertips. Her wings contracted, pinching a nerve between her shoulder blades. She grimaced at the pain. After everything they had fought for—and won—she had failed to save him on the battle-field. Her heart clenched as it played out in her mind, and she shook her head to clear the awful memory.

"Speaking of sharing a nest," said Nutsie. "You should try it."

Snapping out of her reverie, Almond cut a glance at her friend. Her face paled to baby blue. "I couldn't."

"Would it be so bad?" Nutsie systematically shoved seeds into her cheek pouches, keeping count under her breath. "Forty-two, forty-three, forty-four..."

Almond tried not to show that the question needled her. "Of course, I'm grateful that the hedgie witch was able to save Beechnut and bring him back to me—thanks to the healing powers of the royal jelly she sent us on a quest for. And I love the way I feel around him. But, just like you, I want time to myself and my space. I'm keeping my own nest."

"I'll bet he hates that." Nutsie's voice rolled over the seeds in her cheek.

"I don't care," said Almond, watching where she knew the mouth of a tunnel to be. It led from the Dollhouse Inn to the willow's trunk thanks to Beechnut, the self-appointed Knight of the Inn.

Nutsie saw her looking for him and tittered around her cheek-full of seeds. She drew Almond's attention to the nets full of stones suspended from the willow boughs. "Beechnut and Bo have been inventing new boobytraps for any foxes, raccoons, or raptors that might attack. Have you seen?"

Almond squinted up at the instruments of war. "And for the inevitable day when Pepper returns. I can't believe she actually ate Cornsilk."

Nutsie glanced at her from the side of her eye and cleared her throat. "I, um, didn't realize that fairies were cannibals. It was pretty shocking when the Nook fairies brought that news." She removed the seeds from her cheek, one by one.

Almond flushed indigo. "It hasn't happened in a very long time. In fact, I thought it was just old legend. It's embarrassing."

Nutsie pulled the last seed from her mouth and studied the pile she had made. "It's nature, I suppose. Do you think you would ever eat Beechnut?" She gave an exaggerated wink.

Almond puffed out her cheeks, miming being sick, and relaxed that they were laughing about Pepper's indiscretion. "They say now that she's unchecked, every fairy is forced to join her army. More Nook fairies may come here for sanctuary, and I don't know where we'll put them." She gazed at the lawn teeming with fairies soothing themselves with manual labour, and fiddled with her wing ring.

Nutsie reached out to touch the delicate ring woven from tender fern stems and hung with tiny bell-shaped blossoms. "How pretty. Will it hinder your wing wound from healing, though?"

"Actually, it will trigger it to regenerate faster. I just have to take it out at the last minute, or the hole will be permanent."

"You wouldn't keep it?"

"It's clever, but I miss flying higher than the stone wall."

Nutsie chuckled. "I understand." She waved her paw that was fitted in the center with a small nutshell where it had been impaled by Nectar's beak. "At least I can scoop things up." She frowned at her mangled paw. "I hope mine heals."

"It will, thanks to the royal jelly we brought back from the Queen Bee." Almond threw an arm around her friend's shoulders and squeezed. "We're a couple of champions, aren't we? With the battle scars to prove it."

"It won't stop me from winning the foraging contest." Nutsie preened. "No creature at the Dollhouse Inn can touch the capacity of my cheek pouches. Look at this pile!" She swept her arm toward the mound of seeds that had been tucked into her cheek, threatening to topple it. "Sixty seeds in one pouch alone!"

Almond nodded in a show of support as she followed Beechnut's stride across the lawn with her gaze. Nutsie and Blunderman had returned his belt and dagger to celebrate his recovery, and he wore them proudly as he worked on the estate.

"Look what Beechnut found," said Nutsie, scampering down the river stone steps to catch up with him. Almond skipped after her to a fresh hole dug in the soil at the edge of the willow boughs. Beechnut stood to the side, chest puffed out more than usual. "What's in there?"

she asked.

Nutsie reached into the hole and pulled out what looked like a tangerine.

Almond's mouth watered at the sight of the tangy fruit. She squinted, taking a closer look, and then opened her mouth in a shriek. "Nutsie, put that down!" She vibrated her wings, gearing up to zoom in and grab the deadly pod from the chipmunk before she lost her other paw.

Beechnut stepped forward and swiped it from Nutsie, placing it gingerly back into the hole in the ground. "Those are bombs, not snacks." He turned to Almond. "I scouted a monkey-no-climb tree and harvested these ripe pods. I think if we keep them in this pit, they won't be triggered to shoot their seeds. If we need to protect the perimeter, we shake them and throw." He pantomimed lobbing something across the lawn. "Boom."

Almond clapped her hands together. "Brilliant! I never thought I'd be happy to see those things." She eyed the pit from a distance.

Beechnut stepped toward her, and she danced her fingertips down his chiseled torso. He caught her hands in his, holding them to his heart. "I added a skylight to the nest," he said, his lips turning up slightly at the corners.

"A skylight in a tree?" She laughed, but her shoulders tensed at the mention of his nest. He hadn't asked her to move in again since the Great Battle—there had been too much to do. But now, the Inn was recovered and life marched on. Would her need for independence spark another disagreement? Or worse, make him lose interest in her? There were dozens of eligible fairies at the dollhouse now. Maybe she wasn't so desirable to him with other options fluttering about.

"A skylight in a nest in a tree," said Beechnut gravely. "On a clear night, I'll prop it open to look at the stars."

Is this it? Is he asking me to join with him? Almond thought she was prepared for this moment, but her knees shook. She didn't want to nest with Beechnut, but she didn't want to lose him, either.

Silence stretched out between them.

"I also found a velvety, lacy peony bloom for my bed," he drawled.

Almond's wings stiffened and a thrill raced down her torso. *Velvety peony for a bed? Yes please!* She forced her wings to relax. *I can't let myself be seduced into a decision that's not right for me,* she thought, stern with herself. She took a deep breath. "Beechnut—"

Before she could say any more, he cut in. "Perhaps if you're lucky, I'll invite you over on a clear night during a star shower, Nettlesworth." His smirk blossomed into a radiant smile that melted Almond's tension and flooded her with a sweet, syrupy sensation that she couldn't name.

He understood! That meant they had a chance.

She beamed up at him, wrapping her arms around his waist. "Then, until the stars favor me, will you join me in the dollhouse tonight, Beechnut Trufflesnout Dandelion-Bougainvillea?"

He laughed and bent to brush his full lips against her rosebud mouth.

She melted into his kiss for a moment of eternity, and then pulled back, searching his face. "So, you really don't mind keeping separate nests?"

His features settled into a grave countenance as he regarded her. "At first, I thought it was unnatural—and perhaps wasteful."

Almond ducked her head, flushing at her selfishness. But she shook off the ugly feeling, meeting his gaze with equal gravitas. "And now?"

He laced his strong fingers through hers. "Now I understand the wisdom of getting out of your way." He grinned when she punched his arm. "I mean it. You Innkeepers have an important purpose. Maintaining a safe place for creatures who cannot defend themselves is honorable. I would not want to interfere."

She reached up and cupped his cheek. "You are an Innkeeper, too, Beechnut."

His lips curved happily as he covered her hand with his.

Basking in the energy flowing between them, Almond's brow clouded, and she glanced away.

"What is it?" he asked.

She peeked up at him through her curls. "What about eggs? Would you be disappointed if I never lay any?"

He dropped his hand, leaving hers exposed. "I don't know. All fairies hatch eggs—that's all I've ever known. But to what end? I've been thinking about my own time as a pip. Fairy parents don't forge deep relationships with their young. Mine certainly didn't."

Almond shook her head. "Neither did mine."

"All I can tell you for certain is that I don't wish to be a father right now in this moment." He scanned the estate that bustled with activity. "There's too much for us to do as Innkeepers to worry about that now." He caught her chin and lowered his voice. "And any free time I have, I want to spend with you."

She grinned at him. "I'll have to show you how to skydive from a nuthatch!"

His gaze widened, but before he could respond a voice calling instructions rang out from between the far trees. They turned toward it.

"As Chief Farmer, I will instruct you young fairies, and you there, young turtle, on the art of growing food," said the voice belonging to Blunderman. His luminous, sunshine-hued butterfly wings fluttered toward the Dollhouse Inn, followed by three fairy pips struggling to fly while holding their half walnut shells full of seeds. A small turtle trailed the group on the ground, his walnut receptacle balanced on his own shell. Blunderman paused in the air when he spotted Nutsie joining Almond and Beechnut on the lawn.

"I'll never get over your gorgeous wings," said Almond, staring up at him in wonder. "They're like great yellow petals. I'm actually jealous!"

"The prettiest bird I've ever seen," said Nutsie.

"He's a butterfly," Almond corrected her.

Nutsie flapped her intact paw at her, gazing up at their transformed friend. "I'll never get over how you saved Pickles from the mud puddle, Blunderman."

"I guess that's his specialty," said Almond, laughing now that the memory of her own near-death experience in the mud faded into its place in the tapestry of her young life. But she'd never forget that Blunderman saved her, too—even if he'd needed some coaxing at the time.

Blunderman swooped over their heads. "Just a touch of metamorphosis," he said in a voice laced with glee. "It finally happened to me! And just in time. There are many mouths to feed, and much food to grow. The gift of flight helps me scout for the best places to plant our crops."

"Congratulations," said Beechnut, hovering to perform an intricate handshake with the butterfly before settling on the ground by Almond's side. His great metallic purple wing curled around her shoulders, and she leaned into him. Nutsie's warm paw grabbed her hand. Love and lightness shrouded Almond, protecting her from harm—for now.

Pepper was still out there, madder than a yellow jacket now that so many fairies had left the Nook despite her fear tactics. She wouldn't leave them in peace. And those who remained loyal to the Nook were as crazy as she was, from what the fairy refugees had shared with the Innkeepers. With her extremist supporters, Pepper would be more dangerous than ever. But even she couldn't change the fact that the Innkeepers had each other.

And there was no place else that Almond would rather be.

Blunderman grinned down at them, burnished golden wings thrown wide like a bright dawn spreading across the horizon. "What a wonderful start to a brand-new day, my friends!"

ACKNOWLEDGEMENTS

Wing Haven is my sophomore novel, and the product of a lot of love and support. I'm grateful to Amanda and Zak Freedman, Hurchell Greenaway, Monica Kirchmer, Christine Goodrich, Anastasia Kenny, Seth Chapman, Stephanie Barfield, and Ann-Rose Johnson-Lewis for being awesome.

I'm so appreciative of Caroline Bounds for making this book shine, and for my talented editor, Hillary Leftwich.

The title of this book was inspired by Wing Haven Gardens, a magical place tucked away in the middle of my city. I practically raised my son there, and if there were any fairies around, they would be at the gardens.

ALSO BY **NAOMI SHIBLES**

COUNTERBLOW CLEMENCY

It's 2117 and Promo City is blazing with advertising pollution, but all sixteen-year-old Bjorn Bear cares about is having fun, until the city's deadliest assassins attack him. With his motley gang of friends by his side, Bjorn must evade a crime boss with a vendetta, overcome genetically-engineered mini hippos, and race against time to discover and stop whoever is out to get him—all while facing the possibility that the only family he's ever known isn't real.

Praise for Counterblow Clemency

"Filled with heart-pounding action and characters that
will resonate in your soul."
—*Midwest Book Review*

"Fast-paced and action-packed, Counterblow Clemency is an
adrenaline-pumping thriller that never lets its foot off the gas."
—*Readers' Favorite*

"For fans of the fantastical and science fiction,
this book is a must-read."
—*Literary Titan*

ABOUT THE AUTHOR

Naomi Shibles grew up in the U.S. Virgin Islands. She is the author of the critically acclaimed science fiction caper, COUNTERBLOW CLEMENCY. She treasures time with her son, and traveling with a good book.

NAOMISHIBLES.COM

www.ingramcontent.com/pod-product-compliance
Lightning Source LLC
Chambersburg PA
CBHW061339160726
47995CB00001B/95